Eve's Return

Book One of the Book of Eve Series

Crystal Bourque

Dedication

To Mum,
For reading every page I've ever written..

Contents

Acknowledgements vii

Chapter 1 9

Chapter 2 14

Chapter 3 22

Chapter 4 29

Chapter 5 41

Chapter 6 52

Chapter 7 63

Chapter 8 73

Chapter 9 82

Chapter 10 94

Chapter 11 105

Chapter 12 113

Chapter 13 123

Chapter 14 130

Chapter 15 140

Chapter 16 153

Chapter 17 164

Chapter 18 175

Chapter 19.. 184

Chapter 20.. 191

Chapter 21.. 198

Chapter 22.. 204

Chapter 23.. 211

Chapter 24.. 221

Chapter 25.. 230

About the Author.. 234

Acknowledgements

I want to thank everyone who helped read and critique this book. We all lead busy lives, which means: time is precious. I'm honored that you would spend some of yours reading my work. Whether you reviewed several chapters, or the entire manuscript, your comments and suggestions have truly helped to shape this story.

Another big thank you goes to my family. You were the first to know my secret: that I wanted to be a writer. It only made sense that you were the first people I told about this book! I am still blown away by the amount of support and encouragement you continue to give.

I also need to thank AG. The hours (and hours) you spent listening to me spin my dreams into reality will never be forgotten. You believed in this project, even when I didn't believe in myself. You have complete faith in me, but without you there would be no book, and that's the simple truth.

A huge thanks also goes to Kelly Martin for helping with the cover redesign. She's fantastic to work with, and the results are absolutely stunning! Nita Robinson gets all the credit in the world for the wonderful formatting of this book.

Last but not least, I want to thank you, the reader, for giving the Book of Eve Series a chance!

If you enjoyed *Eve's Return*, I'd love to hear from you. You can get in touch with me via email: hello@crystalbourque.com.

Don't forget to stop by my website: www.crystalbourque.com for more information on my upcoming projects.

Chapter 1
In the Beginning

*A*s the taxi approached the house, Jordan pressed her nose against the window.

Damn it, she asked herself, *what the hell did they do?* The house had changed in the time she had been away. Eighteen months ago, the paint on the porch was a color called "Spicy Mustard." Jordan remembered how Mom had selected it because it was named after Dad's favorite condiment.

Now the porch and the window trim were white. *Ghost white*, she imagined Mom would say. Jordan thought it removed any warmth the house once had.

A picket fence surrounded the perimeter of the lawn, likely the result of Dad's handiwork. She wondered how long it had taken him to build, and how much money Mom had collected in the swear jar by the time he had finished.

"That'll be forty-nine seventy-five, miss."

Jordan worried her bottom lip through her teeth and turned away from the window. She noticed the taxi driver watching her through the rearview mirror.

"Sure," she said, keeping her tone light. "No problem." Grudgingly, she pulled two tens and four fives from her wallet, and handed them over. "I hope you don't mind change," she told him.

The driver didn't respond as he folded the bills and slipped them into his shirt pocket.

Jordan turned her attention back to her wallet. *Well*, she thought to herself, *aren't you a friendly one?* She dumped the coins into her hand, and began counting.

After paying the rest of the fare, Jordan dragged her weary bones and

9

fraying backpack out of the taxi. Humid air engulfed her, causing her skin to break into a sweat. She plucked at the cotton fabric of her T-shirt, wishing she had remembered how hot summer was here in The Middle of Nowhere.

The taxi squealed away from the curb as Jordan stood on the sidewalk taking inventory. The Honda wasn't in the driveway, and the door to the single-car garage was closed, which made sense since it was three on a weekday afternoon. Which weekday was it? She had absolutely no idea. Time had lost all meaning back in Chicago. It had been her second seven-hour layover, followed by a two-hour flight and a sixteen-hour bus ride.

Her eyes burned every time she blinked. She smelled awful, and she was certain her stomach had half eaten itself.

Regardless, she was thankful that her parents would be at work for a few more hours. It meant she had time to put herself back together, collect her thoughts, calm her nerves. Jordan groaned, thinking about the moment when she would have to face them. She wanted to put it off for as long as possible. She just wished forever was an option.

Jordan hefted her backpack onto her shoulders, and hoped the straps would hold together until she got inside. *You're here and have nowhere else to go*, she told herself firmly. *It's time to face the music.*

It didn't mean she had to like what her parents had done to the house.

A cicada's hum accompanied her walk to the gate. When the latch gave, she dragged her feet up the porch steps, not wanting to see what changes awaited her on the inside.

Jordan closed the front door behind her. A sigh escaped as a blast of cold air from the AC brushed across her skin. Her nose twitched at the faint sour odor. What a relief. Jordan grinned, willing to bet Mom had forgotten about the trash again. It seemed that despite the changes to the exterior, the tenants remained the same.

The lights were on. She frowned.

"Hello?" she called. "I'm home!"

She set her bag down on the tiled floor. Her spine tingled, pleased to be relieved of its weight.

"Hello?" she called out again.

The house was silent.

I guess Mom forgot to turn off the lights too, Jordan thought, using the toe of one shoe to pry her heel out from the other.

Her keys jangled in her hand. To her right, arranged in neat rows, shoes rested on a rack. She caught her reflection in the mirrored door of the closet, and wished that she hadn't. Her auburn hair hung limp around her shoulders. The dark circles beneath her bloodshot eyes stood out, puffy against pale skin. Her shorts and T-shirt were a wrinkled mess.

No wonder the taxi driver had been watching her so carefully. She looked as though she didn't have a penny to her name. *Actually*, she thought, tilting her head to the side, entertaining the idea, *that's absolutely true.*

Uncomfortable with the thought, Jordan tossed her keys into the bowl on the table by the shoe rack. The only other item on the table was a picture frame, which had fallen over. Her hand hovered over it, and she debated before giving in and righting it.

Hello, Parker, she thought to herself. Looking into his eyes, Jordan saw an exact copy of her own. The nasty twinge that usually accompanied thoughts of him caused her to straighten. *Focus on the present*, she told herself.

Jordan walked past the staircase leading up to the second floor. She caught a glimpse of the living room through the open French doors to her other side. Collector plates with pictures of butterflies covered the walls: painted ladies, monarchs, red admirals, clouded yellows. The range of color made the walls look psychedelic. The plates represented every species, but some, especially monarchs, had a greater plate count. There seemed to be twice as many as there had been when she left. It was one of Mom's quirks that Jordan never understood.

In the kitchen, the beige tiles were cold on her bare feet. There were even *more* butterfly plates in here; a little stack of them rested on the breakfast table.

Ignoring the current of goose bumps running up her legs, Jordan headed to the fridge and opened the door. She snorted at the contents: two apples, a jar with a single pickle floating in brine, and a questionable *something* sealed away in a Tupperware container. Jordan shrugged and plucked an apple from its shelf. *Some things definitely haven't changed*, she decided.

A light flashed, drawing her attention. She moved to the marble countertop. The apple crunched as Jordan bit down. She pressed the button for the answering machine, chewed, and swallowed.

"*Good afternoon,*" the message said.

Jordan held the apple poised in front of her mouth. The voice was feminine, but she didn't recognize it.

"*This is a message for Parker Andrews. My name is Sally. I'm calling from*

Capital Collectors. This is our third attempt at reaching you. You have one week to provide us with payment, or we will be forced to repossess your car. Please call us back at—"

Jordan didn't listen to the rest. Little did Sally know, Parker hadn't lived at this address in years. She tried to shrug the call off like it was no big surprise, except that it *was*. Parker was a lot of things. Careless with money wasn't one of them. Selfish bastard.

The phone beeped.

"*Amy*," a hard, feminine voice said.

Jordan rolled her eyes and bit into the apple again. Aunt Lydia, Mom's younger sister.

"*I wanted to check in with you. Brian told me Jordan was due home this week. I still think you should lock her out. She's too proud for her own good. It's a sin for your own child to be so—*"

An automated voice said, "*Message erased.*" Jordan frowned at the phone, her finger still on the button. *Meddling shrew.*

Her hunger sated for the time being, Jordan wanted nothing more than to take a shower. She tossed the apple core into the garbage, and walked back the way she had come. Taking a closer look through the French doors, she was pleased to see that Dad's "No friggin' plates in the living room!" policy was still holding up.

Coming home might not be such a bad thing after all, she thought with a small smile.

Her foot connected with something and sent it spiraling forward. When she went to pick it up, she realized it was the picture of Parker from the table in the front hall.

"How did you get over here?" she muttered. She shook her head, reminded herself how jet-lagged she was.

Jordan put it back before starting up the stairs. She froze on the last step.

A light shone beneath her parents' bedroom door.

She stared at it, didn't know what it meant. *Did Mom and Dad take Lydia's advice to heart?* she wondered. *Would they be angry enough to shut me out? No. They hadn't changed the lock on the house.*

Jordan's grip on the banister tightened, and she came to a decision. This was ridiculous. So she hadn't met the terms of their agreement. They couldn't ignore each other forever.

She took the last step and strode over to their bedroom door.

She knocked and said, "Mom, Dad, we need to talk." No answer. She opened the door before her bravado slipped away.

What she planned to say next came out in a stuttered mess.

Mom was lying in bed—her neck sliced open, head tilted so far back, her forehead almost touching the pillow. Her lips curled back from her teeth, mouth open wide, but silent.

Jordan threw herself backward.

I can't get away, she thought. *Why can't I move fast enough?*

The gray flesh around Mom's neck and ears was stained red...and her chest, and the cream-colored sheets. Red trailed down the side of the mattress, ending in a wide puddle that had seeped into the hardwood floor. A cascade that had since gone dry.

From her position, Jordan could still see the hand reaching out from behind Mom's torso. It belonged to Dad. Contorted fingers made it look as if he had arthritis. His fingernails were black.

Someone had vomited on the carpet. Jordan realized it was her. She was lying curled around the puddle, clutching her stomach in agony. Her throat was raw. Had she been screaming?

This isn't real.

I need help.

A coherent thought. She grabbed hold of it as she gasped for air. *Phone. I need a phone.*

She half crawled, half stumbled to the top of the staircase. Tripping down most of the stairs, she made it through the hallway and into the kitchen. Her fingers could barely manage to grip the phone receiver. She punched in the numbers. Sank to the floor as the receiver rang. Once. Twice. Three times. Four—

"*Nine-one-one, please state the nature of your emergency*," the operator said.

"Help me. Help me please!" Jordan half spoke, half sobbed into the receiver. Her throat constricted. She choked out the next few words. "My parents are dead!"

Chapter 2
Church and Estate

"'Lord, you have been our dwelling place in all generations,'" Jordan read aloud. She stared out into the throng, shifted on the lectern, and removed her hand from the smooth page of the Bible. She wasn't pleased that the funeral was in a church. She didn't see the point.

Statues of saints she couldn't name looked down at her, pious expressions etched on their faces. It made the skin between her shoulder blades itch. The service should have been held at home. Instead, Lydia had railroaded her into having "the religious service her sister would have wanted." Irritation warred with sorrow as Jordan struggled to continue.

She squinted, trying to see the tiny words. Hushed whispers reached her ears, an irritating white noise. *Why did you let that bitch bully you into reading this Psalm?* She swallowed hard. She would continue, but in her own way. She closed the Bible.

"My parents were always there when I needed them," Jordan said. Her throat felt thick, as if she was having an allergic reaction. "They only wanted the best for me..."

And I left them with a broken promise.

From the front pew, a woman said, "Keep going, sweetheart." Jordan thought that she might be a neighbor, but wasn't sure. "You're doing fine."

Jordan glanced down at her hands, and then took another look to see if she recognized the woman. She almost fell off the lectern. Pointed spikes jutted out from the woman's face at awkward angles. Blood trickled from the wounds, dripped off the sharp edge of her jawline, and blended into the dark fabric of her collared shirt.

"Thank you, Jordan," a solemn voice said.

Jordan recoiled when she saw who approached. "Lydia?" she asked.

The fine lines around her aunt's eyes deepened. "Yes," she said, putting her hand on Jordan's shoulder. "Let me help you back to your seat."

"I...I'm not finished," Jordan said. She glanced back at the woman sitting in the front row.

The spikes and blood had disappeared. A normal-looking woman stared back, a hand pressed to her chest. Confused, but not wanting to embarrass herself any further, Jordan allowed Lydia to guide her to her seat before she returned to the lectern.

Jordan settled in as much as the hard wood allowed, and closed her eyes. Lydia started speaking. Behind closed lids, Jordan saw her mother. Crusted blood stained the flesh around her neck. Jordan blinked furiously to try and shake the image. She decided it was probably best to listen instead of letting her mind wander.

"Parker wished for me to express his sorrow," Lydia was saying. Her lips were painted red, like a frame for her words. Unshed tears glistened in the corners of her eyes. "Unfortunately, he was unable to get time off from his band's tour to be here today. He sends his love, and prayers."

Isn't that interesting, Jordan thought, crossing her arms in front of her chest. Parker hadn't answered any of the messages she had left, nor any of the half-dozen e-mails. Yet Lydia had no trouble making contact with him. Jordan wanted to be angry, but all she felt was misery. His parents were dead, and he still refused to come home.

Jordan felt someone tap her shoulder. "Excuse me?"

Jordan turned her head to see a young woman with bleach-blonde hair and cleavage that rivaled a porn star's.

"So, like, was that chick joking?" the woman asked, without waiting for a response. "Parker Andrews is going to make an appearance at the end, right?"

Jordan forced herself to take a breath. How many of these unknown faces were just pretending to attend her parents' funeral? Groupies, looking for the chance to snag an autograph? Jordan debated punching the woman in the face.

"*What's wrong with you?*" Jordan hissed instead. She wanted to say more, but there was movement all around. Lydia had finished speaking. The priest asked everyone to rise.

Jordan gave the blonde woman a look of disgust before standing up and wobbling down the aisle on the kitten heels she had thought were appropriate enough for the service. She needed a moment to herself. Maybe some fresh air.

As she left the church, a flash nearly blinded her. Another step forward and she was surrounded. Cameras went off around her and people shouted her name. Asking if Parker would show up for the reception. How Parker was handling the death of his parents. When Parker would start working on his next album.

Keeping her head down and fists clenched to her sides, Jordan pushed through the crowd of paparazzi and reporters. They didn't follow. There were other guests. She knew several of them would be more than willing to provide the comments that the media was looking for.

Jordan walked around the stone building until the roar of voices faded, then disappeared. She pulled her cell phone from the pocket of her blazer, and punched in Sheriff Tully's number.

"Someone leaked the information," she snapped when he answered.

Tully's voice was even more nasal over the phone than it was in person. "What?"

She stepped out of the building's shade, into the sun. Took a breath. "Sorry, I know it's not your fault." She lifted a hand to shield her eyes against the glare before stepping back. "You were right. I should have accepted the duty officers you offered. It's like a circus down here."

"I'll get a couple down there right now," Tully said. He put her on hold without another word.

"Thanks," Jordan said when he returned. She ran a hand over her face. "How are you holding up? I know how much Dad meant to you."

"I'm all right. He was a good friend," Tully said. She could hear the slight tremor in his voice. "I wish I could be there."

"So do I."

Tully cleared his throat before speaking again. "In any case, I'm glad I can help, at least in some small way. Which reminds me," he said with a sigh. "I should really wait until tomorrow to tell you this, but I know you. You'd want to know this right away…" He paused. Jordan held her breath, waiting. "It looks like the case might be spinning in a completely different direction," he finally said. "I'm really sorry, but I'm going to have to ask you to come back down to the station again."

Jordan's body collapsed against the side of the building. They were going to make her relive that night again and again. The silent scream. The staring eyes, so intently focused on *something*, but seeing nothing. It made her skin crawl.

It had been only a week since she had found their bodies. Since then,

Tully kept in regular contact with her. Asking if any other details came to mind. If anyone she knew held a grudge. A disgruntled employee. A neighbor. Family members. He forced her to address every angle. To assess everyone she had ever known. Including her parents themselves. Did they have a secret life no one knew about? Was it possible her father was having an affair? Did her mother threaten to leave him now that they had an empty nest?

The process horrified Jordan. She wasn't much help. Everyone became a suspect, and she was left feeling much as she did now. Lost in a confusing mess of emotions.

"Jordan?"

"Sure, sure," she mumbled into the receiver. "I'll stop by the station tomorrow."

"Thank you," Tully said. "By the way," he continued in a lighter tone. It sounded slightly forced, but Jordan appreciated the effort. "I know you've been staying with Lydia. The two of you get along about as well as a terrier and a rat. Why don't you stay with me and Beatrice until you figure things out?"

Jordan scratched the side of her nose but it didn't distract her from smiling. The movement felt foreign and inappropriate. "You're the best," she said, "but I can't impose on you like that."

"It's an open offer," Tully told her. "Let me know if you change your mind."

After ending the call, Jordan waited until the officers arrived before heading back inside. The service was over, so she didn't waste time pushing past guests as she reentered the sanctuary. She had an inexplicable need to reach the table. To touch the urn containing her parents' ashes. Before she could take another step, someone lifted it.

"No!" Jordan shouted.

More than a dozen pairs of eyes turned to stare at her.

Jordan cared only about Lydia, who stood in front of the table with the urn between her hands. Lydia was the first to break the silence.

"There you are," she said, her lips curved upward in a way that didn't affect any other part of her face. Movement broke out around them as they reached each other. Lydia leaned forward. "Why did you leave?" she hissed. "You missed Communion."

It took Jordan a moment to focus past Lydia's red lips and hear the words. "I don't take Communion," she said.

Lydia's nostrils flared. "What are you talking about?"

Jordan decided to avoid the question. "I needed a little air," she said. "The media was outside and—"

"The media?" Lydia's eyes widened. "I told you we would need security."

"I called Tully," Jordan said. Her lower lip trembled. She took a breath. "I handled it."

"A little late, don't you—"

"I really would like to be the one to carry it out," she interrupted. "The urn," she added, pointing to it.

"Oh," Lydia said. "Very well."

When the urn transferred to Jordan, the angle of the floor shifted. She had one clear thought: *It's so strange both Mom and Dad can fit inside something so tiny.*

*****

"Jordan," Dad had said. "We need to talk."

Jordan swiveled around in her desk chair to find both parents standing in her bedroom doorway like a two-headed monster. "I'm going," she told them. "I've already booked the flight."

Together, they entered her room and sat on the edge of her bed. Dad leaned forward, elbows on his knees. "Where is this coming from?" he asked. "You've worked so hard. Why can't this wait until after you graduate?"

"I need a break," Jordan said, letting her head fall back against the chair. "It's just a year."

"Is this about Owen?" Mom asked. "It must be." She turned to Dad, as if he could give her the answer.

"No!" Jordan lied. "Please leave him out of this."

"A year, and then what?" Dad asked.

"I don't know," Jordan murmured.

"Yes, you do." Dad's voice rumbled, a clear warning sign that she wasn't going to like what he said next. "You're going to go back to college. You're going to graduate."

Jordan didn't know what to say.

"One year," Mom said, holding up a finger to illustrate. "Do we have a deal?"

*****

Jordan took a deep breath. She was standing inside the church with her hands wrapped around something heavy and cold. The urn. She moved to stand in the lobby. She found it nearly impossible to focus on anything anyone said. As people approached her with their condolences, she felt as if she was stuck inside a giant humming beehive.

"I'm so sorry for your loss," someone said on their way out the door.

"It was terrible, what happened. So terrible."

"Your mother was one of the kindest people I knew," an elderly gentleman told her as he was leaving. "She didn't deserve this. Neither of them did."

"I'm bringing cake!"

"They'll catch whoever did it," another woman told her. "They always do."

"What's your address again?"

"Chocolate cake. You like chocolate, right?"

The words floated around Jordan as people exited the church. She wanted to respond, to acknowledge that she had at least heard what was said, but it felt safer to stand there and say nothing.

"Let me give you a lift," someone said.

Jordan turned to see Lydia walking toward her. A few people stood near the entrance, watching. Jordan's grip on the urn tightened. *What would they do, Lydia*, she thought, *if I smeared your lipstick all over your face?*

"Sure," she said instead.

Lydia chattered all the way across the parking lot. "Did you know there's this new exhibit opening in Rolling River?" she asked. "Supposedly it's a document, some sort of lost testament, or something of that nature. I can't quite remember."

"Uh-huh," Jordan replied.

"I think we should go and see it together," Lydia rattled on. "It would be a great little road trip, just us girls. It might also help to encourage you to take Communion again. What do you think?"

Jordan gave her aunt a blank stare and thought, *You don't know me at all, do you?*

Once they were in the car, Jordan relaxed into the seat. The urn rested against her stomach. Her hands kept it from tipping in her lap.

"I'm curious," she said, as she watched Lydia start the engine. "What exactly prevented Parker from canceling the rest of the tour to make it to his parents' funeral?"

"I'm not sure," Lydia said with a toss of her head. "Maybe Owen convinced him to finish. They don't have many shows left." Her hand was in her hair fluffing the curls back into place. "Three. Four maybe? Or was it two? Oh, I don't remember. You really should have made the effort to talk to him yourself."

"I did," Jordan said through clenched teeth. "And we both know that Owen would have forced Parker to cancel."

"Have you heard from Owen, then?" Lydia asked, pulling out of the parking lot and into traffic.

Jordan hunched her shoulders and turned to stare out the window. "No," she said.

Lydia let out a grating laugh. "Oh, dear. Neither have I." She went silent for a moment as she made a left-hand turn. "Parker told me he would pass the news along after the show last night." She gave Jordan's shoulder a little pat. "Owen's practically family," she muttered through a sharp right. "Whatever happened between you two anyway?"

"Nothing," Jordan said with a shrug.

"Never mind Owen, what happened between the three of you?" Lydia pressed on. "There was a time when you were like little musketeers, never out of each other's sight."

A muscle in Jordan's jaw twitched. She didn't respond. She wasn't going to, but when Lydia's gaze continued to fall on her instead of the road, she gave in with a sigh.

"We grew up," she said in a quiet voice.

When they pulled into the driveway of the house, Lydia took the keys from the ignition and shifted in her seat so that she faced Jordan. "There's no need to be so upset with me," she said. "Parker misses you, he said as much, but he has obligations that he just can't change at the drop of a hat."

"You actually believe that bullshit?" Jordan snapped. She knew she should shut her mouth, but the words kept coming. "Why do you always defend him? He's twenty-three years old, not four. You don't baby *me*, and Parker and I are the same damn age." She pulled the urn in tight. "*I'm* here. *I'm* his sister. Where the fuck is *he*?"

Lydia pursed her lips. They wriggled as if she was trying to control her reaction. It didn't work. "I'm not sure if you noticed," she began, "but no one at that funeral was there for you."

Jordan's mouth opened slightly before she caught herself and closed it.

"Tell me," Lydia said, a small smile flitting over her painted mouth. "Where are your friends when you need them the most?"

"They're here," Jordan said; her tone didn't do much to convince even herself.

"Oh, please. You don't have any," Lydia told her. "And the ones you did have, you've completely shut out of your life. You think you grew up?" She paused to laugh. "No. Parker and Owen were the ones who grew up. They left *you* behind."

Without another word, Lydia grabbed her purse, got out of the car. The closing door was as effective as a slap across the face.

Chapter 3
The Letter

Jordan felt flushed. The *clack, clack, clack* of Lydia's red pumps against the pavement did nothing to calm her. She slumped in the seat. That woman sure knew how to go straight for the kill.

Jordan blinked at the pressure building behind her eyes. *Don't do it*, she thought. *Feeling sorry for yourself won't bring anyone back.*

Jordan peered at the house through the windshield. It was time to tackle a more immediate problem. Since finding her parents, she hadn't been able to set foot back inside.

It's all yours now, she reminded herself. *The house and everything in it, so you had better figure something out.* It was still difficult for her to process, even though the lawyer had informed her days ago; it hadn't been the only thing he had said.

Jordan didn't know what to do. While the house contained all that was left of her parents, it was also a stockroom full of nightmares.

Flicking the door latch, Jordan got out of the car, still clutching the urn. *Time to get this over with*, she thought. She stumbled up the driveway, through the gate, and up the front steps. The door opened before her hand touched the knob.

"Where have you been hiding?" It was the elderly gentleman who had spoken to her at the church. "Everyone's wondering where you want to put the food."

Jordan couldn't enjoy the fact that at least one person had wondered where she was, nor did she have time to settle into being in the house again. She only had time to put the urn down on the entryway table and turn the picture of Parker facedown before she was ushered past.

"Oh, there you are!" a voice called.

A dozen women, whose features blended into each other, faced Jordan with trays of food.

"The kitchen," she blurted out, placing a hand on her forehead. "Put it all in the kitchen. Thank you," she forced herself to say as she took a tray from a young woman. It was only when the woman walked away that Jordan recognized her. One of Mom's coworkers. *Emily?* she thought. *No, Erin. Or was it Emma?* Jordan added the deviled eggs to the breakfast table with the rest of the casseroles, tiny sandwiches, and canapés.

Jordan wove her fingers together, gripped them tightly. She couldn't take it any longer. She walked away from the table before she gave in to the urge to throw her guests' good intentions back at their heads.

She wandered out of the kitchen to find Mom's coworker staring up at the collection of plates covering the wall beside the entrance to the living room. Jordan watched as the woman's hand reached toward one.

"Can I help you?" Jordan asked, stepping in front of the woman, blocking her just as her fingertips brushed the edge of the ceramic. The staircase loomed menacingly in Jordan's peripheral vision.

"Your mother promised me one of her monarch plates," the coworker said. She started reaching out again. "I thought, since I'm here..." she trailed off, eyes still locked on her target.

"I'm sorry," Jordan said, "you can't have it. I've decided to keep them all."

Where was this coming from? She hated Mom's plates.

"There are more than a hundred," the woman said with a smile. "Surely you won't miss one." When the coworker continued to try and stretch her arm around Jordan's body, Jordan pushed it back down.

"I don't care what Mom told you. I'm keeping all of the plates." Jordan thought the coworker was going to stand her ground, but she gave in, walking toward the living room with a haughty toss of her head.

Taking a moment, Jordan focused her gaze on the hardwood floor before she felt like she could move into the living room. When she did, she sat down in Dad's chair, back straight, hands folded in her lap, legs crossed at the ankles. Just like Mom had taught her.

The scent of Dad's cologne enveloped her. She wished it was his arms instead, closing her eyes to hide her tears. Her guests continued to move around her, as if they were part of some sort of dance that she hadn't been invited to, but had shown up anyway.

"Listen." A hand came down on her shoulder.

Jordan turned her head and blinked up at Lydia.

"I wanted to let you know that I'm heading out now," Lydia said, her tone brisk. "I suppose you'll be staying with me one more night? Should I expect to see you back at my place later this evening?"

"Yeah," Jordan said into the empty room. She wished she had paid more attention as people left. "Sure."

"Great," Lydia said, tugging at the hem of her shirt. She cleared her throat. "You should sell," she said. "The house, I mean."

Jordan looked up to see Lydia glance around the room. Words jammed in her throat as suspicion clutched at her chest.

"I know they left you with nothing else," Lydia said. "They've been broke for years. Do yourself a favor. Sell it." Her hand fluttered, gesturing to several pieces in the room.

"It's none of your business whether I sell or keep the house," Jordan managed to say. The lawyer had told her she was the only person privy to that piece of information. Jordan rose to her feet. "I'll be by later to collect my things. I'll be staying with Tully tonight."

Lydia arched a well-manicured brow. Then she was gone, and Jordan was alone.

It was over. The dreadful buildup, the awkward questions, the redundant sympathy and misdirected pity. It was a relief, but she knew if she let herself relax, even for a moment, she wouldn't make it out of the house in one piece. *Keep busy*, she told herself. *Keep moving.*

I can live here, she thought. *There's nothing to be afraid of. I can do it.*

Leg muscles clenched midstep. Jordan's breath came in gasps as she realized what she had been about to do. Lost in her thoughts, she had intended to go upstairs for some extra clothes. Ones that she hadn't worn out over the past year and a half. Fingers gripped the banister, but her feet refused to make the first move. Jordan forced herself to look up. The steps seemed impossible, as if they had grown into the height of a mountain in one afternoon.

To get to her things, she would need to pass her parents' room; it sent her gag reflex springing into action.

"Screw it," she muttered, turning away. "I'll try again later."

A flutter of movement off to her right caught her attention. She was certain all the guests had left. "Hello?" she called. A shadow lengthened in the living room. Putting on a brave face, she headed over. "Sorry, I didn't realize…" But the room was empty. "Is anyone here?" she yelled. Her question went unanswered.

Jordan wrapped her arms around herself and tried to suppress the urge to run from the house. Her mind was playing tricks on her. That was all. She took a breath, forced herself to walk into the kitchen and take out a garbage bag from under the sink. She tossed all the leftover food inside. CorningWare and all.

She dragged the bag to the curb, feeling all the while like she was being watched. Needing a distraction from the hairs rising on the back of her neck, Jordan mulled over what Lydia had said. *There's no way in hell I can sell the house*, she thought. *It's all I have left of Mom and Dad.* Guilt hit Jordan like a sucker punch to the stomach. She shoved the feeling aside and walked back into the kitchen. *In any case, Lydia can kiss my ass. Lipstick optional.*

What I do need to do, Jordan thought, stopping in front of the cutlery drawer, *is find a little overhead to tide me over until I can find a job.*

Her hand hovered over the handle of the drawer. It felt odd to be standing there, hoping for enough cash to get her to the end of the week, when her parents weren't even buried yet. Thinking about what they would have thought if they knew her predicament made her feel ill.

The house and everything in it is yours, she reminded herself. It still took her a moment to open the drawer and lift out the cutlery tray. She reached in, found what she was looking for. It didn't take long to do the math.

"Twenty dollars?" Disappointed, she tossed the bills down on the table, and pulled out a chair. A piece of paper spun out with it. Jordan picked it up, then had to sit down.

It wasn't a piece of paper. It was an envelope, addressed to her parents. Parker had sent it. She set it down on the table. The urge to open it was irresistible, yet she made herself wait. Was it inappropriate to open mail if the recipients were deceased? *Oh, go on*, she told herself. *Who's going to know?*

Jordan grabbed the letter, tore it open, and slid the single page from the envelope. Parker's familiar scrawl was bold against the stark white paper. He always had a thing for writing with black marker. She started reading.

Mom & Dad,

Sorry. I can't help you out this time. I won't. It's not fair for you to use guilt as your bargaining chip. You both have a problem. I can only hope one day

you can accept that. For now, J just
hope you understand.

"What the..." Jordan trailed off. She had to reread the words to make sure she had understood them correctly. *Parker was sending Mom and Dad money?* It seemed that way, but it wasn't possible. Mom and Dad barely spoke to him. Other than the picture in the entryway, you wouldn't have even known they had a son.

There was more.

Can you let Jordan know J've been
trying to get in touch with her? J've been
sending her e-mails, but they keep
bouncing back. Let her know J have
something for her.

All my love,
Parker

"What does he want?" Jordan asked the letter. She put it down on the table. Drummed her fingers against the wood. They hadn't talked in months, although now it seemed like wrong e-mail addresses had been the culprit. "Damn it," she growled. He hadn't been ignoring her after all.

She snatched the envelope from the table. Flipped it over. There it was. The return address, Rolling River.

Really? Jordan thought, scanning the address again to make sure she read it correctly. Parker was supposed to be on tour. The band only stopped in Rolling River when they were recording. It was a four-hour drive away. Tops.

"What's going on?" she wondered aloud.

Her lips formed a firm line as she made her decision. Screw playing phone tag. Screw deranged aunts. She would go to Parker. Maybe he could even get her a job on tour. The more she thought about it, the better the idea seemed. There was nothing left for her here. For now.

Jordan slid the letter back in the envelope, folded it, and shoved it into her back pocket. She wrinkled her nose as she stuck the bills in another. The kitchen smelled sour, like milk that had been left out for too long. She had just taken out the garbage, so maybe it was just the scent lingering in the air. She waved her hand in front of her face, worrying her bottom lip between her teeth. She was going to need more cash.

There were only a few other places where Mom typically hid bills. *That stupid slut better have left some money somewhere*, Jordan thought. She opened the ceramic cookie jar on the counter. Nothing. She threw the lid across the room, barely heard it shatter against the wall. One more place to try, and then she would tear the house apart. Her skin felt tight over her bones.

She sang to herself like a nursery rhyme, "*I'm going to rip, rip, rip, them out. Rip your insides out.*" Jordan froze with her hand on the cabinet door beneath the sink. *What's going on?* she wondered. *Where had those terrible thoughts come from?* She almost choked on the putrid smell.

Jordan rose, looking around the kitchen. Her body tensed. *Was that a creak on the stairs?* Her vision narrowed as she turned back to the sink and opened the door. *Your mind's playing tricks on you again*, she told herself. *Get a grip. Focus. There's no one here but you.*

Jordan reached under the sink for the empty box of dishwasher detergent. She was disappointed when her fingers discovered it was in fact empty, but was more concerned about still feeling like she was being watched. The sensation crawled its way up her back, sinking its talons through her rib cage. Squeezing her heart.

She turned around slowly. The box fell to the floor with a clatter.

A *thing* was staring at her. It came up to her knees, but Jordan couldn't define whether it was human, animal, or a sick combination of both. Loose skin hung around its frame, as if it were an article of clothing that was too big for its body. It had a round head, and squat body with black eyes that didn't reflect any light. One was much bigger than the other; Jordan gagged when she realized it was bulging out from its socket.

The thing stared at her. It tapped long claws on the tiles. *Click. Click. Click.* Thick yellow saliva dripped from its lower lip, onto its chest. It shone beneath the light like a glaze.

Jordan became aware that she was licking her lips. She wanted nothing more than to kill something. Rip it apart with her claws. Long claws that she loved to sharpen on rocks. She pressed her back up hard against the marble. The creature didn't move. It simply continued to tap its nails. A horrible understanding washed over her.

Her thoughts were not her own.

"W-what do you want?" she shouted, not knowing what else to do.

The creature replied by launching itself at her. Jordan's fingertips scampered across the length of counter, reaching for the knife holder. It was too late; there wasn't time.

Jordan squeezed her eyes shut against the impact. It never came.

She slowly opened her eyes. The creature had vanished. There was no one else in the kitchen.

"What the hell *was* that?" she shouted. The wobbling pitch did nothing to help calm her rattled nerves.

She tried to assess and compare the hallucination to the one she had earlier in the day. There was nothing different as far as she could tell. They had both felt so real. She took a few deep breaths. Forced herself to acknowledge the fact that she had been through a traumatic experience. That it was bound to take time to feel like she was back to normal.

"You are going to see Parker," she reminded herself. Her voice was steadier now, and the sound was comforting in the otherwise silent house. "You are going to find out what he wants to talk to you about." Feeling calmer, she strode from the kitchen. "And," she said as she rushed past the stairs to the front door, "you are going to take a break from this house, until you are ready to come back."

As she bent down to slip on her shoes, something silver caught her eye. Whatever the object was, it was mostly hidden in the toe of Dad's shoe. Curious now, she reached in and pulled it out. It was a set of keys.

How could I forget? A slow smile spread across her face.

She couldn't quite leave just yet. There was one thing she couldn't leave behind.

Chapter 4
Joyride

Jordan used the keys to unlock the garage door and stepped inside. "Hello, gorgeous," she murmured. She let her hand rest on the cloth covering the old beauty. It didn't for a moment seem the least bit silly, greeting her old friend. She yanked the cloth, drawing it to the floor. The fading sunlight haloed the floating dust, but Jordan only had eyes for the car.

Dad's 1965 Dynasty Green Mustang Fastback 2x2 gleamed. Jordan ran her fingertips along the hood, saying, "It's good to see you again." Out of habit, she checked the tires. The chrome. The Luxury Black leather interior. The bumper, and the engine. Everything looked exactly as she remembered. Pristine. Dad really loved this car; hadn't stopped. Even after she left.

The Mustang was finicky, always had been. It was Jordan's favorite thing about her. Dad had spent hours with Jordan, going over what made the old girl tick. She knew her way around the engine better than her own room. A 289-cubic-inch V-8, with 225 horses.

It was hers now.

She made her way to the back of the garage where Dad kept his tools. There were at least fifty mason jars lining one of the shelves. They contained different-size nails, screws, bolts, washers, and other various knickknacks.

"Which one are you?" she asked before she picked up a jar and unscrewed the lid. Peered beneath it. Nothing. She tried another jar. Still nothing. She knew Dad changed the location of the Mustang's key more often than he changed his socks. He used to write it down on a piece of paper, slip it in with her lunch, and expect her to dispose of it appropriately. The days she would find that paper were the days she loved most.

Worried that she would have to open every jar, Jordan was surprised on the fourth guess, when she found what she was looking for. Taped to the underside of the lid was a silver key. Curling her fingers around it, she grinned, feeling like a kid again. The smile faded as the urge to reminisce with Dad overwhelmed her.

How do I reminisce with ash?

She did her best to ignore the thought and inserted the key into the door. Turned it slightly to the right. She brought it back to the left, before turning it the rest of the way in the opposite direction. She slammed her hip against the door, then pulled on the handle. It opened with a slight *pop*. The scent of well-worn leather, in combination with Dad's cologne and the faint spearmint of his aftershave, greeted her with unexpected force.

Jordan managed to get into the driver's seat as she remembered: *Dad smiling at me as I learned to ride a bike. Dad giving me the last pancake at breakfast. Dad waving good-bye after dropping me off at college. The crestfallen look on his face when I announced I was taking time off before my final year...*

Not now, she told herself, blinking her vision clear. *You can fall apart later.* She took a deep breath.

"It's just you and me," Jordan told the Mustang. She buckled herself in. "Let's go." She turned the key in the ignition and ran her palm over the steering wheel.

The old girl stuttered and died.

*****

"Move over," Jordan had said, forcing Parker to slide over to the passenger side. "You're gonna make her choke."

Parker rolled his eyes and ruffled her hair as she got behind the wheel. Jordan smacked his hand away, but she caught his grin and knew he hadn't taken her jibe the wrong way. He was so touchy lately. Conversations that used to be familiar ground were stilted, and occasionally off-limits. A casual comment could cause him to ignore her for hours. It was like walking over coals while someone fanned the flames.

"You sure your Dad won't mind, Jo?" Owen asked from the backseat.

Jordan caught a faint whiff of shampoo and cologne as he leaned forward. A combination of all things she associated with masculinity. The outdoors, spice, sandalwood. Only, on Owen, it made her stomach flutter, hands sweat, and thoughts blur.

Jordan wiped her palms against her jeans before she wiggled the key in the ignition. "Dad and Mom are gone for the weekend," she told Owen. "They won't even know we took her out."

"Lucky," Owen said, leaning back. Jordan watched him rest his arm on the portable amp on the seat beside him through the rearview mirror. "Madison caught me on the way out. I had to accept dish duty and garbage run in return for her silence."

"I thought she had already gone back to boarding school," Jordan said.

"Nope," Owen replied. "I've still got one more week with the squirt." His tone belied his words, betraying how fond he really was of her.

"Squirt? Are you kidding?" Parker exclaimed. "She's turned into one of the hottest..." He trailed off, clearing his throat. "What I mean to say is that little sisters are such a drag."

Jordan laughed at the glare Owen gave her brother in the rearview mirror. "Nice try," she told Parker. "You're only three minutes older than me. It doesn't count."

"Well, since you're so smart, get this piece of junk moving," he replied, putting on his seat belt. "They're expecting us to start at nine."

"Relax," Jordan said. "I told you, you can't rush her. She won't start otherwise."

"It's a car, Jordan," Parker said, gesturing to the vehicle. "I don't get it. You and Dad spend all your free time with this piece of junk, and you still can't get it to start properly?"

There it was. The sudden shift in his mood. Teasing her one minute, snapping at her over the strangest things in the next. It made her feel so lost. She used to know everything he was thinking.

"If you spent more time with Dad instead of in Owen's garage," Jordan began, wiggling the key again, a little harder than necessary, "maybe you'd understand."

"We're working on our *sound*," Parker said, regarding her with narrowed eyes. His tone was dark. "It takes time to develop. Not to mention hours and hours of patience, and don't even get me started on the practice!"

"All right, all right," Owen said. He leaned forward again to give Jordan a smacking kiss on the cheek. He turned and gave Parker one as well. "There. All better. Can we please get going before the neighbors see us?"

It took a moment for Jordan's thoughts to clear. Her cheek still felt warm where he had pressed his lips against her skin. She fought against the urge to touch the spot. If she had turned her head just a fraction more toward him...

She had already decided that tonight was the night she told Owen how she felt, how she had always felt about him. With the summer coming to an end, and college starting in the fall, she knew she didn't have much time left.

Willing to bide her time, Jordan gave Parker her patented apologetic glance. He gave her a raised brow in return, which meant *I forgive you*. She winked, then turned the key. The Mustang roared to life. The boys cheered, making her laugh as they congratulated her ingenuity. As soon as they were clear, she waited for Parker to close the garage door before heading down their street and turning onto the highway.

"How do I get there?" she asked. The highway wasn't really much of one; it was more a dirt road with a "suggested" speed limit.

"It's not that far," Owen said. "Keep going. I'll let you know which turns to make. Here." A CD appeared over her shoulder.

"Tainted Dilemma?" she asked, popping it in the player she had just helped Dad install.

"Like you even have to ask," Owen said. Heavy drums blasted over the speakers, the intro to "Dying Debts." A few bars later, Celestia, the lead singer, came in with the lyrics. "I'd give anything to bask in her presence for an hour." He sighed. "Man, she's got a sweet, sweet voice."

"Sweet rack too," Parker added. "You mind turning it down, though? We need to review our game plan."

Jordan listened as the boys discussed the last-minute changes Parker wanted to make to their set. Owen would cut in every so often with a "left" or "right." She saw the tents and bonfire before they did. The field party was already well under way.

She pulled into the grass beside some other cars, feeling Parker's excitement as if it were her own. She wanted them to do well.

"Hey," she said, grabbing Parker's hand as Owen got out of the car. "I can't wait to hear you guys play."

Parker put his other hand over hers. Gave it a squeeze. "Your opinion is the only one I really care about, you know?"

"Yeah," Jordan said, releasing him. "I know."

Parker looked down and picked at the skin around his thumbnail. "It's going to be really weird in the fall without you and Owen."

"You still have time to accept," Jordan said. "Come with us."

"We've *never* been apart from each other for more than a day," Parker said, his voice quiet. He lifted his head to look out the window. "I've always wondered if I'd still feel whole without you around. I guess it's time to find out, huh?"

Before Jordan could say anything, Parker turned to look at her, his features rearranged in a bright smile. "Listen to me," he said tugging gently at the ends of her hair. The gesture usually made her smile, but not this time. "I'm getting crazy in my old age."

"Hurry up," Owen called. "I want to find out where we can set up."

Jordan and Parker got out of the Mustang and followed Owen through the sizable crowd. Having to push her way through in some places, she wasn't surprised when a girl with long blonde hair backed up into her.

"Oh gosh, I'm so sorry." The girl's hair whipped around as she turned. Her dimples flashed as her green eyes widened. "Jo!" she squealed, pulling Jordan into a fierce hug.

"Hey, Madison," she said, then lowered her voice. "Heads up. Owen's right behind me."

"Darn it," Madison hissed. She released Jordan to face her brother.

Owen scowled at her. "What are you doing here, squirt?" he asked. "Why didn't you tell me what you were up to instead of blackmailing me?"

"I didn't want to take the chance that you'd stop me from coming," Madison told him.

"Since when—"

"Now, Owen," Parker cut in, nudging him aside so that he could stand in front of Madison. "There's no reason to get upset. We snuck out plenty of times when we were sixteen."

Madison's dimples flashed again. What Parker had said in the car was true. In the year that she had been gone, she had filled out in all the places Jordan was still waiting on. "I knew you guys would draw a huge crowd; I didn't think we would run into each other," she said. Her cheeks flushed, giving her a delicate pink glow. "I really wanted to watch you guys play."

"Come on, Maddie," Owen said. "You gotta give me a little more credit." He reached out and tugged on the ends of her hair. Jordan grinned, knowing it was his way of telling her he wasn't really upset. "Nice job, buttering me up with a compliment like that."

Madison beamed. "I thought so too!"

"You can stay, but I'm giving you your chores back," he told her.

Madison made a face. "You know I wouldn't have really let you do them," she said. "I'm a softy when it comes to you."

"Yeah, yeah," Owen said. "Same here, kid."

Parker leaned forward, this time pushing Jordan out of the way to gain Madison's attention. "Listen," he said his tone serious, "if you need anything, if anyone bothers you, you let me know."

Jordan choked back a laugh and ended up coughing. Owen didn't seem to notice. He was too busy glaring at Parker's back.

"Why thank you, but I'm totally safe," Madison said. "It's not like I'd show up here alone. How lame would that be?" As if to help prove her point, someone called out her name. "And there's my cue. I'll see you tomorrow?"

"Be good," Owen said, his voice stern.

"Always." Madison reached for Owen, giving him a peck on the cheek. "Love you. Knock 'em dead."

When she turned to leave, Parker grabbed her arm. Jordan felt Owen stiffen and heard him inhale sharply. "After the first set, come find me," Parker told her. He toyed with her hand, tapping his fingers along her skin. "I'd like to hear what you think."

Madison looked at Jordan who rolled her eyes. "Sure," she said with a husky laugh. She gave a quick wave and disappeared into the crowd.

"What the hell was *that*?" Owen rounded on Parker.

"Nothing, man. Relax," he put a hand on Owen's shoulder and squeezed. "You know I meant nothing by it."

Jordan felt like she was missing something, but figured it was because she wasn't a boy and didn't understand Man Code. She cleared her throat. "Do you guys need help setting up?"

"Naw, we got this," Parker said. "Don't we, Owen?"

"Yeah," Owen mumbled. "Sure."

Jordan hung back as Parker went to the Mustang to get the amp and microphones. When he returned, Owen had found out they would set up near the fire pit. She could see people had already begun to gather around a lone tree in the middle of the field. As Parker worked on connecting the equipment to a generator, Owen joined him, guitar in hand.

Feeling a little out of her element, Jordan headed toward the tree and sat down with her back against its trunk. She was a little outside the perimeter of the flames, but it gave her a better view. Looking around, she realized she knew many of the faces from school, but she wasn't interested in making conversation. She only had eyes for the stage. Owen was tuning his guitar now. His hair, always just a little too long, hung down in front of his angular face.

This is it, she thought to herself, her hands twisting together in her lap. *Tonight's the night.*

When they had finished setting up, Parker said something to Owen which made him smile before he nodded his head a few times, feeling the rhythm before strumming out a chord on the guitar. Jordan's heart swelled as they began to sing. The crowd quieted, attention drawn to the pitch-perfect harmony, notes so tightly intertwined they sounded like one voice instead of two.

The song was a slow one, to draw in the crowd. It worked. There was a beat of silence as the last chord faded away. Roaring applause broke the spell; wide grins unfolded on both musicians' faces. Jordan cheered with everyone else, and when she caught Parker's eye, he blew a kiss into the crowd.

That song was for you.

They launched into the next few songs, each one adding to the energy of the next until all conversation had ceased and most people were on their feet. Jordan watched Parker and Owen through the swaying bodies. It felt strange to know she was watching the beginning of something that didn't include her. She thought back to what Parker had said in the car, and wondered to herself, *Will I feel whole when we are apart?*

After the first set, Parker and Owen helped themselves to a couple of drinks as the crowd surged toward them. Several girls Jordan didn't recognize had Owen surrounded. She felt her heart clench, then release when he looked through them to give her a brief wave. A fresh surge of nerves drenched her palms in sweat. Desperate to distract herself, she looked for her brother. Parker was talking to a group of people, excitement animating his face and gestures. He was so happy, she could feel it from where she sat.

The second set was even better than the first. People were up and dancing now. The steady, rhythmic riff Owen strummed on the guitar was enough to set the stiffest toes tapping. Parker had the crowd in the palm of his hands; his voice was the right combination of smooth and edgy. The words were poetic, accompanied by a catchy hook. Her boys really had something. She had never felt so proud.

At the end of their last set, Parker headed straight back into the crowd, but Owen sought her out. She moved over to give him room to sit, and clenched her teeth against the giddy laughter bubbling in the back of her throat.

"What did you think, Jo?" Owen asked. His green eyes were serious. "I screwed up the chord progression on the last song but otherwise, I don't think we crashed and burned."

Jordan swallowed. "You were amazing," she said. Her head felt light, and her breath came in short gasps. "I understand now. All that time you've put into this..." She trailed off, shaking her head. "You were amazing," she repeated, unable to find the right word.

Owen was sitting so close to her, she could see the flecks of gold in his green eyes. Her back pressed harder against the tree's bark, but she could barely feel it against his warmth.

It's time, Jordan decided. "I—I... can't..." she began, then thought, *Don't you dare back down now*. She leaned forward, and pressed her lips against his.

To her surprise and delight, Owen responded in kind, tangling his fingers in her hair as he pulled her closer. A seed of warmth started in her belly, and grew until every inch of her body hummed from his touch. His lips were softer than she had imagined.

"That was unexpected," he murmured.

"I have no problem with nudity!" Parker's voice rang out from the other side of the fire. "If given the option, I'd choose to be naked all the time!"

Owen laughed. Jordan wasn't as amused, feeling like her moment was ruined. "Looks like he's had a few shots," Owen said. He shook his head, and the both of them watched Parker tug off his shirt.

"I am a fire god!" Parker shouted, swinging his arms in a wide arc to gesture to the flames. "Watch me leap!"

"Not good," Jordan said, getting to her feet.

"I'll help," Owen said, following her lead. "I think it's time we headed back anyway."

They reached Parker as he tripped over his own foot and crumpled into a heap on the ground.

"You can be a fire god another night," Jordan said as she reached down to help her brother to his feet. "Right now, it's time for bed."

"What are you talking about?" Parker asked, bringing his face much too close to hers. His breath reeked of Jim Beam and cigarettes.

"I'm taking you home," Jordan said, keeping as much distance as she could without dropping him. "It's almost three."

"Where's Owen?" Parker's grip on her arm got tighter as he looked at the faces around the fire. "Where is he?"

"I'm right here, buddy," Owen said, slipping his arm around Parker's waist. "There you go, one foot in front of the other."

They made it to the car without much trouble. Jordan was disappointed when Owen insisted that Parker sit in the front. She sighed. *You waited this long to make a move*, she thought. *You can wait one more day to talk about it.*

On the way home, the three of them fell into a comfortable silence. Parker had the window down and seemed to be sobering up. Jordan let the rhythm of the car soothe her as miles of road disappeared beneath the tires. She noticed a pinprick of light in the distance. Another car. She took a breath and refocused.

"Just in time. I was getting bored," Parker said, sitting up straight in his seat. "Let's play chicken."

"I really don't think that's a good idea," Jordan said.

"You never think anything is a good idea," Parker retorted. "Here, I'll help you." He reached over and took hold of the steering wheel. The Mustang slowly edged over into the other lane.

Jordan tried to nudge them back, but Parker's hand remained steady. The car in front of them was getting closer.

"Okay, you've had your fun," she said. An edge crept into her voice. "Let go, he's not moving."

"He's just messing with you," Parker cut in. "Speed up a little. He'll back off, trust me."

Jordan spared him a glance, but did what he said. "Uh, Parker," she said a moment later. "He's still not moving."

"Don't worry. Pick up your speed."

"I don't know how that..."

"Just do it!" Parker screamed at her.

"No," she said, trying to remain calm.

"*Faster,*" Parker yelled, leaning over to push down on her knee.

"Parker," Owen shouted from the back. "Stop it!"

"Are you crazy?" Jordan screeched. She started to pull over to the other lane when Parker grabbed the wheel and held their course.

"Cut it out," Owen yelled.

Jordan wrestled with Parker to free the wheel as the headlights of the approaching car turned into a blinding glare. The sound of blood rushing to her ears drowned out the other car's blaring horn, a long tone that distorted when the light swerved around the Mustang and back onto the lane behind them.

"And that's how it's done!" Parker shouted, letting go of the wheel to raise his fists in the air.

Jordan couldn't bring herself to speak just yet. Her hands shook so badly, she could barely keep the Mustang on the road. She caught a glimpse of Owen in the rearview mirror. A hand covered his eyes.

"That was awesome," Parker was saying. "Well, wasn't it?" He waited a beat. Turned around to look at Owen. "Aw, come on! You guys suck."

"And *you* almost got us *killed*," Jordan said. Her voice shook along with the rest of her. "What the hell is wrong with you?"

When she thought she could trust herself, she looked at Parker. His eyes were much too bright, almost as if he had a fever. But it was his deranged smile that made Jordan wonder who was sitting beside her. It made her skin crawl. The hunger in it, the absolute certainty of knowing that, if he had to do it all over again, he would.

"I'm going to kill you when we get home," Jordan snapped. She turned her attention back to the road.

"Good idea," Owen said. "Would you mind pulling over first, though? I almost pissed myself back there. I don't think I'm going to make it."

"Sure," Jordan said. She eased the car onto the shoulder of the road, still gripping the steering wheel as Owen got out of the car.

"You're mad at me, aren't you?" Parker asked.

"You think?" Jordan muttered as the car light dimmed. She tried to look at Parker from the corner of her eye but it was too dark.

"You used to be fun," Parker said. She didn't have to see him to know that he was crossing his arms. His lower lip would be sticking out just a little too far.

Owen got back into the car. Jordan eased back onto the road. No one spoke until they got closer to the house.

"Hey, didn't we close the garage door before we..." Jordan trailed off. "Oh, shit."

Her parents stood in the driveway, silhouetted by the light from the front porch.

Parker let out a laugh. "Looks like you're in for it now, sis," he said.

Jordan didn't like the malicious undertone to his voice. She was more worried than she cared to admit.

She pulled into the garage and the three of them slunk out of the car.

"Get inside," Dad said, in a voice brewing with fury.

Jordan followed behind Parker, who followed Mom and Dad into the house. Her shoulders just about touched her ears.

"I'm really sorry, Mr. and Mrs. Andrews. This is just as much my fault as it is theirs, but I think I better be heading home," Owen said, holding the door open behind him.

"You're staying the night," Dad said. "Your parents already know. The spare room's ready for you. I'm sure they're busy preparing a lecture for you, so I'll save you the trouble of listening to mine."

Owen shut the door, nodded, and gave both Jordan and Parker an apologetic glance before heading up the stairs.

"I can't believe either of you," Mom hissed. She hated yelling when there were other people in the house, and would proceed to whisper-shout at them until she winded herself. "The neighbors thought you were thugs, stealing the car. You're lucky they thought to call us first instead of the cops! Six hours! We were gone *six hours* and you decided to take the car for a joyride?"

Jordan dug her toe into the arch of her other foot, but said nothing. It was usually best to hear her parents out and keep her mouth shut. They would finish sooner that way.

"We're legally adults now," Parker said.

Jordan stifled a groan.

"Really," Dad said in a dry tone. "Last time I checked, adults don't steal cars."

"You've got to be kidding," Parker shouted. "We went for a drive. We brought the damn car back. How is that stealing?"

Jordan wanted to kick Parker as they all watched Mom's mouth work. No sound came out. Dad finally put a hand on her shoulder and she stopped.

"You, sir, are grounded," he said. "I don't care how old you are, you do not touch the Mustang when I'm not home. That's *my* car." The vein in Dad's forehead pulsed. "Both of you, to your rooms. Now. We'll talk more about this later."

Parker stormed off toward the stairs, but Jordan went to give her parents a hug. She hated going to bed angry.

"How'd she handle?" Dad whispered into her ear.

The tight knot that had formed in the pit of her stomach loosened. "Like a champ," she whispered back.

Her smile faded as she looked over Dad's shoulder to see Parker staring at them. She made a small gesture, one that should have communicated her need for him to wait for her. She wanted to talk to him, figure out what was making him so crazy.

Parker turned and walked up the stairs.

*****

Jordan lifted her head, gasping.

The memory of her parents was so vivid. The feel of Dad's stubble against her cheek. The sound of Mom's voice. The searing anger in Parker's eyes.

It took her a full minute to realize that she was still sitting in the Mustang. Her hands gripped the wheel, knuckles white, arms quivering. Her stomach knotted, feeling exactly like it had that night. The night she thought of as The Beginning of the End. She hadn't let herself think about it in more than four years.

It was Parker's damned letter. Reading it had affected her more than she thought it would.

Jordan stared at the inside of the garage, trying to stop her regrets from seeping into her thoughts. *I should have come back like I promised. I should have been the one to help Mom and Dad with their money problems. I should have told them...*

Exhaustion settled in. Her muscles ached like she had just run a marathon. She wanted to get her things from Lydia's before she fell asleep at the wheel. She needed to get away from the house. It was time to go.

"I'm sorry," she said, readjusting her seat belt. She stroked the dashboard like a cat, not really knowing who she was apologizing to. "Let's try again."

She wiggled the key in the ignition, turned it slowly. The Mustang purred to life.

Jordan spared once last glance at her home before she drove away, with no idea if she would ever be back.

Chapter 5
Burning Bridges

$\mathcal{T}$ully opened his front door on the third knock. He glanced down at the duffel bag Jordan carried. "Need a place to stay?" he asked.

"Yes, please."

Beatrice's face appeared from behind Tully's shoulder. "Oh, hello, Jordan," she said.

"Sorry to bother you, Mrs. Tully. I know it's late."

Beatrice gave a little wave. "Not to worry. The basement's all ready for you."

Jordan looked up. Tully shrugged. "I like being prepared for the inevitable," he said, ushering her inside.

Jordan followed him down into the basement. It was a large, familiar room. It contained a dresser, television, desk, and double bed. Everything looked the same. It was a relief since there were an overwhelming number of things in her life that had changed.

"Are you sure you don't mind me staying with you guys?" Jordan asked, trying, and failing, to stifle a yawn.

Tully's wide frame blocked her view of the bed as he handed her a pillow and a thick blanket. "The basement gets pretty cold at night so you might need these," he said, ignoring her question. "Holler if you need anything. Beatrice and I are right upstairs."

Jordan opened her mouth to ask again, when another yawn took control of her jaw. "I only need to stay the night." She wondered if she was telling him, or reminding herself. "I'll be heading to Rolling River. I'm going to confront Parker."

"You're dead on your feet," Tully said, his tone gentle. He nudged her toward the bed. "Get some sleep. We'll argue about how long you can stay tomorrow. Come down to the station. I'll buy lunch."

"That sounds nice," Jordan murmured, lying down on the bed, still clutching the pillow and blanket. "Wait." She managed to lift her head to look at Tully through bleary eyes. "Thank you." Unable to keep her eyes open, she let her head fall back down onto the mattress.

"Anytime," Tully said.

*****

The weather in Paris had been horrible. Tired of trying to make the best of a bad situation, Jordan decided she had gone on long enough without checking her e-mail. It had been three weeks. Time to put on a brave face.

She sat, hunched in front of her laptop screen, chewing on a thumbnail as she viewed the unread items. There were several from Owen, which she deleted immediately without reading. There were none from Parker, which she had come to expect.

There was only one message from her parents.

> Jordan,
> We had an agreement. School started a few weeks ago.
> Where are you? Your mother and I are at our wit's end.
> I'm disappointed that you think it's acceptable to
> disappear for months at a time without letting us know if
> you're still alive! I expect this behavior from your brother,
> but not from you...
>
> What's going on, Jo? Why won't you come home?
> Dad

Jordan's fingers hovered over the keyboard before she returned them to her lap. How could she tell him the truth?

She logged off, pushed away from the desk, and grabbed her umbrella. Inside or outside, she couldn't possibly feel any worse.

*****

Jordan woke to the sound of bells. A hollow feeling gnawed at the pit of her belly, and it wasn't hunger. Just as she was about to open her eyes, the bells stopped ringing. She burrowed her face deeper into the pillow. Tried to shake off the dream. The bells started chiming again. With a groan, she lifted her head, bleary-eyed and annoyed.

She reached out to the bedside table. Her grasping fingers sent something spinning. It landed on the floor.

It was her cell phone.

She peered over the edge of the bed, down at the call display. Three missed calls from Tully. "What the..." She trailed off, grabbing the phone to check the time. It was two in the afternoon. "Damn it!"

She scrambled to her feet and hit the Call button.

"Jordan," Tully said. "Everything all right?"

"I'm so sorry. I'm coming!" Jordan looked down to see that she was still wearing her outfit from the funeral. Her stomach turned. "I'll be there in half an hour."

She moved the phone away from her ear so she could pull off the dress. She wanted to throw it in the garbage. Or burn it.

"Relax. Take a deep breath," he replied. "No harm done. We can do lunch tomorrow."

"You trying to get out of buying?" she asked and was pleased to hear him chuckle.

"Definitely not. I'm a man of my word."

"Good, 'cause I'm starving. See you in half an hour."

Jordan hung up, letting the dress fall from her fingers onto the floor. If she threw it out, she couldn't afford to replace it.

*****

True to her word, she made it with two minutes to spare.

The station had three doors behind an empty front desk. Two were open: the offices for Tully and his deputies. The third door was shut and locked with a PIN pad.

Jordan walked straight into Tully's office, where he was seated at his desk, pulling napkins and two iced teas out of a brown paper bag.

"Just in time," he said. He held out a sandwich. "Roast beef?"

She took it. "Thanks." She sat down in the chair across from him.

Tully bowed his head, closed his eyes. Jordan watched his lips move as she picked up her sandwich and took a bite.

"Lydia find out about your lack of faith?" he asked when he was finished.

43

"You bet. She was about as pleased as she usually is about any of my opinions." She shrugged. "It wasn't the reason why I found all my stuff outside though."

"What did you say to her this time?"

"I may have implied that I thought she was full of it."

"Ah," Tully said, taking a bite of his sandwich. Silence followed as he chewed and swallowed. "About time someone told her that."

Jordan flashed him a grin.

"How was your trip?" he asked. "Didn't get too much news from, well, when I asked, your parents never quite gave me an answer."

"It was great," she said. The sandwich tasted like sandpaper. Tully watched her as he took a long drink of iced tea. "They left me the house," she said, just to change the subject.

"Oh?"

"That's it. The house." She shook her head. "No savings, no nest egg. They drained their RSPs. Even Parker was giving them money."

"I'm sorry, I had no idea."

"Neither did I," she told him. *And that's what's bothering you, isn't it?* she asked herself with a sigh. "I have no idea how I'm going to keep it..." *And I'm just not ready to give it up*, she finished silently.

When Tully finished eating, Jordan watched him brush the crumbs from his desk, crumple the paper bag, and throw it into the trash. His chair creaked as he leaned back, still watching her.

"What?" she asked, popping the last corner of bread into her mouth. "Do I have something on my face?"

The corners of Tully's mouth tugged upward. It made him look like he was having trouble digesting his lunch. "No, nothing like that," he said. "You..." He paused, before continuing, "You just remind me of your mom. She talked with her hands too."

Jordan leaned back. "Yesterday, you said you had some news," she said in a strangled voice. She took the empty cellophane wrapper off the desk, bunched it up into a tiny ball.

"We can discuss it another time," he said. "You're upset. I shouldn't have brought your mother up like that."

"No, no. Let's talk now," she said, waving her hand in the air. "It's fine. Really."

"Where to start," Tully muttered. He exhaled loudly, scratched his

44

head. "Do you know if your parents were recent pet owners?" he asked. The chair squealed as he leaned forward to rest his elbows on the desk.

The question caught Jordan by surprise. "Pet owners?" she repeated, confused. She frowned, and said, "No. Mom is...was allergic to most animals."

"I thought so." Tully pulled a pad of paper toward him, grabbed a pen from his drawer, and wrote something down.

"Why is that important?" Jordan asked, making a special effort to sound relaxed.

Tully toyed with the pen before setting it down. "Here's the thing. Some of the swabs taken at the scene were tested for DNA," he said. His gaze was direct, yet reading his features told her nothing. "The results we received were a little unusual. They weren't human."

Jordan's breath hitched in her throat. "What were they, then?"

"Canine."

"You're joking." The words came out sounding much harsher than she intended.

"No."

"But the Honda is missing," Jordan said, shifting so far forward, she was barely touching the chair. "Are you telling me that a dog killed my parents and then drove away?" She squeezed the plastic wrap until her nails dug into her palm.

"We found the car. Your dad left it at work. We don't know why, but the video surveillance checks out." Tully kept his voice low, Jordan knew, in an attempt to soothe her.

"None of this makes any sense."

"I know how you feel," he said. "I'm right there with you."

Jordan opened her mouth to protest, but cut herself off when Tully gave her a stern look.

"You're looking for someone to blame, and the answers don't fit the bill," he continued, "but as close as this case is to the both of us, I can't ignore the evidence."

She wanted to scream.

"We're going to do everything we can to find the animal," Tully was saying. "We've got a few leads. It's probably a coyote. You know how they tend to roam in the warmer months out here."

"Yeah," Jordan said lamely. *Coyotes totally break into people's houses all the time*, she thought, staring at the wood grain pattern in Tully's desk.

"Is there anything else?" he asked, interrupting her thoughts. "Anything you've remembered since the incident?"

"Yes, actually," she said slowly, lifting her gaze from the desk. "After the funeral, something attacked me."

"*Something?*"

Jordan watched his brow crease and rushed on.

"I don't remember much about it, the creature I mean. It wasn't human, but I don't think it was an animal either. Especially not a canine. It had claws, about this long." She used her hands to demonstrate. "They looked like knives. Mom's throat was sliced. Sliced open, I mean—"

"Why didn't you mention this before? Did it hurt you?" Tully interrupted, his tone brisk.

"I'm fine," she said. Then she remembered why she had forced herself to forget in the first place. "It, uh, it kind of disappeared," she mumbled.

Tully didn't miss a word. "It disappeared," he repeated.

Jordan pressed her lips together and wished she had kept her mouth shut. "Yes," she said in a small voice.

"Okay, got it," Tully said, picking up the pen. He made a few more notes. "Thanks for letting me know."

"Please don't pretend to believe me. I'd rather have you tell me I'm crazy."

"I don't think you're crazy," he said, putting the pen down. When he continued speaking, his voice was low. "It's not uncommon to see things after experiencing something traumatic. If it happens again, I want you to tell me. You can talk to me."

Jordan nodded and threw out the cellophane ball to distract herself. *You will not start crying now*, she told herself.

"Dang it," he said. "I'm so sorry, I've got to get back out on duty." He stood up, took his hat from its hook on the wall, and placed it on his head. "Did you want a ride?"

She shook her head. "I've got the Mustang."

"Hey, that gives me a thought. You could sell your father's car," Tully told her. Jordan gave him a horrified look, and he quickly continued, "No, no. Not the 'Stang. Anyone with half a brain can tell how much that beauty means to you. His other car. It might help to pay off some of those bills."

"I suppose."

"I'll see you tomorrow morning, then?" he asked, changing the subject.

46

"I'll get the wife to make you pancakes and bacon before you head out."

"I can't resist a good pancake," Jordan lied. After Tully's news, she wanted nothing more than to get the hell out of town. "I'll be there, but I'm leaving straight after breakfast. No more bribes."

"You've got yourself a deal," he said, hooking his thumbs through his belt loops.

*****

What now? Jordan thought. She was back at Tully's house, lounging on the bed, missing her own. She *still* couldn't wrap her mind around the fact that her parents had been murdered by a *dog*.

Glancing at the clock for the fifth time, she came to the conclusion that she was being ridiculous, and that 7:37 p.m. was much too early to go to sleep. What she really needed was to be surrounded by people. People who had no idea she had just lost both her parents.

There's a bar down the street, she thought. She rolled out of bed, dug through her duffel bag, and pulled out a worn copy of *Pride and Prejudice*.

Jordan could hear the bar before she could see it. Speakers blasted out an old rock tune, a pulsing undercurrent to the loud conversations. As she got closer, she saw that the noise was coming from the patio, an option she hadn't considered. There was a table available. She took it, ordered herself a pint, and opened her book.

Five people occupied one corner of the patio. Listening to them for a few minutes revealed that they were backpackers. Jordan felt compelled to watch them; women and men, laughing over shared stories. How long ago had it been since she was in their position? It felt like months, when in reality, it had barely been more than a week.

Jordan winced when, lost in her thoughts, one of the women caught her eye. She buried her face behind her book and wondered if anyone would notice if she ran away.

"Hey there," the woman said. "You by yourself?"

Jordan lowered the book and surprised herself by answering. "I am."

"Why don't you join us?" the woman asked.

Jordan hesitated for a moment before forcing her lips into a smile. "I'd love to."

Introductions were made, a pitcher was ordered, and soon the conversation was flowing as if she had known these people all her life.

This had been what she loved about traveling. Strangers. Meeting them and developing a friendship that only lasted a couple of days before extracting herself and moving on; no hurt feelings, no pressure to keep in touch. The only memories were good ones. They were the only ones Jordan wanted.

"Whoops," Jordan said, a few pints later. She swayed on her feet as she tried to make out the details on her watch. It was one thirty o'clock. Or something. "I'm going to have to call this one a night," she said.

Their waiter was wiping down the table next to them. "Need me to call you a cab?" he asked.

"Naw," Jordan said, giving a last high five and hug to the lady from Denver. No. Wait. Was it Detroit? "I'm staying right next door. I'll be just fine."

Back at Tully's, alone in the basement, she was anything but. She wasn't staying in a room full of happy travelers. She wasn't going home. Her parents were dead. She had found them. Hadn't been able to help them.

Useless, she thought as she struggled to pull off her shoe. *I'm useless.* When the shoe came loose, she lost her balance and toppled over. "How the hell did I end up down here?" she demanded of the ceiling. The fall had scratched the surface of her temper, which, she discovered, had already peaked. She clawed at the wall as she struggled to get to her feet. She ended up half crawling, half stumbling over to the bed.

Lying down sent the beer in her stomach sloshing upward, a direction she did *not* want it to go. She sat up with a groan and cursed herself for having that one last drink. Then she cursed the waiter for giving it to her. The space right below her diaphragm felt like she had swallowed a lump of coal. A ball of heat flamed with each breath.

Fucking waiter. I'm going to go back and rip his heart out, she thought, pushing herself off the bed. *Rip, rip, rip, his heart right out.*

Jordan took a step forward and fell to the floor again. She covered her face with a hand and erupted into a fit of giggles. *Where did that come from?* she thought. *Put a few beers into me and I think I'm Rambo. God. What a night.*

A scratching noise put a stop to the laughter. Feeling abruptly sober, Jordan listened intently. The basement was quiet. Jordan figured she should get herself some water, but collapsed back onto the bed instead.

The scratching started again, louder this time. Jordan propped herself up on her elbows, squinting. *Did the wall move in time with the sound?* She didn't need to second-guess herself. As the scratching continued, a section of the wall a little larger than the size of a basketball began to ripple. Part of her wanted to get closer, to see what was happening, but the other part of her wanted to get as far away from it as possible.

The wallpaper tore, slowly, like a chick hatching from its egg. A large foot came free, hitting the carpet with a squelch. It was gray, with thin trails of green running like vines up its leg. The other emerged along with two long, thin arms. The length and size of the claws protruding from its fingers reminded her of a bear.

Jordan watched as the creature used a claw to peel the wallpaper away from its face. She wanted to scream, but the only sound her vocal chords decided to produce was a squeak. She had seen this *thing* before. The familiarity didn't make it any less grotesque.

Thick yellow liquid dripped from one corner of its mouth onto the floor.

"This isn't real," she muttered to herself. "I'm drunk. I'm dreaming and I'm drunk."

The creature raised its claws.

"Holy shit," she screamed.

Jordan threw herself onto the floor, and scrambled under the bed. She could hear the creature's breath shuddering in and out of its body like a locomotive struggling to burn coal. She tensed, stretching her neck in an attempt to peer out from under the bed. She couldn't see far enough. The creature had to be somewhere. The damn thing was still wheezing. Jordan imagined it was perched on top of the bed. Waiting to leap onto her back as she made her escape.

The volume of the creature's breathing increased. Nerves made Jordan choke on a fit of laughter. She ended up snorting. Horrified, she clapped her hand over her mouth and nose. It was during the silence that followed that she realized the breathing she had been listening to had been her own.

It took several minutes, but she was able to gather enough courage to inch her way closer to the bed frame. She managed to keep her breathing under control, but her limbs trembled. All she had to do was stick her head out, just a tiny bit, to see where the creature was.

It was a horrible plan. The thought of the hideous thing jumping on her face made her joints freeze up. There had to be a way to lure the creature out from wherever it was hiding, without sacrificing any of her major organs.

"I know you're in here, ugly," she shouted. "Show yourself!" She waited a beat. "Come on, you bastard," she said, voice cracking. "Where are you?"

"Jesus Christ!" The nasal-sounding words came from the direction of the door. "What the hell's going on?"

"Tully, be careful." The words came out as a shriek. Her breath seemed constricted now. Her heart felt like it was being ground beneath a heel. She hoped she wasn't slipping into a full-fledged panic attack. "I don't know where it went. It could be anywhere!"

"Come out from under there."

"Have you checked? Where is it?"

"Now, Jordan."

She inched her way out from under the bed and got to her feet. At first, she didn't know why Tully was standing in the doorway, arms crossed. She gasped when she saw what was left of the room.

The television screen was shattered. Pieces of glass glittered on patches of shredded carpet. The top of the desk looked like it had been scratched by an overgrown cat. The back of the chair was resting by the dresser, which seemed to be the only piece of furniture that remained intact. Jordan's leg brushed up against the bed as she surveyed the damage. Even the stuffing had been pulled out of the mattress.

"I was attacked," Jordan told him, her voice tight.

"I see." Tully folded his hand over his wide belly. He tapped his forefinger against the wrist of his other hand as he regarded her, *tap, tap, tap*. "Have you been drinking?"

"I've had a few pints, yes," Jordan said. She didn't like the way he was looking at her.

"Was that before or after you decided to destroy my basement?"

"You think *I* did this?" she asked. "I was hiding under the bed the whole time. It was that creature, the one I was telling you about."

Tully's eyes widened. "Are you listening to what you're saying?" he asked. "You're blaming this mess on a hallucination?"

Jordan's nostrils flared. "Didn't you ask me to tell you if I saw the creature again?" she retorted. "Maybe I didn't state it clearly enough. *I saw the creature again.*"

"Don't get flippant with me. I'm not family. I didn't have to take you in."

The words stung. "I don't understand. You believed me at lunch," she said. "Why don't you believe me now?"

"I don't have time to babysit you," Tully snapped. "I think it would be best if you left for Rolling River. Go find Parker."

"I'll clean everything up," Jordan rushed on, giving her upper lip a nervous lick. "At least let me get some sleep. I'll leave before noon."

"You should leave now. It's almost dawn," Tully said. His eyes were fixed on hers, finger still tapping away on his wrist. *Tap, tap, tap.* "They've been doing a lot of construction on the highway this summer. You don't want to get stuck in traffic."

"Don't give up on me," she said in a small voice.

"I'm not going to say it again. You need to leave," Tully replied. The words sent shivers running up her spine.

"All right, all right," Jordan said. She was pleased that the words came out smooth, confident. Her legs trembled as she turned away from him. "Just let me pack my stuff."

When she had gathered her things, she tried to leave, but found Tully blocking the door.

"I'm sorry this didn't work out," Tully said, putting a hand on her shoulder. Jordan clenched her jaw. "Give me a call when you get there. I'll want to know you made it safely."

"If you expect me to call you after this, you're out of your mind," Jordan said, pushing her way around him.

She left the house without another word. Dawn was rapidly disappearing; she could see the halo of gold peeking above the horizon. When she reached the Mustang, she threw her bag into the trunk and got into the driver's seat. Hands shaking, she started the engine. She could barely see where she was going as she pulled out of the driveway.

A few blocks down the street Jordan pulled over and parked the old girl. She crawled into the backseat. Lying on her back, she placed her feet flat on the leather and stared at the roof.

She choked on the first sob, trying her damnedest to hold it in. The second was accompanied by tears. They were hot, stinging her cheeks even after she had wiped them away. Her chest heaved as a keening sound escaped. It felt like she was throwing it up. Jordan wanted her mom. She wanted Dad. She wanted the comfort that only they could bring. She turned her head into the back of the leather seat and breathed in, her body shuddering from the effort.

She lay there and wept, breathing in memories, until there were none left.

Chapter 6

Finding Parker

ROLLING RIVER, POPULATION 15,000

$\mathcal{T}$he sign was like a beacon for Jordan's weary eyes. It had been a four-hour
drive from Tully's place. "With no damn construction," she muttered to
herself. "Liar."

Jordan drove the Mustang into an empty parking lot beside an empty
parkette. She sat for a few minutes before pulling out her cell phone. Although
her anger had simmered for the entire drive, she had managed to come to a
decision about the house. "It's Jordan," she said when her parents' lawyer picked
up. "Sorry, I know it's early but I was wondering if you could do me a favor?" she
asked. "I want to sell Dad's car. That's right." She nodded. "Put the money
towards the mortgage. That should be enough to keep it, right?"

By the time she hung up the phone, her fist was clenched up against her
stomach. *What the hell am I going to do with a house I'm afraid to live in?* she thought,
then decided to let it go for the time being. Feeling the need to stretch her legs,
take in some sights, and avoid seeing Parker for a while longer, she started
walking.

The parking lot was tucked into a side street, one lined with Victorian
homes, manicured lawns, and high-end cars. Jordan tugged at the day-old shirt
she was wearing and wrinkled her nose. She smelled like a brewery. *It doesn't
matter*, she told herself. *This isn't going to be a picture-perfect reunion.* She frowned
and shoved her hands into her pockets as she headed toward Main Street.

She knew she was getting close when the breeze picked up, and she could smell fresh water. It came from the town's namesake, Rolling River, known for being almost as wide as the Mississippi. Half a block later, she found herself walking down a bustling sidewalk trying not to get jostled between strollers, couples holding hands, and gaggles of teenagers. It seemed everyone was heading to Old Port.

It was stunning what the town had done with the old shipping port. The docks had been transformed into a mile-long boardwalk, where a person could lose themselves in the sound of wind, laughter, and conversation. Several groups of teens were spread out along the riverbank, baring skin, throwing Frisbees to each other. Swimming was designated to one area of the strip; however, Jordan could see several heads bobbing in the distance.

A sharp crack made Jordan whirl to her left. A roar of cheers greeted her gaze. Beyond a metal fence, there was a baseball diamond. She could see the stands; the crowd faced the river, and cheered as the players darted around on the field.

At the end of the boardwalk she came upon a massive building with tinted windows and a large sign made of tiny lightbulbs. RIVER SIX, she read, and wondered how they would look in the evening under a dark sky. *It's so quiet*, she thought to herself. It was odd that it felt like the sounds and the energy of the bustling town didn't fit in here. *There's no one around*, she told herself. *That's the difference*. It seemed as though no one else had the desire to walk as far as she had. With the sun as high as it was, she couldn't blame them for wanting to stick closer to the shade. There was nothing else here except the building and the river.

Jordan's curiosity grew. *I wonder what this place is?* she thought. *It's too big to be a restaurant...*

She walked closer, but the windows were so dark she couldn't quite see what was inside. Worrying her bottom lip through her teeth, she debated pressing her face up against the glass.

"Great building, isn't it?" The voice was rich and full-bodied, like a well-aged wine.

Already captivated, Jordan looked up at the man who had spoken, and pressed a hand to her heart. He had dark-brown eyes and just a hint of stubble peppered over a very well-defined jaw. His slight smirk made her wonder if he could hear her heart's erratic beat.

"I, uh, well..." She cleared her throat and almost choked when she remembered her appearance. "Yes, it certainly is," she said weakly.

"I'm sorry," he said with a slight chuckle. He ran his hand through his thick, dark locks.

Jordan wondered if it would be inappropriate to ask him if she could do it for him. She mentally shook herself.

He was saying something. "That was my sad attempt at trying to start a conversation with you. I should have just started with hello."

Tingles shot up through Jordan's arms, and a warmth spread across her cheeks. "Hello," she said in a husky voice. *Well, at this point, you might as well literally throw yourself at him*, she told herself.

"I'm Levi," he said, holding out his hand.

She grasped it, indulging in its warmth, and the coarseness that told her that he probably wasn't afraid of doing a little handiwork. "Jordan," she managed.

"Well, Jordan," he said, "can't say that I've seen you around town before."

"I just got in today," she told him with a smile she hoped came off sweet, rather than starry-eyed.

"Do you plan on staying?"

She shook her head, and for the first time wished she could give a different answer. "I'm just visiting." A gust of wind sent her hair flying in all directions. She managed to get most of it under control, but let out a nervous laugh.

Levi grinned, reached out, and tucked a strand behind her ear. "I hope you change your mind." There was something about the gesture that tugged at her. "If you do," he continued, "there's an exhibit in town, an old book from the first half of the—" He cut himself off and gave her a sheepish look. "Sorry, I haven't done this in a while. How am I doing?"

"You're asking me out?" The words, loudly spoken, hung in the air between them. *Just give me a shovel*, Jordan thought, *I'll bury myself.*

"I'm hoping you'll at least consider it." Levi's gaze was locked on her face. It made her want to consider it. Hell, it made her want to do more than consider it.

"I've got to get going," she murmured instead, trying to make sense of her reaction. She hadn't been this attracted to a man since, well, she couldn't remember the last time she had been this attracted to *anyone*. "It was nice meeting you."

"You've brightened my day," he told her. "Even if you leave me feeling a little disappointed."

Jordan had to tear her eyes away from him. She took a few steps back in the direction she had come from before giving in to temptation. She glanced back at Levi over her shoulder, and felt a little satisfied that he was watching her.

When she got back on Main Street, she could see its end about six blocks away. The blinding-white church steeple that rose above the other buildings on the street marked the town limits. After that, the road curved off to the left, the route back onto the highway. Each side of the street was lined with quaint little stores, bakeries, ice cream shops, and restaurants. The bells of the church started to ring. *I wonder if anyone stops to pray anymore, or if everyone just thinks it's lunchtime.* The streets bustled with activity. *I guess that's my answer*, she thought as she entered the crowd.

No one paid any attention to her as she walked, looking into the windows of each shop. The smell of freshly baked goods filled the air. Jordan stopped, closed her eyes, and breathed in. Her stomach grumbled. She hadn't eaten anything since the sandwich in Tully's office, which felt like years ago. She stopped, having reached Main and Liberty Avenue. Thoughts of the funeral forced her to make the left.

It was time to see Parker.

The length of her stride shortened as the numbers on the houses decreased. When she saw the place, she sucked in a breath of air. It was a lovely building. Modern, with three stories, cheery red brick, and large bay windows.

There was no doorbell. Jordan went ahead and tried the knob. It opened with a tinkling sound. She looked up in time to see a little bell ring again as she closed the door behind her. Confused, she walked into the middle of the room and turned in a slow circle.

Jordan was standing in what appeared to be a waiting room. It was nicer than any other she had ever seen. There were mahogany chairs with thick green cushions lining the walls to each side. At the other end of the room was an open doorway.

She was about to leave, thinking she had the wrong address, when she heard movement.

"Hello," a masculine voice called. Jordan's eyes were drawn to the shadow nearing the open doorway. "Give me a sec, Scotty. I'll be right there with the tracks."

"Damn it," Jordan muttered. She hadn't considered that Parker wouldn't be the one to greet her; a significant miscalculation on her part. Jordan laced her fingers together to prevent herself from reaching for the voice's owner.

A lanky man walked toward her, busy capping what looked to be a memory stick. "Any news?" he asked. When he looked up and saw her, he jerked to a stop. The corner of Jordan's mouth quirked upward. She had to admit, surprising him like this was almost worth the jolt to her system.

Owen met Jordan's eyes through a curtain of hair that was long overdue for a trim. He seemed to have regained his senses. "Jo?" He took a step toward her, his long legs bringing him much closer than she would have liked. Jordan didn't move to meet him. He stopped where he was, his hand outstretched. Jordan's remained where it was.

"I didn't know you were back," he said. His hands disappeared into the back pockets of his jeans. "It's nice to see you."

It's true, she thought. She felt her nostrils flare. *He doesn't care that he missed the funeral.* Jordan kept her distance and squirmed under his gaze. She felt like he was running through an inner catalogue of details, assessing what had changed, what hadn't. *It doesn't matter what he thinks*, she reminded herself. *It's clear that he only cares about himself.*

"Is that all you have to say?" she snapped. "What happened to 'I'm sorry for your loss,' or 'How are you holding up?'" She frowned when he stared at her, his expression blank. "Never mind. Forget it. I'm looking for Parker. Is he here?"

"Whoa, hold on, back up," he said. "What are you talking about?"

It was Jordan's turn to stare at him. *Oh, shit*, she thought, feeling her stomach plummet. *He doesn't know.*

"Who died?" His voice was insistent, his gaze sharpened.

Jordan looked away. "I'm sorry, I thought—"

"Who died, Jo?" Owen repeated, urgency loud and clear in his tone. When she couldn't bring herself to answer, his eyes searched her face as if the answer were tattooed to her flesh. "Don't do this to me."

"Mom and Dad," she whispered.

"No." He took a staggering step forward. "No. You're lying."

"I thought you knew," Jordan heard herself say in a rush. "Lydia said Parker was going to tell you."

"If I knew about it, I would have been there!"

Jordan clenched her fists. *Let him be*, she told herself. *Give him space.* She watched him pace as he tried to maintain his composure.

"I need a minute," he said.

Jordan watched Owen's back as he retreated into the room he had come out of. The door slammed shut behind him.

Jordan closed her eyes and pressed the heels of her hands against her lids. Coming here was a mistake. She turned to leave, and then groaned. She dropped her hands from her face and sat down in one of the chairs. Owen would have questions, and he deserved to know the answers.

She lost track of time staring at a dark spot on the floor. The only sound came from the growling of her stomach. There was nothing to indicate what Owen was going through on the other side of the door. She was immediately aware of him when it opened. Jordan rose to her feet.

"When?" Owen asked, leaning against the door frame.

"About a week ago."

"How?"

"Murdered," Jordan told him. "Tully's investigating. They don't really have any solid leads."

Owen let out a noisy breath of air. "Why didn't you call me?" he asked. "I would have been there for you. You know what? Screw that. I would have been there for *them*." His jaw moved forward as his mouth tensed. He looked like he was about to say something, then thought better of it before asking in a voice almost too quiet to hear, "Do you hate me that much?"

The blood drained from Jordan's face. "It wasn't intentional," she said, her tone cool. "I had so much on my mind, trying to get ahold of Parker, trying to get all the arrangements together." She had almost told him about the creatures that haunted her dreams, the strange hallucinations. She had learned her lesson with Tully.

"I know how much they meant to you," she said instead. She became very interested in a hangnail as tears welled in her eyes.

"Thank God you weren't there."

"Don't. You know God had nothing to do with it."

"Right." Owen sniffed, then let out a forced-sounding chuckle. The whites around his eyes were red. "I meant it, though. What I said earlier." He gave her a small smile. "I'm glad you're here."

Jordan could only stare at him and wonder how she had been able to go without seeing him for so long. Her thoughts were interrupted by a low rumble. She covered her stomach with her hands as her vision skewed. She blinked furiously, trying to get rid of the black spots that were clouding her vision.

Jordan lurched forward, reaching out for something to break her fall, knowing there was nothing close enough to grab on to. She cursed herself for not eating before coming here. She was going to faint, and the thought horrified her.

You are not going to pass out in front of Owen. Her vision narrowed, ignoring her command. *Hold it together!*

"Jordan?"

Her name was the last thing she heard before she collapsed.

*****

Jordan's eyes fluttered open. A pair of vibrant green eyes looked down at her.

"Are you all right?" Owen asked. He was crouched over her, his brow lined with worry. His body was much too close for comfort.

Jordan resisted the urge to brush the loose strands of hair behind his ear. She placed her hands firmly on either side of her body. Propped herself up with her elbows. When he didn't move, she said, "Give me some space. You're hovering."

"Good lord." He inhaled loudly. "When's the last time you've seen the inside of a shower?" Jordan gave him a cold glare, and Owen clucked his tongue against the roof of his mouth. "Now, now," he said, his mouth forming a lopsided grin. It appeared as though he had used her fainting spell as an excuse to tuck his emotions away where she couldn't see. "You could give me a little credit," he continued, as he helped her into a seated position. "I did stop you from breaking your face all over the floor."

Jordan snorted, pressing the heels of her palms against her closed lids. Her vision was still a little spotty. "I guess you're going to expect a thank-you then." She snuck a peek at him. He raised a brow. "Thank you," she said, in a flat voice.

"How are you feeling?" Owen asked.

Her stomach rumbled again.

Owen glanced down at it. "When's the last time you ate?" he asked.

"It doesn't matter," she said, pushing his arm away as she got to her feet. Jordan made it halfway up before the spots overwhelmed her vision. "Oh, help me back down," she hissed. "I think I'm going under again."

"Head between your knees," Owen said as he guided her. "That's it. Deep breaths now."

Jordan's fingers gripped the skin beneath her thighs as she grudgingly listened to his instructions. *You didn't come here to make up for lost time, damn it,* she thought.

"Where's Parker?" she said when she could lift her head without much trouble. It felt clearer. The room no longer slanted at a dangerous angle. "I need to talk to him."

"Don't you want to know how *I'm* doing?" Owen asked, his tone dry as he stood and sauntered back through the doorway he had come through when she arrived.

"Jesus, Owen," she yelled after him, and waited a beat for him to reappear. He didn't. Taking a deep breath, she slowly rose and took a step forward. And another. As she closed the distance between her shuffling feet and the doorway, her head began to swim again.

Making it to the door frame, she leaned against it, trying to make it look like she wasn't gripping it for support. The room beyond was an office, decorated in a style similar to the sitting room. There was an oak desk, bigger than the one in the waiting room, that filled half the space. A guitar was propped up against the chair closest to the window. Shelves lined the opposite wall, and two chairs adorned the space on the other side of the desk. Owen was rummaging through one of its drawers. A leather jacket hung over his arm.

"What are you doing?" Jordan asked.

"I'm taking you out for lunch," he replied. He tossed a set of keys into the air, slammed the drawer shut, and caught them.

"No," she said, wishing she sounded a little more convincing. "I need to talk to Parker."

"Do you still love pasta as much as you used to?" Owen asked. He took hold of her elbow and led her toward the door before she had time to respond.

A strangled sound escaped Jordan's lips as they walked down the steps and onto the sidewalk. "I don't want to have lunch with you," she said, trying to wrest her arm away.

Owen turned to face her, and blocked her path, so that all she could see was him. "Still stubborn as ever," he said, his voice soft. He looked down at her, but didn't touch her. "I know you. You're in trouble."

Jordan opened her mouth to deny it, but stopped when Owen gave her a level stare.

"Is it really *that* hard to accept my help?" he asked. "You used to do it all the time."

"It's different now. This is family business," Jordan muttered, but her resolve was wavering. She was *hungry*. "All right," she said, resigned. "Let's go."

Owen grinned, and nodded in the direction they had been heading. "This way."

*****

He guided her back onto Main, toward Old Port. The sidewalk was still crowded, yet the distance seemed ten times longer than the short half block it was. They stopped in front of the *Amore Perso*. The royal-blue awning was welcoming, but it was the smell of fresh spices and herbs combined with other heavenly scents that had her reaching to open the door.

Owen anticipated her move, and got there first. "After you," he said, pulling it open and giving her a slight bow.

"I wish you wouldn't do that," she murmured as she moved inside.

The restaurant seemed much too fancy for the state Jordan was in. Cozy booths with red velvet cushions lined the perimeter. The middle housed tables for larger groups, and dangling chandeliers provided a brightly lit atmosphere.

Despite the small crowd, Jordan still wished she could crawl inside of her shirt until someone doused her with a hose. She couldn't help but think that the waitstaff were staring at her. Of course, the more likely scenario was that they were staring at Owen. He was in a famous band, after all.

The hostess led them to a booth at the back of the restaurant. "Enjoy your meal," she told them. Jordan wanted to tell her it would be a stretch, but she would do her best to try; but a snarky comment like that would only make Owen laugh. Jordan clenched her jaw, and slid into her seat.

"You're still mad," Owen said as they settled into the booth. "I don't blame you."

Jordan snatched the menu that had been placed in front of her and opened it, blocking her view of him. "It really doesn't matter anymore," she said, scanning the items listed. "It's been what? Four years? I'm over it."

She could feel his legs stretch out beside hers, and tried to ignore the flutter in the middle of her belly as they accidentally grazed hers. Owen's fingers appeared over the top of her menu before he grabbed and pulled it down.

"You're still mad," he repeated.

"I didn't come here to force an apology from you," she said, but the heat

60

was gone from her voice. "I told you, I came here to see Parker."

"Right," Owen said, letting her menu go to pick up his own. His eyes skimmed the page, but she caught him tucking his tongue under his upper lip. He didn't believe her.

The waiter came by at that moment with two glasses of water, and asked if they wanted anything else to drink. Owen got a beer. Since Jordan didn't want to prolong the lunch any further than was absolutely necessary, she told the waiter that water was fine, and gave him her order as well.

When the waiter left, Jordan had nowhere else to look except at Owen. He took a breath, opened his mouth to say something.

"Enough," she said. "I told you I'm not mad, and I really don't have the time to sit here and catch up. Let's have lunch. Then, I want you to take me to see Parker. Can you do that for me? Please?"

Her plea did nothing to dissuade Owen. "If you want me to believe you, you're going to have to wipe that sour look off your face," he said. "Look at me. No, not like that," he chastised her when she gave him another glare.

She relaxed the muscles around her eyes.

"That's better." He leaned forward, eyes locked on hers. "You can see that I'm genuinely sorry, can't you? And I don't mean that in the completely arrogant way you're interpreting it."

Jordan didn't know whether to kick him or burst out laughing. Owen hadn't changed a bit. "I've missed you," she said instead, and was instantly mortified. The words came out all sultry, in a tone usually saved for lovers.

Owen dropped his menu and broke out into a lopsided grin as he grabbed her hand. "I'm so relieved," he said. It was good to know he was still thickheaded as well. "I don't have anyone I can talk to about this."

"What do you mean?" Jordan asked, instantly alert at the odd change in his tone. She watched him tense, then become very interested in drinking his water.

The waiter chose that moment to return with Owen's beer, and requested his order.

"Owen," she hissed when they were alone again. "Why don't you have anyone to talk to? Where's Parker?"

Something wasn't right. She let out a gasp when she realized what he wasn't telling her. She couldn't believe she hadn't caught on sooner.

"You cagey son of a bitch," she said. She knew she was shouting, but was unable to stop. "Parker isn't even here, is he?"

"No," Owen told her, scrunching up his face. "He's not."

Chapter 7
Unrequited

"You've got to be kidding," Jordan said, snatching her hand away from Owen's.

"I know, I know," he said. "But the news about your parents caught me off guard. Seeing you caught me off guard." He bowed his head and trailed a finger through the ring of condensation left behind by the water glass. "I really meant what I said. I've been trying to figure out how to get in touch with you. There's something you need to—"

"What about the band?" Jordan interrupted.

Owen's hands fell to his lap as he leaned forward; the crease in his brow deepened. "We're playing it off as if we're working on our next album." His voice was hushed, eyes scanning the tables beside them. "Our manager, Scotty, he's insisted on hiring private investigators to find him, instead of the cops. We don't want word getting out that our lead singer's lost his mind. Apparently it's bad for our image," he said. "I've been working on some tracks even though I think we're over. But no one asks the guitarist for his opinion."

"Lost his mind? What are you talking about?" Jordan asked. "The band is everything to Parker."

Owen leaned back in his seat, crossed his arms over his chest. "When's the last time you talked to him?" he asked. "I mean *really* talked to him."

Jordan waited until he met her eyes. "About four years ago."

"Fair enough," he said. There was tension around his mouth. "About six months ago Parker started acting differently."

"How so?"

"He started showing up late to shows, getting into fights with our crew, with me."

"I thought you said he was acting differently."

"Don't be a smart-ass," Owen said before continuing. "I talked to Parker about taking some time off after the tour. You know, so he could sort out whatever it was that he was going through."

"Wait," Jordan said, holding her hands up above the table. "When did the tour finish?"

"Two weeks ago. We cut the last city," he told her.

Owen folded his hands, rested them on the table before continuing. "Our manager wanted us to regroup. Banished us here to sort ourselves out and write some new material." He paused. "It made Parker even more erratic. He was convinced that the break would ruin everything we've worked for. He's obsessed with staying…relevant." He frowned. "I tried to get him to write some new material with me. He refused. Told me he thought our sound needed to go in a new direction. A direction that only he could take us."

The last tidbit of information took Jordan by surprise. Parker and Owen wrote all their songs together. Always. It was how they had become so successful. Separately, they were decent musicians, but together, they were magic. No matter how angry she was with both of them, she couldn't deny the truth. They had something special.

"We ended up having a huge fight." Owen chuckled, scratching the side of his nose. "It was worse than the one we had in grade two when I didn't want to share my action figures with you. Remember? Parker told me then that if I wanted to be his friend, you were part of the deal." He paused. "He really loves you, you know."

"So I've been told," Jordan murmured. "So you two had a big fight, then what? He was gone the next day without a word?"

"Pretty much."

"How long ago?"

Owen went silent for a moment. "Six days."

Jordan drummed her fingers against the tabletop. *None of this makes any sense*, she thought. "Lydia spoke to him recently. She announced it to everyone at the funeral."

Owen gave a one-shouldered shrug. "I guess one of us is lying."

Jordan pressed her fingers against the burn building in the middle of her chest. *The truth doesn't matter*, she thought. *Parker should have shown up to his parents' funeral.*

The waiter arrived with their food. Jordan's mouth watered as the smell of fresh basil and cream hit her. She picked up her fork and loaded it with noodles. "You're absolutely sure you have no idea where he went?"

Owen finished chewing a mouthful of linguine before he replied. "I tried calling a couple of friends after he left. No one's heard from him. I wanted to call your parents, but, well, you know what things were like between them."

I guess you don't know about the money he was sending them, Jordan thought, slouching over her plate.

"I've been ordered to stay here in case he makes an appearance," Owen said as he poked at a cube of chicken. "I call his cell every night. Leave a message." He speared it. "It's frustrating as hell."

The conversation stuttered, then died, as they both turned their attention to their lunch. When they were finished eating, they stared at each other for a moment.

"Well, thank you for lunch," Jordan said. "I better get going."

"Where are you staying?" Owen asked, rising with her as she stood to leave.

Jordan panicked. "Oh, you know, one of those motels off the highway," she said, walking around him.

"Are you serious?" he asked. "No, no. I've got space. We've got an extra room, you won't have to sleep on the floor."

She didn't want to look at him, but she forced herself to. The fact that he had said "we" stung more than it should have. "That's all right," she said. "I prefer my own space." She paused, running a hand through her hair. "Thanks again."

Jordan rushed away, cutting Owen off from whatever it was that he was going to say next. She slipped through the front door and out onto Main, her thoughts tumbling. She had no money, no gas to get anywhere. Not that she knew where the hell she was supposed to be headed. Resigned, she crossed her arms over her chest, kept her head down, and made her way back to the parkette where she had parked the Mustang.

She got inside the old girl and cracked open a window. Coming to Rolling River was a huge mistake. *What's the sense in trying to find someone who doesn't want to be found?* She snuggled against the leather. She needed to figure out what she was going to do.

Her mind turned to a memory instead.

*****

The only thing that had made being grounded bearable was that at the end of it, Jordan would have her first date with Owen. He said he wanted to surprise her, that he had something really important to tell her.

She spent the week daydreaming about it, and had even practiced for the moment when he told her how much she meant to him. She would take his hand in hers, and look up at him through her lashes until his fingers laced with hers. He would kiss her then, Jordan was certain of it. The anticipation of experimenting further with what she had only a taste of that night at the bonfire brought a smile to her lips.

When the day finally arrived, Jordan spent most of it in her closet, trying to figure out the perfect combination of flirty and sexy, but not slutty.

"What are you doing?" Parker asked. Jordan shifted her gaze from the full-length mirror to find him leaning against her bedroom door frame.

"I'm getting ready to go out," she said, throwing the skirt back onto the pile of clothing on her bed.

"Yeah, I know that," he said, rolling his eyes. "What I don't get is why you're putting so much effort into it. It's just Owen."

"I'm a girl. It's what we do."

"You've never done it before."

Jordan turned to face him. "What is this about? Are you still pissed because I was only grounded for a week?" she asked. "I told you. If you would've just kept your mouth shut—"

"Whoa, whoa! Relax," Parker said. "You're awfully defensive tonight."

"And you're acting awfully weird."

"Sorry," he said with a frown. "You leave in a couple of weeks. I was just trying to spend a little time with you." He disappeared into the hallway, leaving her to figure out what the hell she was going to wear, and feeling like a complete jackass.

Owen picked her up promptly at eight. "I asked to borrow my parents' car, so don't worry. There's no chance of getting grounded a second time."

Jordan linked her arm through his and smiled up at him. She was so happy, all the words she had carefully prepared slipped from her mind.

"Are you okay?" he asked with a frown.

"Yeah. Yes," she told him. "I'm fine."

She spent the majority of the ride in the same dazed state, until they pulled into the parking lot of the local bar.

"Charlie's?" she asked.

Owen grinned. "I don't want to ruin the surprise," he said. "Let's go inside."

Charlie's was really a barn, redesigned to look like a bar. The establishment was eighteen plus on Friday nights, and they were able to pull in some pretty decent bands. Music filled Jordan as they walked in. The floor was already full, but it didn't matter. The woman singing onstage had her complete attention.

Jordan clutched Owen's arm. "Holy shit," she hissed. "That woman looks exactly like Celestia."

He gave her a wink. "That *is* Celestia."

"Owen, this is amazing," Jordan said. "How could I not have known they were playing? How did you manage to get tickets?" She thought she was going to die from joy. They had spent hours listening to Tainted Dilemma; of course he would take her to see them on their first date.

He grinned. "We didn't get tickets," he said. "We were invited."

"We were?"

"Not you, silly," said another voice. Jordan turned to find Parker standing behind her. He draped an arm over her shoulders. "Owen and I were invited."

"What are you doing here?" Jordan asked through clenched teeth. Parker appearing in the middle of her date hadn't quite been what she had envisioned. "Mom and Dad will kill you if they find out."

"The only way they'll find out is if someone tells them," Parker said with a smile. Jordan wondered if Owen could see how it was laced with an unspoken threat. "I had Owen invite you here because I didn't want to ruin the surprise. I wanted the three of us to be together when we broke the news."

"What news?" she managed to ask in a weak voice.

"Parker and I are going to be opening for Tainted Dilemma on their next tour," Owen said, his eyes shining. "They had the time off and wanted to meet us. Celestia came up with the idea of doing a sort of test run tonight."

"September first, Owen and I are flying out to New York," Parker said, bringing Jordan's attention back to him. "What's wrong, sis? You look upset. Aren't you happy for us?"

"Of course I am," Jordan lied, "but Owen, what about college? We were going to drive down together."

"You seriously think he would choose college over the band?" Parker scoffed.

"What about *us*," Jordan said to Owen, "going *together*?"

He turned to Parker. "Do you think I could have a moment alone with Jo?" he asked.

"You two wouldn't be keeping any secrets from me now, would you?" Parker said, giving Jordan's shoulder a painful squeeze.

Jordan looked to Owen, who was looking very intently at something on his shoe.

"What's gotten into you?" she asked, removing Parker's arm. "You know you can trust us."

"I'm just joking around," he said. His eyes said otherwise. "You're so touchy lately." He glanced at Owen. "I'll start setting up. Don't take too long."

Owen gave a mumbled response before he led Jordan by the elbow to a dark corner of the bar.

"Listen," he said. "There's no easy way to say this. I know you think…" He trailed off as his eyes focused on something beyond Jordan's shoulder.

Jordan turned in time to see Celestia breeze past her in a skintight black leather skirt, with matching leather corset. Her legs went on for miles, ending in a pair of red, six-inch spiked heels.

"Owen," Celestia said, her voice like silk. Jordan watched as she wrapped her arms around him and pressed herself up against his chest. "I'm so pumped to hear you play. Did you manage to catch our set?"

"Of course," Owen said. "I told you I wouldn't miss it."

Jordan crossed her arms over her chest and tried to stand up straighter. She cleared her throat. Owen didn't notice, but Celestia did.

"Who's this? A groupie?" she asked, leaning her head on Owen's shoulder. "Oh, she's so cute. Her dress looks like it belongs on a little doll, don't you think?"

Owen scratched the back of his neck, and blushed before letting out a barking laugh. Jordan's mouth worked, but Celestia's attention was back on Owen.

"So listen, we're going to The Felix after this. I know the bouncer, he'll let you in no problem." She tugged at the edges of Owen's collar, gave him a slow, sultry smile. "I'll see you there?"

She was already walking away, but Jordan wasn't watching her. She was watching Owen, whose shining eyes were now following Celestia across the room.

"Asshole," Jordan said, glad she was finally able to put sound to the word.

"Don't do this," Owen said. "Parker and I are finally getting some traction. You should be excited for us." He sighed. "I didn't know how else to tell you."

"You could have just *told* me," she said, hating the quiver she heard in her voice. "I thought, when we kissed, I mean——"

"It was just a kiss, people do it all the time. It doesn't mean anything." He wouldn't look at her. "Look, you're going to college. There's going to be a hundred guys throwing themselves at your feet." Owen put a hand on her shoulder. Jordan batted it away.

"And a thousand girls throwing themselves at *yours*," she said. "I guess at least one of us gets what we want."

"Shit, Jo, it's not like that." He shoved his hands in his pockets. "Damn it, this isn't going to work, is it?"

"What are you talking about now?" Jordan asked through the lump in her throat.

"Us. We can't just go back to being friends." Owen raised a brow. "Can we?"

Jordan didn't respond.

"Right," he said, running a hand through his hair. "I don't think we should talk to each other for a while."

"You don't..." Jordan felt her knees wobble, and braced her hand on the table beside them.

"I think it would be best if we didn't talk to each other," Owen repeated in a firm voice.

"Owen." Parker's voice carried out to them over the speakers. "Buddy, we need you for a sound check."

"I've gotta go," Owen said. "You take care of yourself, all right? Have fun at college."

"Owen, sound check please."

Jordan watched Owen walk away from her. She held her breath until she thought she had her emotions under control. Someone laughed. It sent her rushing for the exit.

Jordan wanted to be as far away from Owen as she could get. Despite everything, before she pushed the door open, she leaned on it for a moment, willed herself not to turn. She couldn't help herself. She looked back and saw Parker standing alone onstage, staring at her.

The door crashed against the wall as she flung it open and stormed out. Jordan told herself she didn't care, but couldn't help feeling betrayed by the smug grin she had seen plastered to her brother's face.

*****

A knock against the window made Jordan's eyelids snap open in time to watch the sun slip past the horizon. The knock came again. She turned her head. Owen stood outside the Mustang with his hands on his hips. Jordan got out and slammed the door.

"Why are you following me?"

"I thought you said you were staying at a motel."

"I am," Jordan said with a slight lift of her chin. "I was just taking a nap before heading over."

"You're a terrible liar," Owen said. "I was about to tell you as much when you ran out of the restaurant."

"I didn't run," she snapped.

"Enough already. Let me help you. Please."

"I'm not a charity case," she told him in a soft voice. "I can take care of myself. How many times I have to tell you before you'll understand?"

"I've got a fridge full of food," Owen said. He gave her a small smile. "Not to mention running water. I bet you'll feel more like yourself after a hot shower."

Jordan raised her eyebrows. She felt uncomfortably warm. In fact her entire body felt much too hot. A tight ball of flame took root in her chest, increasing in pressure with every beat of her heart. *How dare he try and smooth-talk me into staying with him?*

"Whoa. Hold it," Owen said, taking a step toward her. "I wasn't being snarky about the whole shower thing. I'm trying to help you, and you look like you're thinking about tearing me a new one."

"Listen to me," she said. She shivered despite the fact that her blood was like fire pumping through her veins. "I'm going to shred your flesh and break your bones."

"What the hell?" Owen said, taking two steps back. "If you're trying to be funny, it isn't working."

Jordan's esophagus burned. Her hands rose to her neck as she tasted a familiar bitter acid in the back of her throat. A rush of understanding nearly sent her sprawling to her knees.

"Are you all right?" Owen asked. She felt his arm slip around her waist. "Say something. You're starting to scare me."

"I...I'm fine. Really," she said. "I've been having these really intense hallucinations. It should pass in a moment."

Something crashed down onto the Mustang.

Both of them jumped back. Jordan looked up, and gripped Owen's hand. A long, sinewy body covered the length of the dented hood. Catlike eyes embedded in a narrow face swung toward them. Its neck stretched until a forked tongue almost brushed against Jordan's face. The creature stared down at them as it crouched low on four squat, muscular legs. Jordan tugged at Owen's arm, a silent scream filling her open mouth.

"What *is* that thing?" Owen shouted.

The creature widened its mouth to display a pair of gleaming white fangs. Owen shoved Jordan out of the way. The creature leapt down, and missed him only by inches. As it shot past, something thin and metallic twisted around Owen's forearm.

The creature skidded to a stop, claws scratching along the pavement like nails on a chalkboard. Scaled skin shimmered with an odd orange hue when the creature's head swiveled back to face them. The length of its body was coiled in a semicircle around itself. Several yards of what appeared to be silver cord stretched out between Owen's arm and the creature.

"Get it off," he screamed. "Get it off of me!"

The creature bared its fangs and swung its rear to the left. Owen jerked forward. It was then Jordan realized that the cord was actually the creature's tail.

Bright-red blood welled from beneath the section of tail wrapped around Owen's flesh. He tugged at it with his other hand, and managed to get his fingers beneath it. The creature pulled its tail away, slicing Owen's palm open. His cry filled the air.

Jordan couldn't focus. In fact, she was pissed. It was late, and she was hungry. But before she could eat anything, though, she had to destroy the male-smelling one. He was a distraction to the female, a problem to her master. She had to shred his flesh and crush his bones...

71

"Watch out," Jordan cried. The creature flung itself at Owen. They fell to the ground in a tangled heap.

Jordan did the only thing she could think of. She kicked the creature as hard as she could. To her surprise, she heard a crunch, and the creature was sent sprawling, landing a few feet away. She somehow knew it had twisted one of its limbs, landing on it in a way that was both painful and infuriating. There wasn't, however, any time to be impressed by her own strength.

The thing was getting back on its feet.

Chapter 8

Madison

*J*ordan grabbed Owen's sleeve, and dragged him to his feet. Together, they half limped, half ran to the Mustang. She jammed the key into the lock on the driver's door. "You can see it?" she asked.

"What do you think?" Owen hissed back. His face was pale.

The creature's tail whizzed past her hands, cracking against the door like a whip.

Jordan tried to turn the key. She could hear the creature winding its tail back into its body like a fishing rod. The door didn't open. The monster scratched the pavement. Jordan jiggled the key. Turned it again.

I can't attack with my claws, she thought. *Not with the tall one so close to the female.* Confused, she paused, fingers hooked under the handle.

"Watch out," Owen shouted. He pushed her aside as its tail lashed against the car again.

"Other side," she snapped, and ran toward the old girl's hood. When she reached the passenger's side, the creature tackled Owen from behind. He fell to the ground as the beast raked its hind claws down his back.

"No!" Jordan rushed toward them, cocked her leg back, and slammed it into the creature's side. The jolt of the impact ran up the length of her thigh.

The creature screeched as it smashed into the ground. Jordan had to cover her ears. Owen scrambled back and out of its way, clutching his arm to his chest. The creature writhed on the pavement, kicking up chunks of asphalt with its wide feet. It continued to scream. Jordan wanted it to stop.

Stupid thing, she thought. *Doesn't know when to keep its mouth shut.*

She marched over to it and kicked it in the jaw. A dark liquid sprayed from its mouth, and splattered her clothes. The screeching stopped. She kicked it again. She felt giddy. A surge of adrenaline had her smashing her foot down on the creature. There was a crunch. *Was that its skull?* She hoped it was.

"You got him," Owen said. He seemed far away, nothing but a blur in her periphery. Jordan lifted her leg. "Enough!" he said, wrapping an arm around her waist to pull her away.

Jordan turned on him. *How dare he tell me what to do? Does he have any idea who I am?*

Owen's eyes widened as she wrenched herself from his grip. He lost his balance, and fell to the ground.

"Hold on. Calm down!" he said, trying to get to his feet.

Jordan lurched forward. *What have I done?* "I'm sorry," she said, vision blurring. "I didn't, I mean, I don't know what..."

"Let's just get out of here," he said.

"Are you all right?" she asked, dropping down beside him. "Can you stand?"

"I'm fine." Owen winced, but got to his feet. "Nothing a few Band-Aids can't take care of."

Jordan frowned, and watched him limp toward the Mustang. "You don't look fine to me."

"Well, to be honest, I've been better," Owen snapped. "Would you mind taking me home now, please?"

This time the doors opened without any trouble. Cursing the creature under her breath, Jordan slid the keys into the ignition. Ran the palms of her hands over the wheel.

"Come on, darling," she murmured, sparing a glance at Owen, who was still fumbling with his seat belt. "Give me enough juice to get where we need to go." She started the car. It rumbled to life. "Thank you," she said, smacking her hand against the dashboard.

She backed up fast. Her shoulders met her ears even though the shocks absorbed most of the bump. She closed her eyes. It did nothing to block out the sound of tires crushing bones. She turned a sharp right onto Main.

"So. Where am I going?" she asked. Her nerves were still jumping; it was hard to keep the Mustang in her lane.

Owen was cradling his arm, his upper body hunched against the door. "Left. Next light."

Jordan made the turn. As the wheel straightened, she tried to get a good look at him. There wasn't enough light. A tiny shiver of concern made the back of her neck itch. "You doing okay?"

"Yeah. Turn right here," he murmured. "Third building."

She turned into the huge empty driveway. "You live in a warehouse?"

He grunted. "Converted it."

"Of course you did," Jordan said. She killed the engine, shoved the keys into her pocket, and got out of the car.

Owen's forehead banged against the passenger-side window. She darted over. A dark-red smear coated the inside of the glass. "Oh, no. No, no, no."

He pitched sideways when she opened the door. Jordan managed to lift him most of the way out before his weight became too much for her. They both fell to the ground.

Jordan untangled her limbs from his. She leaned over him, and patted his cheeks. "Owen. Wake up!"

Owen coughed, which sent blood dribbling down the corner of his mouth. She wasn't an expert, but she sure as hell knew that this wasn't a good sign.

Popping the trunk, Jordan rummaged through her bag for her cell. "Shit." The battery was dead. She shoved it into her pocket. Pressed her hands against her temples. *Calm down*, she thought. *Think.*

She remembered the "we" Owen mentioned when he asked her to stay with him. *I don't care who she is*, Jordan thought, *as long as she's home and has a working phone.* Clenching her teeth against the panic attack threatening to cut her lungs off from her brain, Jordan scrambled to her feet and ran up the steps leading to the door. She rang the doorbell, then slammed her fist against the wood.

He can't die, she thought. *I can't lose him too.* Images of her parents flashed through her mind. She rang the doorbell again. *I can't lose him.* She pounded both fists against the door. Owen's bleeding body joined her parents. Wide eyes. Open mouths.

When the door opened, Jordan fell forward with a sob.

A woman caught her by the arms. "Jordan?" she asked. "It *is* you! Holy smokes, what are you doing here?"

"Madison?" she asked. *Owen's sister*, she thought. *It's just his sister.*

"What's going on?" Madison asked. Her bubbly voice took on a crisp edge. "What happened?"

75

"Owen's hurt."

Jordan was almost knocked down the stairs as Madison pushed her aside. Jordan caught up with her as she was kneeling down by Owen.

"What have you done now?" Madison muttered.

"Is he going to be all right?" Jordan asked. Her eyes scanned Madison's face for any sign of worry, or fear.

"The big oaf is fine. Or at least he will be when we get him patched up." Madison moved toward his feet. "Do you mind giving me a hand? He's a heavy one."

"Shouldn't we call for help?" Jordan asked, hooking her arms under Owen's armpits. "I mean, an ambulance, the police, a neighbor? Someone?"

"Deep breaths, Jo," Madison said. She put her hands behind Owen's knees. "I'm premed. This isn't anything I can't handle. Pinky swear."

"Oh," Jordan said, relieved that at least one of them knew what to do.

Together they were able to lift Owen and move him inside. Jordan followed Madison's lead, through the entryway, down a hallway, and into a bedroom. She assumed it was Owen's. It reminded her very much of the office she had seen earlier. It was filled with sturdy wooden furniture.

As soon as they put Owen down on the wide bed, Jordan's body started to shake. It felt like she had done fifteen shots of espresso. "It came out of nowhere," she told Madison. She wrapped her arms around herself and started backing up toward the door. "I don't know what it was, but it was huge. It attacked us. *It attacked us!*" Her gaze darted about the room. "There isn't enough space in here," she said between panting breaths. "Why would you bring me into a room where there isn't enough space?"

Madison rushed to Jordan's side and put her hands firmly down on her shoulders. "There's enough room in here for all of us," she said in a soft voice. "Hey. Look at me." Her voice came at Jordan again, a little sharper. "I need you to look at me."

Jordan did as she was asked. "I'm shaking," was all she could manage to say.

"Yes, you are. You're going into shock," Madison told her. "The thing is I need your help with Owen. I can't manage on my own. Do you understand?"

Jordan gave a few quick nods.

"You're doing great, hon," Madison said. "Now. I need you to take a few deep breaths. Can you do that for me?"

Jordan closed her eyes and put her hands over Madison's. Her blood felt like it was racing through her veins, but she forced herself to take slow, deep breaths.

"Better?" Madison asked.

Not trusting her voice to work right, Jordan nodded again.

"Good. Now. Down the hall, to your left, is a bathroom. Under the sink, there's a first aid kit," Madison said, using her hands to outline the shape. "Would you mind grabbing it for me?"

"Sure," Jordan said. "I can do that." She darted away, skidded into the bathroom, and grabbed the kit. She ran back just as quickly.

Madison was just behind her with a bowl of water, and several towels. "Let's start with the worst of it, shall we?" she asked. She put the bowl down on the nightstand beside the bed, then bent down to take a closer look at his arm. "Excellent. This is good. The lacerations are deep, but not deep enough to need stitches." She tucked her hair behind her ears and opened the toolbox that Jordan had retrieved. "You're not shaking anymore. That's also a good sign. Have a seat, there on the bed beside Owen."

Jordan didn't want to ask why, but sat where Madison pointed.

"I'm going to keep talking to you, all right?" Madison continued. "It'll help to concentrate on something other than what happened." She opened the first aid kit. "I have to say, I almost freaked out seeing you on our front step. I mean, after all this time..." She trailed off with a warm laugh as she searched through the contents. "It's been forever since I've seen you."

She pulled out a bottle of antibacterial ointment and some Q-tips. She set them aside, drenched a towel in the water, and then dabbed at the blood on Owen's arm, a combination of dried and fresh.

"The last time I saw you was at that field party," Jordan said. The normalcy of the conversation helped her relax. "You were always away at boarding school."

"Don't remind me," Madison said. "That place tried to strip the originality right out of me. It was awful." She straightened. Reached for the ointment, opened the bottle, and held a Q-tip against the opening. She spread the ointment liberally along one of the raw gashes in his arm.

He moaned, and his head lolled back and forth, but he didn't wake.

"Oh boy! Owen, it's all right." Madison brushed a hand across his cheek. "You're safe."

Jordan took his hand in one of hers. "Let me help," she said. She gripped his wrist and braced herself. Madison continued to apply the ointment, her lips pinched together. Owen fought against Jordan, but she managed to hold him still.

"It's my fault. I should have known he was lying," she said. "He said he was fine. I believed him. I should have taken him to the hospital."

Madison snorted. "So he's got a little bit of common sense left in him." She reached for another Q-tip.

Jordan watched Madison work on a different section of Owen's arm. "What do you mean?"

Madison paused to look at her before applying ointment to the last wound. "I'm doing my residency here." She put the used Q-tip with the others on the side table, and started rummaging through the first aid kit again. She pulled out some bandage dressing. "It wasn't easy to work out, but it had been so long since Owen and I had spent any time together." She grinned as she began to bind his arm. "I totally made it happen."

She doesn't know how lucky she is, Jordan thought. *Not that it matters. Getting shut out of Parker's life was the best thing that ever happened to me.* She let go of Owen's hand.

Madison was busy securing the dressing. "Anyway, a couple of days after I moved in, Parker and Owen went to the River Six." Finished with Owen's arm, she grabbed a pair of scissors and started cutting down the length of his shirt. "It's the only club you'll find in Rolling River. Pretty swanky."

"I walked past it earlier today," Jordan said. "It was hard not to notice the sign with all those little bulbs. It's a great building..." She trailed off, remembering Levi and his perfect smile.

"That's the place," Madison said. "Anyway, Parker got trashed, and started running his mouth. He insulted someone's girlfriend and ended up taking on three guys at once. Owen jumped in to save the day and took most of the punches." She repeated the process of coating a Q-tip with ointment and applying it to the scores on his chest. "They both ended their night with a trip to the hospital. The cops threatened to lock them both up if either of them caused trouble again."

"Did Parker listen?"

"What do you think?" Madison asked.

"He didn't."

"Bingo. Got himself thrown in jail too."

"That idiot," Jordan exclaimed, bringing her fingers to her temples. "What happened? Wait. Why wasn't any of this in the news?"

"You have Owen to thank for that. He paid off the local guys, and the rest was taken care of by the fact that this little town really doesn't want the attention."

"Those boys have horseshoes up their asses."

"Not this time. At least not for Parker," Madison said. "Owen refused to bail him out of jail." She finished cleaning the wounds and started binding them. "There. That should do."

You left out a pretty key part of the story, buddy, Jordan thought to herself, glaring at Owen. *I thought you said he ran away. Were you ashamed to tell me you left him there?*

Much to Jordan's relief, the rest of Owen's wounds looked worse than they actually were. The blood Jordan had seen dripping from his mouth turned out to be nothing more than a gash from where his teeth had cut the inside of his cheek.

"All he needs now is a little rest," Madison said when she finished.

He's not the only one, Jordan thought, stifling a yawn. She helped Madison tidy up, and put the first aid kit back under the sink.

When she returned, Madison was no longer in Owen's room. Jordan wandered into what she assumed was the living room. It took her a moment to register the fact that all the furniture was white and supersized: a large floor rug, matching love seat, and two chairs flanked the white-tiled fireplace. She finally spotted Madison sitting on a long sofa. The only object that wasn't white was a glass coffee table in the middle of the room.

Madison rose to her feet. The sofa lengthened, morphing into a giant serpent. "How are you feeling?" she asked. The serpent's mouth widened. Pointed fangs glinted in the firelight. Its head slowly lowered above Madison. It looked like it was ready to strike...

Jordan cleared her throat. The sofa looked like a regular piece of furniture again. Madison was still standing in front of her. *Another hallucination*, Jordan thought while her heart pounded.

"Are you okay?" Madison said.

"Yeah, I'm fine. It was good to see you," Jordan said. "I wish it was under better circumstances."

"You can't possibly be thinking of leaving?" Madison said. "You can barely stand."

She gestured to the door with a thumb. "I really need to get going."

"There's no way I'm letting you leave here without getting you cleaned up first," Madison said, taking her by the arm. "You're covered in blood."

Jordan looked down at her clothes. "Oh."

Madison led her back toward the entrance. There was a staircase that led up to a loft, which Jordan hadn't noticed when she passed it the first time. When they reached the top, Madison opened the door, and flicked a light switch to reveal a carpeted room with a double bed already made up.

"Soap's in the shower," Madison said, taking Jordan into an adjoining bathroom and turning on the taps. "Towels are under the sink."

Jordan undressed and stepped into the tub. Hot water sluiced over her body, making her eyelids feel heavy. She scrubbed her skin until it was pink, and the water ran clear. When she was finished, she opened the curtain. A pair of cotton pants and T-shirt had replaced her clothes. She tugged them on before reentering the bedroom.

Madison was turning down the bed covers. Jordan noticed her cell phone charging on the nightstand; the Mustang's keys rested beside it.

"Thanks for everything," Jordan said, "but I really should get down to the police station."

Madison continued to fix the covers. "Why?"

"To get Parker out of jail," Jordan said. "Don't you think he's been there long enough?"

The crease between Madison's brow deepened ever so slightly. "Oh, hon, Parker's not in jail," she said, straightening from the bed.

"I thought you said…"

Madison shook her head. "I said *Owen* didn't bail him out. *Someone* did, though, a Mr. Smith." She arched a brow. "Want to take a guess how many Smiths there are in Rolling River?"

"Has Parker been in touch at all?"

"No," Madison said. "Owen's really torn up about it too."

"I'll bet he is," Jordan muttered. *He hadn't lied after all.* "It doesn't matter. I'd better get going if I'm ever going to find Parker."

"Jo, you're exhausted and emotional," Madison said. She put her hands on her hips. "To top it all off, I suspect you're still in shock. Take a nap, you'll feel better for it."

"Don't you want to know what happened?" Jordan asked.

Madison pulled her hair back over her shoulder. "Absolutely," she said. "But it's late. I can wait."

Jordan rubbed the heel of her palm against her closed eyelids. "All right," she said with a sigh, and moved over to the bed. "I'll just set the alarm on my cell."

"No need," Madison said, taking the device from Jordan's hands and placing it back on the nightstand. "I'll wake you up in a couple of hours. Sweet dreams." She made her way over to the door and paused with her hand on the light switch as Jordan got into bed. "By the way, I'm glad you're here."

Chapter 9
The Yearbook

It was dark. Jordan tried to get her legs to move away faster. From what, she wasn't sure. She couldn't see a damn thing.

In the distance, Jordan could make out two figures. They stood side by side, the pitch surrounding them like ink. Jordan squinted until the figures became distinguishable.

"Mom?" she called. "Dad!"

The sight of her parents propelled her forward. The sound of her own heavy breathing flooded her ears. Her parents stood still, their faces like stone masks. They didn't move to acknowledge her cries.

A great rumbling shook the ground beneath Jordan's racing feet. Mom's arm raised slowly into the air. Her finger pointed at Jordan like the barrel of a gun.

Mom's voice was a ghost of a whisper, but it reverberated around Jordan's head like a gong. *"It's coming."*

Dad's voice followed. *"Open your eyes. It's coming."*

"I miss you," Jordan shouted, wishing to hear the words herself.

Mom and Dad's flesh began to melt. Jordan's eyes were riveted to Mom's face. Mouth gaping, Jordan watched the first trickle of liquefied skin run down her face, dripping from her chin and onto her sweater like wax.

Jordan could hear herself screaming. "Hold on, Mom!" She pushed herself to run even faster. "Dad! Just hold on." Her thighs burned from the strain. Her next scream was cut short when whatever it was she was running from caught her from behind.

It swallowed her whole.

*****

Jordan woke with a start, sunlight warming her sweaty face. The shock of opening her eyes in an unfamiliar room after a nightmare made her feel like her heart was trying to punch its way through her chest.

Monsters were her first thought. Owen and Parker were her second. Getting the hell away from everything was her third.

Jordan reached toward the nightstand for her cell phone. With shaking fingers, she pressed a button to turn the backlight on. Six thirty a.m. *Surely no one else will be up at this hour.* She stared at the time until the light went out. That third thought was damn appealing.

Snippets of what had happened only a few hours before, the day before, the week before, ran through her mind. She squeezed her eyelids shut, as if she could pause the slide show of memories she would rather forget. *I should have been there to help Mom and Dad*, she told herself. *But I was there last night. I got Owen the help he needed. Made sure he was safe.* Her thoughts added a disjointed soundtrack to the images flooding her mind. *There's no reason to stay.*

Jordan swung her legs over the side of the bed, clenching her jaw when she felt her limbs tremble from the effort. She slid her phone into the pocket of her borrowed pyjama pants. Her mind was made up. She would leave immediately. With the rest of her things still in the Mustang, and her clothes from the night before nowhere to be found, Jordan made a silent promise to return the clothes she was wearing as soon as she could.

The bedroom door shut behind her with a quiet click. When she reached the stairs, she recalled that they were creaky. Jordan placed a foot on the first step. She shifted her balance, winced, then raised her other foot and set it down on the next.

A shadowed figure glided around the corner before Jordan could put the rest of her weight down. She fought against her body's desire to fall down the rest of the stairs, wet herself, or complete a simultaneous combination of both. Jordan tensed, prepared to run back the way she had come. The light to the entryway switched on.

"Good morning!" Madison said. "I hope you slept well. I know, I know." She waved a hand in Jordan's direction. "You only wanted to take a nap, but you looked so worn-down I just didn't have the heart to wake you."

She walked toward Jordan on long, lean legs, exposed by the baby-blue short-shorts she was wearing. Her hair bounced in time with each step, and it wasn't the only thing that was full of spring. Jordan tugged at her T-shirt and wished she had taken the time to at least comb her fingers through her hair. And grow boobs. The woman belonged on a billboard.

"Coffee?" The smile slipped from Madison's face. "Oh, man," she said, retracting the offered mug. It was then that Jordan noticed her nails were painted neon yellow. "I totally wigged you out, didn't I? Sorry."

"That's all right," Jordan told her, taking another step. She tried to keep her tone as light as possible.

Madison offered the coffee again. "Here. This will fix everything. Seriously. It's not that instant crap." Jordan took another step and watched the tendrils of steam waft upward. "Ground the beans myself."

Madison's voice was so...*pleasant*. Jordan forgot she had been trying to leave. The aroma was now overpowering all of Jordan's other senses. Her hands itched to take the mug. *Is that hazelnut?* she wondered.

"No thanks," she forced herself to say. There was no way she could accept the coffee and then disappear. She had accepted enough hospitality already. "I've been trying to cut back."

"Good for you," Madison said with a sigh. She brought the mug to her lips and took a sip. Sighed again. "I can't seem to shake the habit."

Don't ask any questions, Jordan told herself. *Cut yourself loose. Nice and simple.* "I was going to get my things from the car," she told Madison.

"Oh, you don't have to do that now. Have some breakfast first. I'll help you bring everything up after."

"No," Jordan said a little too quickly. She skipped the last step, and started tugging on the shoes that she had left in the entryway. "I really prefer using my own stuff. You know how it is." She rose to see Madison looking at her with a frown. "I mean, shampoo, you know? Finally got something that takes the frizz right out of my hair."

Madison's eyes lit up. "What brand?" she asked, clasping both hands around the mug like a kid who's just seen the display window of a candy store.

"Ah, um..." Jordan began. *Why the hell did you have to mention a beauty product?* "I...found it in Europe. Can't for the life of me pronounce the name."

"Oh, gosh, I'm so rude. Why don't you show it to me at breakfast. I make pretty awesome waffles," Madison said as she started back down the hallway. "It'll be ready in an hour, so take your time."

*****

Outside, Jordan tried not break into a sprint when she caught sight of the Mustang.

She glanced up at the warehouse. It wasn't as if Owen could watch her from his room, and she had plenty of time before Madison came looking for her. Even so, she rushed over.

Slipping behind the wheel, Jordan continued to glance out the rearview mirror. *Get a grip. No one's going to stop you.* She wiggled the key in the ignition, turned it. The engine rumbled, stuttered, died. Jordan tried to ignore the knot forming in her chest. The feeling that someone was watching her, and getting closer. She turned the key again. And again.

The old girl wasn't going to start.

"You had enough gas to bring me here. You could have saved a little to get me the hell out again," she said, resting her head against the seat. *Why did you come here?* she asked herself. *Why did you let that letter sway you?*

No money. No Parker. No gas. Looked like she was good and stuck.

"Well, shit."

Jordan got out of the Mustang, slammed the door shut, and walked away before she gave in to the urge to kick it. After a few deep breaths, she turned back, and got her things out of the trunk.

Her string of curses was interrupted by a vibration in her pocket. She shifted her bag to her other hand, pulled out her cell, and held it to her ear. "Hello?"

"Oh, thank God. Are you all right?" Tully's nasal voice blared in her ear. "When you didn't come home last night, I thought—"

"It's none of your business how I'm doing," Jordan interrupted.

"What are you talking about?" Tully blustered on. "The wife and I woke up yesterday morning only to find you and your things gone, and the basement torn apart."

Jordan wanted to hang up. She took a deep breath. "Is this a joke, Tully? Because I've got to say I'm really not in the mood."

"Did you leave to find Parker?" he asked. "I mean, that's swell and all. You can do what you like, but at least leave a note."

"You kicked me out. Why are you acting like it never happened?"

There was a pause. "What are you talking about?" Tully finally said. "Why would I do that?"

Jordan sagged against the Mustang. "You don't remember?" His response was silence.

"Hello?" Jordan stood upright. Looked at the cell's screen. Put it back to her ear. "You still there?"

"*Your service has been disconnected,*" a female voice told her. "*To reinstate your services, please contact us at your earliest convenience.*"

"Oh, for crying out loud," Jordan said, turning her phone off and on again. She tried to redial Tully.

"*Your service has been disconnected...*"

"Gah!" she yelled at the voice. She shoved her cell back into her pocket, picked up her bag, and headed back inside.

*****

In the apartment, she could hear the metallic clang of pot hitting pan. Dragging her stuff behind her, Jordan struggled up the stairs to the loft and shut the door.

She grabbed the portable phone from the nightstand, and made another silent promise to pay Madison and Owen back for the charges as she punched in Tully's number.

"You swear you don't remember?" Jordan said when he answered. She bit her lower lip to stop it from trembling.

"Scouts' honor," Tully said. "What happened? What did I say?"

"You told me..." she started, then hesitated. "It was nothing. I guess I overreacted."

"Do you need help?"

"No," Jordan said. She closed her eyes and mouthed the word *yes*.

"You let me know if you do," Tully told her. "Listen, there's something you should know." He sounded tired. "I got a tip this morning. Someone saying they saw Parker entering the house a few days before you came home."

Jordan flopped backward against the bed. "Jesus," she said in a low voice. "Please tell me this doesn't mean what I think it means."

"I'm afraid so." Tully cleared his throat. "We need to bring Parker in for questioning."

After telling Tully what she knew about Parker's whereabouts, Jordan hung up. This wasn't what she had envisioned when she decided to come home. After traveling for so long, she craved normalcy, and had come back to chaos. Death and guilt. Anxiety gutted her peace of mind. *Damn it, Parker*, she thought, *where* are *you?*

"Hey." Madison's head popped out from behind the door as she opened it. "Breakfast is ready."

Jordan followed Madison down the loft stairs, and through the hallway. Jordan sped up as they got closer to Owen's room. She was grateful that the door was closed. They walked past another room. Jordan assumed it was Madison's. She had never seen so much pink contained in such a small space before. It was a little overwhelming. The only part that wasn't blinding was the wall behind the desk. It was covered with a huge map of the world, dotted with many pins.

"You look refreshed," Madison said when they entered the kitchen. It was distinctly masculine in design, with dark-stained cabinets and black-speckled marble counters. "Help yourself, hon!" She gestured to the little round breakfast table occupying a corner of the room.

As promised, there was a plate piled with golden waffles. Strawberries cut into quarters filled a bowl, and there was an assortment of jam, honey, and maple syrup lining the table.

"Did you find everything okay?" Madison asked.

"Yes, thank you," Jordan said, taking a seat. She ran a hand over her curling hair and tried not to stare at Madison's pin-straight locks.

"Owen's awake."

"He is?" Jordan said. She stabbed a waffle, but was grateful for the news. It meant she didn't have to ask. "Good to hear." She added several chunks of strawberries and unscrewed the top from the maple syrup.

She cut off a piece of waffle, speared a strawberry against it, and brought it to her mouth. "Mmm. You weren't kidding, this is amazing," she exclaimed around the mouthful of food.

"Thanks," Madison said with a beaming smile before the mirth slid away from her face. "Owen told me about your parents. You should have said something. I'm so sorry. If you need any help with anything, you only have to ask."

"Don't worry about it," Jordan said, pushing the waffle with the tip of her fork. "I don't plan on going back home for a little while yet. I need a little…space."

"You don't have to talk about it," Madison told her. She pushed her hair back from her face with her free hand, stared at the ground, pursed her lips, and then sat down in the chair across from Jordan. "I know how nosy I can be, so I'll change the subject. What happened last night?"

The tension went out of Jordan's shoulders. This, she could talk about. She poured herself a glass of orange juice, and launched into retelling what happened the night before.

"What do you think it was?" Madison asked when she was finished.

Jordan stared at what was left of her waffle. "Honestly?" She looked up at Madison. "I have no idea. It was dark. Owen was screaming. Everything happened so fast…"

Madison plucked a berry from the bowl. Popped it into her mouth. "Let's go see it."

"What?"

"You kicked its ass and backed over it. The remains should still be there, right?" Madison asked. "Let's go take a look, maybe we can identify it."

"I don't know if that's a good idea." Jordan dropped her fork onto her plate. Her bowels clenched as she envisioned showing Madison the body, only to have it come back to life and claw her face off. "I really need to find Parker."

"It's a great idea," Madison said. "We have to hurry, though. I have to head out to work in a few hours."

*****

"Maybe the SPCA picked it up," Jordan said, crouching down beside a dark puddle of black slime.

They had walked to the park, but the creature's body was nowhere to be found.

"We could always call to find out," Madison said, joining Jordan. She rummaged through her oversized purse and pulled out a plastic vial. Using one hand, she scooped up some of the substance.

"What are you doing?" Jordan asked, slightly amused.

"I can sneak a sample into the lab at work. Get my friend to run a few tests to see what sort of DNA we're dealing with," Madison said. She capped the tube with a rubber stopper and slipped it back into her purse. "Mystery solved."

"Maybe," Jordan said. She knew what she had seen wasn't like any animal she could name.

"Sorry to cut this field trip short, but I've got to get back and get ready for my shift," Madison said, leaning forward to pat Jordan's arm. "I can't convince you to stay?"

"Actually, yes." Jordan said. "For a little while at least," she said without looking at Madison. They rose to their feet together.

"That's great! We're glad to have you," Madison said. "When I get home, I can get started on some research. I've got a few books on reptiles somewhere. Let's see if we can't figure this out." She laughed. "It'll be fun. Promise."

"Right," Jordan said. Research wouldn't provide the funds she needed to find Parker.

"Do you mind checking in on Owen while I'm gone?" Madison asked as they headed back to the warehouse.

"Um, okay."

"You know what?" Madison said with a slight frown. "On second thought, I really shouldn't impose on you like that. Don't worry about it. I'll call and let work know I can't make it in today."

"No, no!" Jordan said without thinking. "I can look after him for a few hours. It's not a problem."

"Are you sure?"

"Of course," Jordan said, wishing Madison wasn't so damn good at making her feel guilty. It darkened her already bleak mood.

After Madison left for work, Jordan went back to the loft to make her bed. An excuse to put off checking up on Owen for a little while.

What the hell am I going to do? she thought to herself as she tugged the sheet toward the headboard. *I should have sold the damn house. I should have stayed away from this place. From Owen.* She tossed the duvet on top of the sheet and began straightening it out. *Instead I'm stuck here. Completely broke, with no family I can turn to.* She picked up a pillow, thought about Tully. *Or want to turn to.* She picked up the other pillow and tossed them onto the bed.

"Damn it, Parker," she said aloud. Her voice sounded tiny in the large room. "Why can't you act like a normal person and be where you're supposed to be?"

Jordan sat down on the edge of the bed for a split second before getting to her feet. She reached for her duffel bag and went through her things, checking pockets, bags, and crevices for cash. There wasn't any.

With nothing else to do, Jordan looked around the room. There was a walk-in closet. The door was half-closed, and pitch-black on the other side. Her hands immediately balled into fists. She didn't want them to start shaking.

It's just a closet, she told herself. *There isn't a monster waiting to slash you open on the other side.* A trickle of laughter escaped before she cut it off. *Listen to yourself. You handled whatever it was that attacked Owen. If there's anything hiding in there, you can handle that too.*

Jordan counted to three, held her breath, then flung the closet door the rest of the way open. A length of string dangled from the ceiling. She pulled it, and light filled the space.

The closet was empty, except for a single cardboard box tucked against the corner.

"See?" Jordan told herself. "Nothing to be afraid of." She wiped her hands on the back of her jeans.

A mark on the box caught her eye. Curious, she knelt down and pulled the box toward her. Along one side, "Parker" had been written in thick black marker.

Monsters forgotten, Jordan carried it out of the closet with little difficulty. She sat on the floor beside the bed. "Please," she muttered to herself. "Let there be something in here I can use to find you."

She opened it, and peered inside. All it contained was a yearbook.

Jordan stared at the cover. "Graduating year," she murmured. She didn't have many memories of that year that didn't include Parker. It had been the best year of high school, until the summer at least.

She flipped through several pages, noticed that the corners of several of them had been turned down. As she went through, she couldn't stop smiling over the pictures, the bittersweet memories they held. She also recognized a pattern. All the marked pages were pictures of her and Parker, Parker and Owen, or just of Parker himself.

"You always were a vain bastard," she said. Her fingers gently smoothed one page, lingering over a photo of her and her brother, covered in bits of food. Identical grins stretching from ear to ear.

*****

"Can you see it?" Parker had asked. He pointed to a spot on his forehead. "Huge zit. Right there."

Jordan squinted. "What are you talking about?" She gave his arm a gentle smack. "I don't see anything." She turned back to her backpack, pulled out a banana.

"It's still growing in," Parker said, rubbing at the area with the palm of his hand. "I'm going to grab a soda," he told her. "You want anything?"

"Nope," she told him. "You should try a fruit sometime. Maybe then you won't have to worry about huge phantom zits."

"Just taking advantage of my metabolism while I still can," Parker told her before heading toward the vending machine on the other side of the cafeteria.

"Hey, Red." The voice came from behind her. The tone made Jordan cringe. She knew who it was without even looking.

"Creeping up on your prey now, Henry?" she asked, with as much nonchalance as she could muster. "Practicing for college?"

Henry sauntered around the table. His curly hair was slicked back with gel. Thin lips were curled back in a grimacing smile. Jordan could barely breathe. The scent of cheap cologne trailed after him like a cloak.

"I've been wondering, since we're graduating in a couple of days, if you'd answer a question that's been burning in the back of my mind," he said. He licked his lips, and didn't wait for her to respond. "Does the carpet match the drapes?"

Jordan debated throwing her banana at him, then thought better of it. She didn't want to waste perfectly good fruit on the school's chairman of the Douche Bag Club. "Did your mother teach you that one?" she asked instead.

"Why don't you put that down?" Henry continued. "I've got something tastier you can wrap your lips—"

"Shut the fuck up," someone said. "Right now."

Jordan's gaze shifted. Parker stood a few feet away. A can of soda was clenched in his hand.

"Aw, come on, man," Henry said, taking a step back. "You keep hovering like this and your sister'll be a virgin forever. Just trying to help out."

Henry was too stupid to see that he was about to get punched in the face. Parker's bicep tensed, his nostrils flared. The punch would land before Jordan had time to stop him. Parker would get suspended. He wouldn't be able to attend graduation.

"Food fight," Jordan screamed, launching her banana at the table across from her.

The reaction was instantaneous. Students picked up their sandwiches, fruit cups, pudding, cakes, fruit, chocolate bars. Food was launched in her direction. Parker shook his can of soda, opened it, and let it explode in Henry's face. He was finally taken down by a Jell-O assault.

Jordan snatched her backpack and ran from the table, delighted laughter bubbling from her lips. She grabbed Parker's hand. A piece of processed cheese landed on her head as they made their escape. A camera flash went off.

Outside the school, Jordan collapsed against the wall, still laughing.

Parker's face was serious. "You should have let me punch him," he said, sitting down beside her. "He had *no* right speaking to you like that."

"He isn't worth it," Jordan told him with a shrug.

"I mean it," Parker said in a heated voice. "That asshole has been pissing us off all year. Owen would agree with me. You should have let me get in two shots. At least."

"Naw," Jordan told him, leaning her head on his shoulder. She wanted to lighten the mood, get him to relax and enjoy the spectacular way in which they had retaliated against Henry. "A fight would have gotten you suspended. And what would you have done if he had given you a nice shiner, right before grad?" She sighed for dramatic effect. "I bet you prefer that zit now, huh?"

Parker didn't respond.

*****

Jordan quickly flipped the yearbook page. Her hands stilled. She brought the book closer to her face. Ran her finger along the binding. Yes. There was a rough edge. Parker had removed a page. But why?

She went back to the beginning of the book and flipped through it again, looking for other missing pages. There weren't any. It seemed there was something about page fifteen that Parker didn't like. *Come on, Jordan, think. Why would he take everything but the yearbook with him? Is the ripped page a clue?*

"You're in some serious shit, aren't you?" she asked, jabbing a finger at a picture of Parker. She and Owen were there too. They looked so happy.

Jordan left the yearbook on the floor and rose to her feet, thinking. She combed her fingers through the length of her hair until it crackled with static.

"But I can't go back there. Not yet."

She paced the small length of carpet beside the bed, trying to figure out how the hell to get her own yearbook without having to go back to her parents' house. *Her* house. There just wasn't a way. Unless...

Jordan gazed down at the photo of the three of them. *Perhaps it's time to check on Owen.*

Chapter 10
Unfiltered Truth

Jordan knocked on the door, opened it, and stuck her head inside Owen's room.

He was lying in bed, his left arm stretched out beside him. His right, which Madison had wrapped the night before, rested across his stomach. A sheet covered him up to the waist.

She crept farther into the room, debating. *Should I wake him up?* She considered her options.

"Owen," she whispered.

He didn't stir. His breath continued in the same steady rhythm.

"Can't say I didn't try," she muttered under her breath. With no bookshelf in the room, she turned to the closet. The door was open. A mess of shoes, clothes, and hats littered the floor and shelves. With the tips of her fingers, Jordan lifted a shirtsleeve near the bottom of the pile to see what lay beneath. More clothes.

A snarky remark rested on the tip of her tongue. She bit the inside of her cheek, and let the sleeve fall back into place. *Who am I to judge?* she thought. *I'm the one snooping. Now, if I were a yearbook, where would I be?*

She looked up. Several books were piled in a haphazard fashion on a shelf above his ties and belts. Lifting her weight onto her tiptoes, Jordan saw a book with dark binding, propping up several other books. Embossed in gold was their high school's name.

Without thinking, she reached for the book. It wasn't until she had it most of the way out that she realized what a poor plan it was. The surrounding books toppled over, raining down on her head. She didn't have enough hands to stop them all, so when a second one hit her head, she yanked the yearbook out and jumped out of the way. The rest of the books thudded to the floor.

Please be the right year, Jordan thought to herself, ignoring the mess she had made. She hunched over the book to get a better look at the cover. Nope. It was the wrong one, of course.

Her hands stilled as she heard movement from the direction of Owen's bed.

"Can I help you?" he asked.

Damn you, clumsy fingers, she thought.

"You're looking well," she told him, straightening.

She didn't know how to drop the book without drawing even more attention to the fact that she had been going through his things.

Owen propped himself up so that his back was resting against the headboard. Jordan noticed that the color had returned to his face, although it was a little on the red side at the moment. *Don't you dare look at his abs*, she warned herself.

He watched her with eyes that shone like dark glass. "What are you doing?" he finally asked.

"Oh, hell," she mumbled. If she talked fast, maybe she could squeeze in her question about the yearbook before...

"Jesus, Jo," he said, wincing as he adjusted his position. "I get it. You're keeping secrets, that's fine. But going through my things while I'm sleeping? Why did *that* seem like a good idea?"

"I was going to ask you," she said, her tone defensive. Well, at least she wanted to sound that way. Petulant was probably a better description. She cleared her throat. Tried again. "I didn't want to wake you. You need to rest."

"Really."

"Yes," Jordan said. Since she was talking to him, it was now or never. She held out the yearbook. "I was looking for the one from our graduating year. Do you still have it? Here," she said when he reached out to take it. "You're going to reopen a wound or something." She brought it over to him.

He glanced at the cover, then put it aside. "This is the only one I've kept," he told her. "I'm not sure where the rest are." He moved to cross his arms over his chest, tensed, and then rested his hands in his lap instead.

"I found Parker's yearbook in the loft," she said, sitting on the edge of the bed. "There's a page missing."

"So?"

"So?" Jordan repeated. "You had a rough night. I'll throw you a lifeline. I think that whatever is on that missing page is important. Maybe it can help us find Parker."

Owen gave her a blank stare, then tossed the sheet aside. Jordan shot to her feet.

"What are you doing?" she hissed. He slowly swung his legs over the edge of the bed. She cringed when he grimaced, felt her muscles tense as his began to quiver.

"We're going out," he announced. He was grinning, but a thin sheen of sweat covered his forehead.

"You're insane," Jordan told him. "We aren't going anywhere. Now get back into bed." She moved to try and get him to lie down, but he got hold of her arm and used it to pull himself to his feet.

"Thanks," he said with a wink. Limping heavily on one side, he made his way over to his closet. "Since you're here, why don't we catch a game of hardball? Rolling River's got a pretty good team."

"I don't watch baseball anymore."

"Now that's too bad," Owen said pulling on a pair of sweatpants. "You were always my favorite heckling buddy." It took him a little while to pull a T-shirt over his head.

"I'm not going," Jordan told him.

"All right," Owen said, pulling a ball cap onto his head. "I'll see you in a couple of hours then. I need to stretch, and lying here isn't stretching."

*****

Owen held the bag out, shook it. "Peanuts?"

Jordan's response was a glare. When she was satisfied he understood, she leaned forward on the metal seat, resting her elbows on her thighs. She wouldn't admit it out loud, but the game was fantastic.

The view of Old Port from the stands made her wish she had made the effort to see a game here more often. The stadium was open, with a short metal fence separating the field from the boardwalk. It meant she could watch the sun transform Rolling River into a sparkling backdrop. It also made her feel warm and romantic, so she tried not to let her attention wander from the game for too long.

The crowd groaned when a sharp crack ripped through the air. A player from the opposing team had hit the ball deep into center field. The ball landed and bounced against the fence before it was caught and sent shooting toward second base.

"Come on," Jordan shouted when the umpire made his call. "Are you blind? He's out!" She frowned when she heard Owen chuckling. "Shut up," she muttered. "It was a terrible call."

"Remember our first game?" he asked. Out of the corner of her eye, she could see him looking down at her. "We were what, ten years old?"

Jordan remembered. It was the first time something inside her had shifted, made her realize that what she felt for Owen was something more than friendship.

"I was up to bat, and this loudmouthed kid on the other team started laying into me." Owen shifted. The narrow seats didn't give much in the way of room. His knee brushed hers. She waited to see if he would move it; he didn't. "I struck out and he let me have it. I still get embarrassed thinking about it."

Like anything could embarrass you, Jordan thought, and she snorted without thinking. Owen grinned. "You walked right up to that punk-ass kid and jabbed your finger into his chest so hard he almost fell over."

"I think he was just surprised that something so tiny could be so loud." She looked at Owen, and frowned for letting herself get drawn in.

"You got kicked out of the game," Owen said.

"We *both* got kicked out of the game," Jordan retorted, before she realized it was exactly what he wanted.

"And I loved you for it."

She went very still.

He continued. "You were always so brave when it came to Parker and me—"

"All right, that's enough," she said through clenched teeth. "What game are you playing now? Is it the one where you get me all doe-eyed and nostalgic to try and make me forget that you tossed me aside like a piece of trash?"

"That's not what I'm trying to do," Owen said. He had the gumption to look hurt.

"You *kissed* me," she hissed. "You had to know how I felt about you. You're not exactly the sharpest crayon in the box, but you aren't *that* clueless." She stood up and noticed that they had gained an audience. The people seated around them were openly staring.

"Listen, I've been trying to explain." Owen tried to grab her arm. "For *years* I've been trying to explain. Why won't you give me the chance?"

Jordan looked over her shoulder as she started walking down the stairs.

"Because it doesn't matter what you have to say now," she said. "It's what you said in the moment that counts." She could feel more eyes on her as she made her escape.

"Jo, please," she heard him call after her, but she didn't want to deal with the whispered conversation and speculative looks from the crowd. It was enough that her face felt as though it were engulfed in flames.

Jordan didn't stop walking until she was behind the stands, near the concession booths. They were oddly deserted, so it was strange to hear the sounds of stomping feet and muffled conversation coming from above her.

"What are you doing?" she asked herself. She tangled her fingers in her hair and tugged. She wanted to go back. She wanted to ask Owen what it was that he had been trying to tell her. She just couldn't do it. She was too scared of what he might say.

I will uncover his secret.

Before the voice in her head had finished speaking, Jordan was running back the way she had come. Something was wrong. When she was about halfway there, the air in front of her changed. Her hand punched through it first, and the momentum of her legs carried her the rest of the way before she could stop herself. Her legs buckled and she fell to the ground. It felt like she had run straight through a wall.

"No." Her voice sounded muffled to her ears as she tried to get her arms under her body. She pushed herself up, and staggered to her feet. *Something's wrong. Something's not right. Something's wrong.* The words repeated themselves in her head, like a mantra. A horrible, gut-wrenching tune.

She took tiny, cautious steps as she moved forward. The late afternoon sun shone brightly, not a cloud in the sky. It set her senses off like an alarm bell. Keeping her body low, she reached the side of the stands. Holding her breath, she peered over the edge of the wall.

The players had disappeared from the field. The crowd had vanished from the stands. Two figures stood facing each other in the middle of the pitcher's mound. Even from a distance Jordan recognized Owen. His attention was focused on a figure hovering in front of him.

The figure looked like a man; it was certainly shaped like one, but its feet weren't touching the ground. He floated in midair. Jordan shifted to try and see his face. As if the figure had heard her thoughts, he pivoted to face her. She had to clamp a hand over her mouth. He had no features. His face was blank, like an empty canvas.

Owen turned beside the figure. His movements were strange, as if he were a puppet, and someone was pulling the strings. In slow motion, his head began to tilt backward, like someone was pulling on his hair. He didn't show any outward sign of struggle, but he did start to scream.

Jordan stifled a sob. She didn't know why. It was unlikely she would be heard. The sound lingered in the air as Owen's head moved back to a more natural position.

Owen's lips moved, and yet it wasn't him speaking. His voice wasn't gritty, nor that deep. "I know you are here. Do you enjoy watching your friend suffer?"

Owen's head tilted again, even farther back this time. The thin column of his throat was pronounced against his stretched skin. He screamed again, but the sound was cut off as his hand gripped his own flesh. Owen's face turned red, his lips gaping like a fish.

An image of Jordan's mother flashed through her mind. Head bent back on the pillow. Blood pooled on the sheets.

"Stop it. Please, stop hurting him," Jordan yelled, stumbling out from behind the bleachers.

Owen's head snapped forward. His hand fell away from his neck. He gave her a smile, so very unlike his own lopsided grin. It was more of a grimace, a baring of teeth.

Heat began to build in the pit of Jordan's stomach. She started forward, clenching her fists to stop her hands from shaking.

The hovering man, she thought, *he's like the other creatures. Where are these things coming from? What the hell am I supposed to do?*

She wanted to turn tail and run. The only thing stopping her was that this man was somehow able to control Owen. It was worse than watching him get sliced apart.

When she reached the pitcher's mound, Jordan let out the breath she had been holding. Owen's hand shot out to grip her arm, fingers digging into her flesh as he pulled her toward him. "What do you think you're doing?" he asked, sounding like himself again. The way he was looking at her was a different story. His eyes were narrowed, and his lips formed a sneer.

Jordan glanced behind Owen and saw the figure, still hovering. *If I could only get closer, maybe I could...*

Her vision blurred. When it cleared, she was looking down at herself and Owen. *I look rather composed for being scared out of my mind,* she thought. Then she was flooded with a surge of resentment. The emotion tousled her around, pushing her farther and farther into what felt like a corner, until she was shoved violently. She shook her head, and blinked. When she could see again, she was looking back up at Owen.

"Are you even listening?" he asked, tightening his grip on her.

"You're hurting me," she replied. The strange switch was forgotten as she pushed him, struggling to get her arm back. She debated kicking him, but she didn't want to hurt him.

"Am I?" he asked, in a tone dripping with sarcasm. "Maybe I think it's the only way you'll listen."

He started dragging her. Away from the mound. Toward the fence with the boardwalk and the river on the other side.

"This isn't you," she said. Her voice betrayed her fear. "You would never treat anyone like this." She tried to dig her heels into the gravel, but Owen continued to pull her along with him. "That...that man is *controlling* you!"

When Owen didn't even register that he had heard her, Jordan decided that hurting him was the least of her worries. She swept her leg behind both his knees. Owen tumbled backward but kept his grip on her, forcing her to fall with him. She scratched his arm, and bit the fleshy part of his hand. *This isn't possible*, she thought. *He shouldn't be able to hold on to me like this.*

He threw his body on top of her. Pinning her down like a deadweight. "You bitch," he wheezed.

"You need to listen to me," she yelled.

"No. *You* need to fucking *listen*." He rose to his feet, yanked her up. He started toward the fence again. They were on the grass now. "Do I finally have your attention?"

He was too strong. He was resistant to pain. Jordan was out of options. "Help!" she screamed, turning to scan the field. It was still empty. In front of her, the boardwalk was deserted.

In the distance, the figure became visible again behind Owen. Jordan's throat clenched shut.

"I'm teaching you a lesson," Owen said, drawing her attention back to him.

"What are you talking—"

"Don't you dare pretend you have no idea what this is about," he snapped, interrupting her question. He lifted her and pitched her over the fence. Jordan scrambled to her feet, but he was already in front of her, blocking her escape. He grabbed her hand and started stalking toward the water.

"I don't know what you're talking about," she yelled, hitting him between his shoulder blades. She tried to push him off balance. To get him to stop moving.

"Then let me tell you," Owen said, his voice breaking. "I'm in love with Parker."

Jordan felt like the wind had been knocked from her lungs. She stared at Owen, searching for clues. A part of her hoped that the silent figure was making him say the words. One look at his face told her that while his actions were being controlled, his words belonged to him.

"I thought he loved me too. We were happy together," Owen went on to say. "But he left me. He left me and you wouldn't listen."

The figure had disappeared. There was nothing behind them now but dark shadows. Jordan screamed for help again, knowing all the while that no one would hear her. Owen dragged her forward. With each step, the darkness lapped at her heels. Water kissed his feet. Hers. When the water was up to her knees, Owen tossed Jordan in.

When she resurfaced, he was there. Before she could catch her breath, he pinched her face between his hands until her lips puckered. "I can't look at you without thinking of him."

Jordan tried to get her feet under her. He only squeezed harder, until her molars cut into the sides of her cheeks. Her eyes watered. A metallic flavor filled her mouth.

Forgive me, she thought, shifting so that her weight was on her bottom. She brought her knee to her chest and let it spring forward. The heel of her foot caught Owen right between the legs. He stumbled back, letting go of her face as his body told his hands they were needed elsewhere.

Get up, she told herself. *Run. Now!*

Her limbs wouldn't cooperate. She caught a glimpse of Owen reaching for her. *That's not possible*, she thought. *There's no way he could have recovered so fast.*

Jordan's head snapped back as his fingertips caught her hair. She fell into the water and came up sputtering. Bile rose to the back of her throat. *If you don't get your ass back to shore right now...You. Are. Going. To. Die.*

"Parker is mine," she heard Owen say. He screamed the words like an animal. "*Mine!*"

Jordan didn't have time to respond. He pushed her underwater. Panic set in, and she struggled, flailing her arms and legs about, attempting to kick

Owen, to get him to release her.

He pulled her out by the hair. She tugged at his hand, not caring if she ripped half of it out to get him to let go. She was submerged again.

Owen yanked her out. Jordan could barely make out what he was saying. She gasped for air, trying to take in as much as she could before he inevitably put her under again. "Are you listening now?" His voice came from behind her. He put a hand on the nape of her neck. "Are you?"

He held her under a long while this time. Jordan's lungs burned to exhale. She felt helpless. Angry. Murderous. She felt a strange heat emanating from Owen's palms. Her skin felt irritated at first, like she had been stung by a jellyfish. It soon increased to an uncomfortable burn.

Jordan's eyes were closed, but she saw herself. Her body floating underwater. Her thoughts didn't make sense. *Why did he leave me? My lover. My life.* There was so much pain. So much hurt. Amid the jumbled rush of thoughts, Jordan needed air. Now. There wasn't time. She needed to *do* something. Anything.

She forced her body to relax. Let her arms and legs drift. Owen loosened his grip, giving Jordan enough slack to twist around. Carried by her momentum, her hand connected with the center of his chest. There were two distinct heartbeats. *Is the figure inside him?* she thought. There wasn't any time to debate how illogical the thought was.

Owen shoved her under again but Jordan gripped the material of his shirt in her fist. As she struggled, she tried to pull him down with her. At least that was her intent. Instead, she felt something icy slide around and down her forearm, over her shoulder, and across her chest.

Owen released her, and as her head broke the water, she screamed as the thing tried to force its way inside her pores. It felt like hundreds of thousands of needles pricking her skin at the same time. She squeezed her eyelids tight against the pain, and gasped for air.

The pain grew sharper as whatever it was dug deeper. Wanting nothing more than to make the pain stop, Jordan clawed at herself. The thought of some unknown entity forcing its way into her body triggered her gag reflex. Her stomach spasmed, and it took all her energy to keep from buckling over. Whatever it was surrounding her knew she was weakening. She was trapped. She was going to drown.

Desperate, she dug her nails into the skin of her arm and dragged them down. Spots clouded her vision; for a terrifying moment, the thought she was going to keel over face first.

Whatever it was that had been clinging to her flesh let go with a slight suction sound. Her eyelids flickered open. A cloud of swirling darkness floated in front of her. She blinked trying to make sense of what she was seeing, and remain conscious.

The shadow swirled, moving together, then apart, twisting around until she stumbled backward. For an instant she had seen a hollow face, with a gaping mouth, bottom teeth overgrown and curling out and over its top lip. When she looked again, the sun was out. There was a commotion on the field. A player had hit a home run. The crowd was going wild.

Jordan stood knee-deep in the river shivering and confused. "Owen," she called. She waited, turning, scanning the water with her eyes. No response.

"Oh, shit," she said when she spotted him. He was floating facedown. She swam over to him, flipped him over, and pulled him toward the riverbank. Her muscles ached, her lungs wanted more air. She should have called for help. She wasn't going to make it.

Someone was taking Owen from her. Helped her make the last few strokes to shore. Jordan managed to drag herself onto the grass where she collapsed.

"Deep breaths now." A pair of pale-gray eyes peered down at her. Jordan didn't know when she had been so happy to hear the sound of someone's voice before.

"Great timing," she said. Her throat felt tight, which explained why her voice sounded so weak and hoarse. "Owen," she started to say.

"He's breathing," the woman said. Water dripped from her short cap of white hair, onto Jordan's face.

She tried to laugh but it came out sounding more like a sob. She sat up to the sound of sirens screaming in the distance. A crowd of strangers who hadn't been there a moment earlier had them surrounded. She looked over to where Owen was lying in the grass. She could see the rise and fall of his chest, but his eyes were closed.

"I don't have much time," the woman whispered. Her gray eyes scanned the crowd before she brought her lips close to Jordan's ear. "Apophis."

"I don't..."

"Apophis," the woman repeated.

"Wait," Jordan reached for her, but she had already gotten to her feet, slipping into the crowd without so much as a backward glance.

"Let me through." A paramedic broke through the circle. He knelt down beside Owen and began checking his pulse and airways. Another paramedic crouched down in front of Jordan.

"Ma'am, can you tell me what happened?"

"There was a man," she began as the paramedic checked her over. She frowned. *But it wasn't human, whatever it was. Something was* inside *Owen.* "H-he tried to…" She couldn't finish the sentence. "Will he be all right?" she asked instead.

"He's breathing, and his vitals are strong. That's a good sign. We'll have to wait until he wakes to find out for sure."

If he wakes, Jordan thought. There was no point in voicing the thought out loud. She could tell by the look on both paramedics' faces that they were thinking the same thing.

Chapter 11
Unconditional

"He was trying to save your life?" the officer asked for the third time. When his pen hovered over his notepad, Jordan wondered how many times he would write down the same answer before he let her go.

"Yes," she said. "I thought it would be nice to cool off. I got pulled too far out. Owen tried to save me."

The officer's eyes flicked from her face to her arms. Jordan folded her hands in her lap so she wouldn't give in to the urge to cover the bruises dotting her arm.

"Do you have any other questions for me?" she asked. "I'd really like to see how he's doing."

The officer closed his notepad and shook his head. "If you remember anything else, you be sure to let me know," he said. "In my opinion, you're a lucky girl. You must have one heck of a guardian angel looking out for you."

"I'm pretty sure that's impossible," Jordan murmured.

She averted her eyes as the officer escorted her down the hospital hallway. She hoped he couldn't see how badly her legs were shaking.

You did what you needed to do, Jordan told herself. *Did you really want them to arrest Owen? He wasn't the one who tried to kill you. It wasn't him.*

She held on to those words when the officer blocked her from entering Owen's room. "You sure there's nothing you want to add to your statement?" he asked.

Jordan hoped her face didn't give her thoughts away. "I'm sure," she said.

When she entered the room, Madison lifted her head from the chair. Her bare feet were tucked up beside her, while her stilettos rested on the floor. The steady *beep* from Owen's heart monitor felt like a jackhammer pressed up against Jordan's temple.

"How is he?" she asked.

"There isn't a thing wrong with him," Madison whispered. Her eyes were red, her cheeks splotchy. "He's not in a coma, he's not sleeping. I just don't..."

"I'm going back to your place to get my things."

"Please stop saying that. Where are you going to go?"

"I have a few ideas."

"Liar." Madison sighed. "Let me at least call you a cab, you really shouldn't be walking by yourself this late at night."

"No thanks," Jordan said. "I'll be fine. I always am."

*****

At the warehouse, Jordan held the yearbook steady in her lap. She had been staring at a picture of her and Owen for a while, thinking. She hated every tear that stained her cheeks, but couldn't stop weeping. *Why didn't they trust me enough to tell me?* she wondered for the hundredth time. *Why didn't I figure it out on my own?*

She was so absorbed in her thoughts she didn't hear Madison arrive home.

"Whoa," Madison said, her blonde hair fanning out behind her as she rushed toward the couch. "Are you okay?"

"Yeah, of course," Jordan said, quickly turning her face away, and wiping at her eyes. "I was just about to head upstairs to take a nap."

Madison caught her by the shoulders. "Are you finished pretending to be fine, hon?" she asked. Before Jordan could respond, she was enveloped in a warm hug.

"Why didn't they tell me?" Jordan asked, releasing Madison. Her throat felt raw. "Why didn't you tell me?"

"About what?"

"That *your* brother is in love with *my* brother."

Madison's hands went to her hips, nails a deep forest green. "If it makes you feel any better, I didn't know either," she said. She flipped her hair behind her shoulder. "I was never at home long enough growing up to notice anything, but even when I started living here I had no idea. Owen only told me after Parker left and I demanded to know why he was acting like a crazy person."

The field party, she thought. *That night at Charlie's...The signs were there! If you weren't so blinded by your own misplaced feelings...*

"They should have told me," Jordan muttered, feeling like an idiot.

"Owen told me he's been trying to tell you they've been together for *years*!" Madison said, green eyes flashing. "If you would have just given him a few minutes of your time, you could have avoided—"

"Avoided what?" Jordan shouted back. "Feeling like this? Again?" She buried her face in her hands. "I never really knew either Parker or Owen, did I? I never knew them at all."

The anger faded from Madison's eyes, but Jordan shrugged away from her reaching arms. "I traveled the world trying to forget them. I left, and instead of..." She paused. "I need some air."

Madison caught her hand and stopped her. "I'll be here when you get back," she said. Jordan squeezed back before letting her go.

She didn't pay attention to the direction she was headed. She kept her head down and let her legs lead her. The scent of fresh water almost made her gag. She stopped and realized that she had walked straight to Old Port. It was deserted, a fact that brought a sense of relief to her aching muscles.

She closed her eyes and faced the river. *Nothing can hurt you now. You're safe. It's just water.* Her arms came up around herself, and she forced herself to look.

"I see you've decided to stay," someone said. "Is everything all right?"

Jordan jumped and spun around. "Levi." She used the back of her hands to wipe her face. "Nothing's wrong. I'm fine."

"I don't believe you."

"Yeah, yeah," Jordan mumbled. "I'm fine. It's just been a rough day."

"You almost drowned," Levi said, his features turning serious. "I think 'rough' is a bit of an understatement, don't you?"

"How did you...?"

Levi shrugged. "News travels fast here." He took a step toward her. "Are you sure you're okay?"

"Not really," Jordan heard herself say. She bit her lower lip. *Oh, what the hell*, she thought before continuing. "Strange, messed-up things keep happening to me. I can't find my irresponsible brother. The man I've loved all my life will never love me back." She laughed. "Listen to me. I sound insane."

"I understand. Better than anyone." Levi was staring at her in a way that was anything but unpleasant.

Her stomach fluttered, and she was suddenly aware of how alone they were. "I'd better head back," she said.

"Let me walk you." Levi got in step with her.

The walk back to the warehouse was, without a doubt, perfect. Levi was full of good humor, and when he looked at her, Jordan felt like they were the only two people in the world.

"I would really like to take you to see that book. Dinner would also be a bonus," he said. "Have you decided to stay?"

"Maybe," Jordan said, looking at him through her lashes. She found she was more than a little disappointed to notice that they had reached her destination. "This is me," Jordan said, pointing to the warehouse.

Levi moved so that he was facing her, and brought his hand to her cheek. "Do you mind?" he whispered. "It's been so long…"

Jordan had time to nod her head before Levi lowered his. She couldn't think. His lips brushed against hers, and then he was kissing her. *Well, this certainly is one way to take my mind off things*, she thought to herself.

His hands slid down her back. She fell against his chest, and let herself sink into him. His scent, his warmth, his caress. As the kiss deepened, Jordan couldn't help but feel a sense of déjà vu. Despite how much she wanted to enjoy what was happening, the sensation grew stronger as his mouth moved over hers. The ease with which her body clung to his made her think they had kissed a thousand times before. It made her shiver with an anticipation she couldn't explain.

From behind closed lids she saw flashes of skin, and limbs. She could smell dew, and the hint of honeysuckle, and lavender. Her skin flushed with pleasure. It felt as if Levi were doing more than just kissing her now. She could see two people intertwined, a man and woman. The man lifted his head and looked right at her.

It was Levi.

Jordan pulled away and the cool night air brought her to her senses. She pushed herself from his embrace. "W-who are you?" she asked.

Levi reached out for her, but drew his hand back. He looked like he wanted to devour her. She admired his self-restraint. *She* still wanted him, and didn't know if she would be able to pull away a second time.

"I told you who I am," he said with a sad smile. "I should go. Sleep well, lovely."

Jordan could feel his eyes on her until she was inside. She collapsed against the door and brought her fingers to her tingling lips.

"You're back!"

At the sound of Madison's voice, Jordan jumped, feeling like she had "I've just been thoroughly kissed" written all over her face.

"What's wrong?" Madison asked. "You're shaking!"

"I want to tell you what happened," Jordan told her, ignoring the question. She didn't want to give herself time to change her mind. "Chances are you aren't going to believe me, but, I need to tell someone." She rubbed the back of her neck with her hand. It was hard to suppress the urge to scream every time she thought about Owen shoving her underwater.

"I'm going to make us some tea while you talk," Madison said, leading her to the kitchen and into a chair. "Go ahead, I'm listening."

Jordan told her everything. From finding her parents, to the hallucination at their funeral, about the ugly imps, Tully's memory loss, and finally what happened at the game. She decided for the time being to keep Levi to herself.

"I can't believe it," Madison said when Jordan was finished. All color had drained from her face. "Owen would never, ever harm anyone…" She broke off with a sob.

"It wasn't him trying to hurt me," Jordan said. "You know him better than anyone. It was the faceless man. He was controlling Owen somehow."

Madison looked skeptical. "I don't know…"

"You'll just have to go with me on this one, then," Jordan told her. "There's one more thing. The woman who saved us, before she disappeared, she whispered something to me. Ap-poth…no, that isn't it." Jordan shook her head and closed her eyes. "Apophis." She looked at Madison. "Any idea what that means?"

"Nope," Madison said, "but it's a starting point. I can head to the library a little later to try and see what I can find."

"Library?"

"I'm a little old fashioned," Madison replied with a smile before tossing her hair over her shoulder. "So, I'm curious about something. How did you manage to stop him?"

"I'm not sure," Jordan told her.

Madison was watching her carefully. "I think it's something you should think about."

"Maybe," Jordan said. She looked into her empty cup, thoughts of

109

Parker weighing on her mind. "By the way, do you think you could take me to the owner of the River Six? He's the last person to have seen Parker; I'd like to talk to him."

Madison frowned. "I'm not sure how much help he'll be."

"What if we called it *research*?" Jordan asked.

Madison grinned. "Clever..." she said, and was interrupted by the ringing of the phone. "Hold that thought."

Jordan propped an elbow up on the table and rested her chin in her hand. She was feeling a little better. It was nice to have someone like Madison to talk to, even if she didn't totally believe her. It certainly made her feel less crazy. *She could turn out like Tully*, she thought to herself. *Pretending to care one minute, kicking you out of his house the next.*

"Jo!" Madison called. She sounded alarmed.

Thought forgotten, Jordan rushed into the living room to find Madison standing by the fireplace, staring at the phone. "Is something wrong?" she asked. "Is Owen okay?"

"He's better than okay," Madison said. "He's awake."

*****

Owen wanted to see her alone. Jordan would have protested, except Madison had already slipped from the room.

There were dark circles under his eyes, as if he hadn't just spent the last eighteen hours in a deep sleep. She had never seen him with stubble, but there it was, and damn him if it didn't make him more attractive.

They stared at each other, not saying a word. Jordan didn't notice if Owen was feeling shy, or awkward. She was too busy trying to hide her own feelings. Anger, sadness, confusion, all currents flowing beneath a bigger wave. Love. She had spent so much time loving him that she wasn't sure if she knew how to stop.

"I'm sorry," Owen finally said. Then he let out a burst of air; half sigh, half strangled laugh. "Jesus, Jo. There isn't a word for how shitty I feel. When I think about what I almost did..." He paused, shaking his head. "I would never have been able to forgive myself."

"Well, everything worked out." Jordan said. She clasped her hands together and moved to stand beside his bed. "I'm fine."

"It's not *fine*," he said in a low voice. "I need you believe that it wasn't me. I would never hurt you like that. Ever." His voice broke on the last word, his lips quivered.

"You remember, then?" Jordan reached for his hand. Their fingers laced tightly.

"Everything."

"Then you know I don't think you had anything to do with what happened."

"But you're wrong," Owen said. He lifted his head to look at her. "The jealousy and anger, that part *was* me." He pointed to his chest. "It was like someone gave me permission to say all the things I would never dare to speak aloud."

"It still wasn't you. You were being controlled."

"And now you know the truth," he continued. "You know what I've never been able to tell you."

Jordan's heart constricted. *Damn it*, she thought to herself. *Did you actually think he would wake up and tell you it was all a joke?*

"Say something," Owen pleaded.

"I feel like someone's standing on my chest and all I can do is lie there until the weight snaps my ribs like popsicle sticks," she told him. She wished she could switch her heart off. She wished it were that simple. "Why did you kiss me that night?"

"I was young and stupid," he murmured. "I was so pissed off at Parker for flirting with Maddie…" He trailed off. Furrowed his brow and sighed. "I should have told you instead of acting like a prick. I'm so sorry. God, that doesn't even begin to describe how I feel."

"How did you manage to keep it a secret?" she asked. "I mean we were always together except for the summer before I went to college…" Her gazed sharpened on his face.

"We kissed for the first time maybe a week before you and I, well…Damn, I acted like a total shit." He swallowed and shook his head. "Have I mentioned how sorry I am?"

"You might need to mention it a few more times for it to really sink in."

"Point taken," he said. He fiddled with her fingers before continuing. "Parker was adamant that we keep our relationship a secret. My parents' garage was the only place we would even risk holding hands. No one ever bothered us when we were down there." Owen's Adam's apple bobbed as he swallowed hard. "We wanted to be rock stars. He convinced me that if we wanted to be successful, we needed chicks to believe we could fall in love with them." Owen's eyelids fluttered closed. "He lost his mind when he found out what happened between us. All I cared about was making him happy, so I did what he asked. I told you to stay away from me."

"It's always been him. Hasn't it?" The seed of envy that she had fought so hard all her life to contain sprouted. Parker had it all. An endless supply of money. A talent that seemed to pour out from within him like water from a faucet. Owen.

"I've loved him forever. I thought he loved me too until he left."

"*I've* loved you forever," she whispered.

Owen stiffened. "Jo, I..."

"I'm glad I know the truth now," she said. "I'm tired of being angry with you. It's exhausting."

He sighed and pulled Jordan forward and down until she was lying next to him. "I'm sorry. I've wanted to say the words for years." His voice was thick with emotion. "I'm so sorry." He cleared his throat and slipped his arms around her. "I do love you. I know it's not in the way you want, but I always have. I always will."

Jordan closed her eyes against the pain in her chest. She felt as though the breath had been knocked from her lungs.

"I've lost Parker," he whispered. "I can't lose you too. Please tell me that my friendship is enough. Please."

She signed and bent her head so that it rested on top of Owen's. "It's enough," she said.

Chapter 12
River Six

"*I*'m beginning to have second thoughts," Jordan said as she looked at herself in Madison's full-length mirror. She tugged at the hem of the borrowed silk dress.

Madison laughed. "About what? The dress, or going to the River Six?" she asked.

"Do I have to choose just one?" Jordan muttered. Speaking with Owen in the hospital had really dampened her desire to search for Parker. She wasn't sure she even *wanted* to find him now, but Madison had arranged everything before she had a chance to say so.

Jordan tilted her head to the side and tugged on the dress again. *This isn't a skirt*, she thought, horrified. *It's a belt!*

"You look fine," Madison said. She sat down on the edge of her bed and slipped her feet into a pair of strappy stiletto heels.

"Are you sure this is the only way to meet Mr…what did you say his name was again?"

"Murphy. And yes, I'm sure. His assistant made it quite clear that if we wanted to speak to him, we had to do it during work hours."

Out of the corner of Jordan's eye, she caught sight of Owen limping through the door with a piece of paper in his hands. It had been a week since the doctors had released him. "That's an interesting choice of…*attire* for asking Mr. Murphy a few questions," he said.

"Like we need an excuse to get all dressed up," Madison told him, leading him toward her bed. "Don't worry. After we shake our booties, do drugs, and have sex with complete strangers, we'll start with the questions."

Owen walked up to the huge map covering the wall behind her desk and pulled out a pin. "Please don't say things like that. I really don't need those kinds of mental images," he said. He didn't sound upset, but he didn't seem pleased either.

"Put that back!" Madison snagged the pin from him. She pushed it back into place, muttering about longitude and latitude, and having to redo her entire system.

"Hate to break it to you, sis," Owen said. "But no one plays with maps anymore." He paused. "I really wish you'd let me come with you."

Madison rolled her eyes. "Hate to remind *you*, but do you remember participating in all that brawling and debauchery?" She gave him a kiss on the top of his head. "Mr. Murphy would have you arrested in three seconds flat." Then, she swatted him. "And I'm not *playing with maps*. I've marked all the places I want to go, and am working on memorizing their coordinates so I can work out the most efficient way of visiting them all. So stop messing it up!"

"Well," Jordan said before Owen could retaliate. "If we're going to talk to Mr. Murphy, we better get going." She did her best to sashay past without flashing him. Madison followed.

"Can I at least tell you what I found before you go?" Owen asked, trailing behind them.

"Sure," Jordan said, pleased to be slipping on a pair of black flats.

"Apophis. I found him," Owen said, and passed the paper to Jordan.

Jordan took one look, then laughed. "Nice one," she said as Madison took it from her.

Owen frowned. "I'm serious. Look," he pointed to the picture on the page. "This is the creature that attacked us."

"Is it?" Madison asked.

"It can't be," Jordan said. "Owen, did you even read what you printed?"

"'Apep, also known as Apophis, is an evil Greek god, the deity of chaos and darkness. His physical form is that of a great serpent,'" Madison read aloud. She lowered the paper. "He certainly matches your description."

Jordan snatched the paper back and scanned it again. "Here," she said when she found what she was looking for. "It says Apophis is a *demon*. It bears a striking resemblance, but if I were to look through a bunch of images on the Internet, I'm sure I could find plenty more."

"It's a start," Madison said. "Great work, Owen! Although, I really wish you would rely less on the Internet and more on books." She pulled out a tube of lipstick from her clutch. "You know, those heavy things, shaped like a rectangle with lots of words inside? They tend to be a much more accurate resource." She swiped the bright pink onto her mouth.

"How about I use the World Wide Web to find a book that proves my point?" Owen's eyes were twinkling.

"Whatever it takes to find out the truth, dear brother," Madison told him before smacking her freshly painted lips together. She held the tube out to Jordan. "Want to give it a try? I think the color would look great on you."

Jordan's jaw clenched. "I can't believe you're buying into this demon theory."

"Sorry, hon," Madison said putting the lipstick back into her clutch. She gently took back the paper from Jordan, then handed it to Owen. "We can't ignore the evidence. You've been having hallucinations, and we found an unidentifiable black substance at the scene. Until you come up with some research of your own, I'm willing to hear him out." She took a look at her cell. "Yikes! We should probably get going. I'll call the cab."

Owen's lips pinched together as he gave his sister a hug. "I'll do a bit more digging tonight on demonic attacks to see if there are any other connections I can make," he said. "Have a great night, Maddie." He then turned to Jordan. "Be careful."

She tugged on the ends of his hair. "I will."

The taxi dropped them off at the entrance to Old Port. Jordan worried her bottom lip between her teeth as she watched Madison pay the fare.

Madison's heels clicked sharply against the boardwalk as they walked toward the club. They weren't the only ones. The boardwalk was alive with moving bodies, all headed to the River Six. The building was like a beacon in the distance, all the little lights blazing against the night sky. Murmured conversations punctuated by bawdy laughter floated around them against the undercurrent of the river.

Jordan was still busy worrying her bottom lip.

Madison looked at her and sighed. "You're upset with me."

"Do you seriously believe that demons exist?" she blurted out.

"Sherlock Holmes."

They reached the entrance to the River Six. "Do I even have to tell you I have no idea what you're talking about?" she asked.

Madison held open the door and Jordan walked through. "It's a principle used in logic or problem solving," she said. "To summarize, when all logical possibilities have been eliminated, whatever remains, however improbable, is correct. I believe in doing the research, and examining the facts." She flashed the bouncer a smile and her ID. She waited for Jordan to get her ID back before continuing. "If the *only* possibility is that demons exist, then yes. I'll believe that they exist."

Together, they stepped through a velvet curtain and into the club. The lazy sounds of a jazz tune enveloped Jordan as her eyes adjusted to the dim light. Madison turned and grabbed both of her hands. "Let's not talk about this for the rest of the night, okay? We might as well try to enjoy ourselves."

"You're right," Jordan agreed. She *really* could use a few hours of normalcy.

"Come on," Madison said, tugging Jordan along. "This way."

The club seemed larger on the inside. It was already full of people mingling. Flashes of skin reflected beneath a huge disco ball hanging in the middle of the ceiling. The space around the dance floor was littered with small, round tables, large enough to hold a couple of drinks and easy conversation. A brightly lit stage took up most of the space against the far side of the room. Five men with matching purple bow ties were responsible for the music.

"There's nothing I love more than a five-piece band," Madison shouted over her shoulder. "Give it half an hour, and we are going to have ourselves one heck of a party!"

Oh. Great, Jordan thought, following Madison farther into the club. Not knowing what else to do with her hands, she let them fidget at her sides. Without even trying, Madison moved through the crowd with a sultry grace that attracted attention from every man in the room. Jordan tried to mimic the sway of her hips, but nearly crashed into a waitress with a tray full of complimentary hors d'oeuvres. When Madison reached a table and put her clutch down, Jordan leaned on it heavily in relief.

Before she could ask where they were supposed to meet Mr. Murphy, the lights dimmed, the band went quiet.

"Well, hello there, gorgeous," Madison said in a low murmur. She nudged Jordan with her elbow. Jordan had already seen what caught Madison's attention. Her mouth went bone-dry. A man wearing a tailored suit had stepped onto the stage.

"Levi?" she whispered.

"Good evening," he said. He didn't need a microphone; his voice carried just fine over the hushed crowd. More than a few women moved closer to the foot of the stage. "It's my pleasure to personally welcome you to the River Six," Levi said. His voice was like a warm caress. "It won't be long before the band is ready, so get started on some refreshments. Cheers to another Saturday night."

There was a round of applause. Jordan was certain that several women actually swooned as he jumped off the stage and into the crowd. Jordan craned her neck, hoping to catch another glimpse of him herself.

"Hot damn," Madison said, fanning herself with a hand. "That man is exactly the kind of fun I was talking about. It's too bad we're here to talk strictly business, huh?"

"*That's* Mr. Murphy?" Jordan hissed.

As if on cue, the band started to play. There was a blast of horns followed by the hi-hat from the drummer, who sent bodies swaying. A few couples took the floor, spinning and whirling in time to the syncopated rhythm. Their energy was infectious. At least it should have been. Most of the women in the club had found a much more enticing form of entertainment.

Levi reappeared by the bar. He said something to the bartender before turning his head in Jordan's direction. He gave her a slow smile as they made eye contact. Her hand went to her stomach as it quivered, and then fluttered uncontrollably. She didn't realize he was moving toward her until he was past the dance floor. He seemed to have little interest in talking to anyone, especially the women who were daring enough to drape themselves around him as he passed. He was getting closer.

"Down, girl," Jordan muttered, fiddling with her earrings.

Madison turned her head away from the dancing to watch him approach. "This is fantastic!" she said.

Jordan's hands fluttered to her hair. "It is?" As she lowered them to smooth out her dress, she forced herself to drop them back down by her sides.

"You get first dibs," Madison said out of the side of her mouth.

"On what?" Jordan was having a difficult time concentrating on anything. She needed to figure out what to say or she would end up babbling.

"On *him*, silly. We can turn business into a little bit of pleasure!" She nudged Jordan with her elbow. "He's clearly interested. I'm a great wingwoman. He'll totally be eating out of your hand by the end of the night."

And what if I've already let him have a sample? she thought.

A waitress stopped in front of them. She held a tray with two tumblers filled to the rim with bright-pink liquid. A tropical umbrella clung to the side of each glass. "On the house," she told them. "Courtesy of Mr. Murphy."

They took the drinks as Levi reached them.

"Thank you," Madison said, giving him a sultry smile as she brought her glass to her lips.

Jordan felt like a dirty rag beside her, but Levi's eyes never left Jordan's face.

She felt stripped bare in front of him, like he already knew everything there was to know about her. Her lips broke into a startled smile. Even though she knew she didn't know a damn thing about him, her mind kept trying to convince her otherwise.

Madison gushed, "Mr. Murphy, it's a pleasure to meet you. I'm Maddie."

He finally looked at Madison. "Please, call me Levi," he said. Jordan tried to catch Madison's eye, but both were riveted on Levi's face.

"Do you dance?" Madison asked, putting a hand on his arm. Jordan wanted to slap it away, but she knew she had lost her chance. *There's no way I can compete*, she thought. *I should never have let him kiss me.* Before Levi could answer, Madison handed what was left of her drink to Jordan, slipped her arm through his, and led him onto the dance floor.

Jordan felt a tug of resentment laced with amusement. She finally felt attracted to a man, one who wasn't Owen, and she had passed him to Madison like a hand-me-down. She stood by herself in the middle of the room, sipping her drink as she watched Madison spin out and then back into Levi's arms.

There it is, Jordan thought. His hand slid slowly down to the small of Madison's back. *Next up, big, green doe eyes.* She paused, waiting. Levi turned Madison so that she was facing Jordan. *Ladies and gentlemen, we have a winner.* Jordan raised her glass, saluted her astute observation, and indulged in a healthy swallow.

The music changed tempo, slowing to a seductive pulse. The sax gave a long, low note before the band took up a softer melody. Levi leaned in to whisper into Madison's ear. She took his hand. Jordan stirred the puddle of pink liquid left in her glass with her straw. *There's your cue*, she thought, trying to suppress the bitter jealousy she felt. *By the time you finish your drink, they'll be in a cab.* She sighed, brought the drink to her lips.

A velvety smooth voice startled Jordan out of her thoughts. "Your turn."

She was vaguely aware that Madison was taking her drink back. Her attention was on Levi. He held his hand out to her, palm facing upward.

"Sorry," Jordan said, shaking her head. She gave Madison a puzzled look. "I'm not much of a dancer."

Madison rolled her eyes from behind Levi's head. "Don't be silly," she said. "Here, I'll hold your glass."

Jordan didn't realize it had been taken from her until Levi had already led her out onto the dance floor. His fingertips moved around her, grazing her skin. Her hand automatically moved to his shoulder. When he took her other hand in his, she wished she'd had the foresight to wipe away the dampness on her palms.

He didn't give her much time to dwell on it. He gathered her to him as he took the step around the dance floor. Too nervous to make eye contact, she kept her gaze focused on the curve of his neck. Their languid movements lulled her. The sound of the music, the gentle swaying, and the scent of dark spice and spring, of him, had her nerves tingling.

"I have to admit, I'm a little disappointed," he said.

"I told you I was a bad dancer," Jordan said, lifting her head with a jerk. She tried to pull away, but ended up pressed closer to him.

"Now, now. Don't be offended. That's not what I meant." He gave her a slow smile. "I can't stop thinking about you. Do you remember me yet?"

"Should I?" Jordan asked, still feeling a little ruffled and now, confused.

"No," he murmured. "I suppose you wouldn't." He spun her around in a lazy circle. When his hand returned to her back, she decided to look him in the eye.

"You look stunning tonight, lovely," he told her.

"Is that what you tell all the women you dance with?" she asked him in a sarcastic tone. "Did it work on Madison?"

He laughed; she could feel the sound rumble through his chest. "Don't tell me you're jealous," he said.

Jordan flushed, "I, w-well...What I mean was—"

"Don't be embarrassed," he told her. "I'm flattered, actually. Your friend is sweet, but I only danced with her to be polite."

"Oh," Jordan said.

Levi's head swiveled to look at something behind him as if it were a response to something only he could hear. "I'm afraid I have some business to attend to," he murmured into her ear. "Save another dance for me."

"Wait. I need to ask you something," Jordan said. Her voice sounded breathless to her own ears. "My brother, Parker Andrews, got into a fight here and was arrested. He went missing after someone paid his bond. You're one of the last people who talked to him. Do you know anything about where he might have gone?"

Levi didn't reply. He released her as the last notes of the song faded into the noise of the crowd. He still held her hand. Before he released it, he gave her a slight bow, and pressed it to his lips.

In that moment Jordan smelled sweet honeysuckle, and she saw Levi, poised over a woman with long auburn hair...

It's me. The woman is me!

The realization stunned her. She tried to pull him back toward her, but he slipped out of her grasp, disappearing behind a twirling couple. She took a step forward to try and follow him, but the scenery around her blurred like a thick fog. The music became muted, even though the horns were blaring. She shook her head. Dread seeped into her body.

"Madison," Jordan called. Her voice sounded hoarse, as if she had gone for days without water. She spun around, in the direction she had left Madison. The space was occupied by two chatting couples.

Jordan was jostled by several dancers keeping in time with the fast-paced music. She stumbled off the dance floor, head lolling in each direction, eyes scanning for Madison. She finally caught a glimpse of long blonde hair disappearing through the bathroom doors on the other side of the dance floor. It took determination, mixed with a healthy dose of fear, for Jordan to make it there. Inside, she stumbled over her own feet but managed to make it to the counter. She leaned all her weight on it.

"Madison," she called.

A moan echoed against the tiles.

Jordan clenched her jaw and concentrated on lifting one foot, putting it down in front of the other. When she reached the stall, she slammed it with the palm of her hand. It felt like she was underwater.

"I need you to open the door," she said. She pushed against the door. "I need you to focus."

Jordan waited a moment, resting her head against the door. She couldn't hear any movement on the other side.

"Shit," Jordan muttered. Her legs gave out from beneath her, which she supposed was just as well. She put her forearm down and used it to pull herself forward. Head under the stall now, she saw Madison. She was sitting on the toilet, her body tilted so far to one side that she was only being supported by her head resting on the wall.

"We need to leave," Jordan told her, pulling herself forward until she was inside the stall with Madison. She got her feet beneath her and used

Madison's thighs to pull herself the rest of the way up. "Cut out the theatrics," she said, tapping Madison's cheek with the palm of her hand. "We need to get out of here." She tugged Madison upright and slapped her. "This isn't the time to pass out on me, damn it."

"Jordan?" The whites of Madison's eyes were lined with red. Her pupils were twice their normal size. "Something's wrong with my head."

"I know. Mine too. Put your arm over my shoulder. There you go." Jordan continued to murmur nonsensical words of encouragement as she steered them both out of the washroom. She didn't want to risk going back into the club. Instead, she turned away from the sounds of revelry, and went out the employee exit.

"Give me a second," Jordan told Madison once they were outside. Jordan propped her up against the brick wall of the club. "I need to get my bearings."

"I don't like this," Madison said.

"Neither do I." Jordan closed her eyes and willed her mind to see clearly when she opened them again. It didn't work. Everything was just as blurry as the moment before. "Call Owen," she said, turning in the general direction of the wall and Madison. "He needs to come get us."

Jordan could hear Madison fumbling in her purse for her cell. She was looking at something completely different. It was dark. She was running through an alleyway. At the other end she saw a woman, teetering back and forth. Another was up against the brick, digging into something.

She caught a glimpse of her long claws as she ran. *Smack, smack, smack.* The sound of wide feet hitting the pavement. Thick yellow strands of saliva dripped from her mouth, onto her extended belly.

I'm going to rip, rip, rip it out, rip your heart right out.

Back in her own body, Jordan saw that she had vomited near Madison's feet. The stench of the creatures brought on another wave of nausea. The sour odor reminded her of death.

She pressed a fist against the little ball of heat building beneath her diaphragm. It wasn't the same creature that had attacked Owen. It was the creature she had seen back in her parents' house. In Tully's basement. But this time, there were more of them.

"He's not answering," Madison said. "But, I don't know if I was calling the right number. I can't see a thing!" she covered her mouth with a hand. "What is that smell?"

"I need you to run." Jordan couldn't see anything in front of her face. She grabbed Madison by the arm and pushed her forward. "Now, Madison."

"I can't!"

"You don't have a choice," Jordan said, as much for herself as for Madison. Her limbs weren't cooperating either.

She tripped over something she couldn't see, and dragged Madison down with her. They collapsed in a tangled heap. The smacking sound increased in volume, ricocheting off the alley's walls. Closer. Closer still. Jordan shoved at Madison. She wanted the chance to at least defend herself before she was torn to shreds. Madison's body felt like a bag of sand on top of hers.

She turned to try and gauge how much time she had left. A figure wearing white blocked her view. "Help," Jordan called. She couldn't quite make out the features on the stranger's face. "Please. Help us!"

The figure stood motionless for a moment before reaching behind its shoulder. Jordan squinted in an attempt to see. A metallic ring echoed around them. A flash of silver gleamed in the dim light. Jordan didn't need her complete vision to recognize that the figure was wielding a sword, and the tip was pointed directly at her.

Chapter 13
Dinah

At the same moment that Jordan opened her mouth to scream, Madison tried to get to her feet. She placed a hand on Jordan's back and squashed the air from her lungs.

"Who is that?" Madison asked, as Jordan struggled to get away from the weapon.

"Stay here," the figure commanded. It had a deep, female voice.

Jordan almost collapsed in relief as the tip of the sword swung in the opposite direction. The figure sprinted toward the squat imps. She didn't slow, didn't stop, even when she met the first creature. Her blade swung down, cleaving the creature's head from its body. She plunged the sword into the belly of another. It came away clean. A ring of blue flame surrounding the weapon lit the alley up like a torch.

Jordan lay on the ground, watching the woman slice her way through the pack of imps. It was eerily quiet. There was only the dull thunk of metal meeting flesh and bone. A shiver ran through Jordan's body.

They're dying, but they aren't making a sound.

An icy calm settled over her. It was a stark contrast to the heat she felt when the imps appeared. She knew she could destroy them all, she just had to focus. Her muscles felt fine; her vision cleared. Rising to her feet, she took a step forward, searching the ground for something she could use to send these little devils back to hell. Back where they belonged.

Something grabbed her ankle. Jordan looked down to see Madison looking up at her with an odd expression on her face.

"What do you think you're doing?" Madison hissed. "Are you trying to get yourself killed?"

The desire to fight left Jordan as rapidly as it had appeared. She stumbled, put off-balance by Madison, who was still tugging on her. Her eyelids drooped, and although her brain was telling her body that it was a terrible idea to pass out, her body wasn't listening.

Her legs gave way, but instead of hitting the ground, she fell into someone's arms. A large green eye looked down at her. Jordan blinked. There were two now.

"Owen?" she asked them.

"You're going to be fine," he told her.

She shook her head. "How do you know?" she asked. "What's happening to me?"

"I've got you," he said, in the same soothing tone. "Everything's going to be all right."

*****

Jordan's memory took her back home, back to when Owen and Parker included her in everything they did.

"Where'd you get that?" Jordan had asked. She hoped she was acting cooler than she felt seeing Parker produce a bottle of vodka from his backpack. They were camping out in Owen's backyard. His parents were gone for the weekend. *Please*, she thought. *Don't let anyone check in on us tonight.* It was already a perfect evening to be outdoors. Not a cloud in the sky, and only a hint of a breeze.

"I'm afraid I can't say, little sister," Parker said. "If we get busted, I don't want you taking the blame."

Owen snickered. "You stole it from your aunt, didn't you?"

Jordan gasped. "Aunt Lydia drinks?" she asked.

"'Course she does," Parker said, handing them each a cup. He poured them each a shot. "To turning eighteen."

"To our last summer before college!" Jordan said. She peered into her cup, and swirled the liquid around.

"One minute to midnight," Owen said. He held his cup out toward Jordan and Parker with one hand, and kept an eye on his watch. "Three, two, one...go!"

Jordan downed the vodka. When she tried to take a breath, she found that she couldn't. "That tastes like gasoline," she wheezed. "Not that I've ever tasted gasoline before. Pretty damn sure it would be the same."

Both Parker and Owen seemed to find that hysterical and leaned on each other for support while they laughed.

"Here," Owen said after catching his breath. "We got you this." He held out a bottle of Baileys.

"We just wanted to see your face," Parker said in between fits of giggles. "Totally worth it."

"Jerks," Jordan said, giving Parker a playful shove.

"Would a jerk bring this?" Owen said, holding out a jar of chocolate powder. Jordan grinned. "I didn't think so."

With a fair bit of arguing, Parker and Owen got a fire started. Jordan was impressed they had even thought to bring a kettle, and soon they were sipping steaming mugs of hot chocolate and Baileys.

Jordan couldn't remember how she ended up lying in the grass, sandwiched between them. It didn't matter. She was amazed at how clear the sky was, how many stars she could see.

"It's so perfect," she whispered. "This night. Everything. It's amazing." She felt a wonderful glow when Owen turned his head to look at her, and she snuggled closer to his side.

"You say that now, but this," Parker said, gesturing to the sky, "this moment. It isn't worth it. We'll never have it again. We'll only look back on it when we're old and wish we were young again."

"Dude," Owen said, shifting away from Jordan to look at Parker. "Are you serious?"

"I'm going to tell you guys something that I want you to remember," Parker went on. He pulled Jordan's arm until she was forced to move closer to him. "That's not going to be me. I'm going to live life to the fullest."

"Isn't that what you're doing now?" Jordan asked.

"Don't encourage the man," Owen muttered.

Parker eyed the both of them before answering. "I want it all," he said. "Don't you?"

*****

"Hmm," a female voice said. "Once more should do."

The scent of ammonia was sharp on Jordan's nose. Through the crack in her heavy eyelids, she saw a woman kneeling beside her. There was something in her hand; she brought it closer to Jordan's nose.

"Smelling salts?" Jordan murmured, trying to bat the vial away with her hand. "Who the hell carries smelling salts with them anymore?"

"Perfect." Owen was there too. "The attitude is how you know she's fine."

"Where's Madison?"

"Where's Madison?" Jordan asked and tried to get up, but was pushed back down by hands that wouldn't take no for an answer.

"She's okay," Owen said. Jordan felt his weight settle down beside her. The pressure on her shoulders disappeared. "She's actually doing a heck of a lot better than you. Here. You need to drink something."

He helped Jordan raise her head so that he could tip a glass of water to her lips. The cool liquid was welcome on her parched tongue. She gulped it down as fast as she could. When it was gone, Owen helped her lie back down. She could see his face now. There were creases between his brow. Shadows beneath his eyes.

"Just when we've kissed and made up, you go and almost get yourself killed," he said in a tone only meant for her ears. "I'd prefer it if you stopped doing that. It's getting rather annoying." He waited until she lifted her head. "What happened?"

"I was dancing with Levi," she told him. "Mr. Murphy," she clarified when he gave her a blank stare. She rushed on when he looked like he was about to interrupt. "He said he had a few things to take care of, and the next thing I knew, I could barely walk."

"That bastard," Owen hissed. "Did he touch you? Did you eat anything, drink anything?"

Jordan licked her dry lips. "A waitress gave us drinks," she said, "but I don't—"

"That conniving son of a bitch." Owen stood and limped around a few paces. "He said he would let everything lie if I didn't show my face near his club again. I haven't! Why would he do something like that?" He tugged at his hair. "We can't bring attention to this either. The smarmy ass would probably smooth-talk me straight into jail."

"He is not to be trusted," the woman said. "It would be wise to refrain from having any contact with him without taking the correct precautions."

Owen stopped pacing to look at her. She was just watching them. Jordan had completely forgotten she was there. "What precautions? No, wait," he said, tilting his head to the side. "Who are you?"

"I am known as Dinah," the woman answered, filling the silence. She didn't hold out her hand, she simply stood with her thumbs hooked through the belt loops of her jeans. Jordan pushed herself up into a seated position. She squinted, trying to get better control of her blurry vision.

Dinah was tall. Jordan could tell she towered over Owen, even though he wasn't standing next to her. She sucked in a breath when she realized that it wasn't the woman's height that seemed so familiar. It was the short white hair and the cool gray eyes that made everything click into place.

"I'm Owen," he said clearing his throat. "Thank you for helping us get back here in one piece. Did you need me to call you a cab?"

"No, wait. It's her," Jordan said. She felt as though she could breathe normally again. "Owen, this is the woman who saved us from...drowning."

Owen straightened. "Then I owe you my thanks," he said. "Did you want anything to drink before you leave?"

Jordan struggled not to roll her eyes at him. "She's not going to call the police," she said.

"She's not?" Owen asked, then turned to face Dinah. "You're not?"

Jordan didn't give Dinah the chance to answer. "I'm fairly certain she doesn't want them to know about the sword she's carrying."

Owen's brows shot up his forehead. "What?" he took a step back. "Are you sure?"

"I take it you missed the show," Jordan said in a tone that belied the fact that she had witnessed Dinah decapitate some very real goo-monsters.

Dinah was frowning. At least Jordan thought the expression could be called a frown. Her lips turned down, but the rest of her face was as smooth as marble. "I don't know what you're talking about," she said.

"You saved my life twice, and I am grateful for it," Jordan told her. "The thing is, I don't know who you are, and, well, considering everything that's been happening to me, what you are."

"Totally understandable," Owen said, moving closer to the couch without taking his eyes off Dinah.

"Thank you," Jordan said. She pushed herself into a seated position. "So. What I'm dying to know is—"

Madison's voice came from the entryway. "Who are you, and what do you want with Jordan?" Even with the three of them facing Dinah down, the woman still didn't move. She stood her ground, facing them with a vacant expression.

"Both of you would be fools to stay and listen," she finally said. There was a steely edge to her voice as she addressed Owen and Madison.

Jordan glanced at them and saw her confusion mirrored in their expressions. "You can leave if you want," she told them. As expected, neither budged.

"Very well," Dinah said, breaking eye contact. "I will not give another warning. Their lives are in your hands now."

Jordan's hand moved to her stomach. *What is that supposed to mean?*

Dinah tilted her head back, lifted her hands toward the ceiling. A slight blast of air tousled Jordan's hair. The wind picked up until strands whipped around her face. It buffeted her back and forth until she was forced to bury her face in the couch.

As quickly as the windstorm had started, it was over. Jordan raised her head and caught sight of a figure dressed in white. She slowly got to her feet. Dinah was wearing formfitting pants, and a white, long-sleeved cotton shirt. Both displayed how lean she was. A thick, tan leather strap crossed her chest. The hilt of a sword jutted out from behind her back.

"See?" Jordan said, pointing dumbly to it. "Sword."

"I am an Authority," Dinah said, giving Jordan a withering glare. "I am here to act as your guide."

"A Warrior Angel," Owen said in a hushed voice. "I read about you last night."

Dinah's eyes flicked to his face and then returned to Jordan's. "He is a clever mortal."

"Stop it," Jordan said. She clenched her hands in her lap to stop them from shaking.

"You were right," Madison said, taking Owen's hand. "Apophis. It's really a demon."

"Are you listening to yourselves?" Jordan said a little louder. "She's crazy."

Dinah was nodding her head. "He was sent from hell to kill Adam's Rib. Those imps I disposed of earlier had the same mission. So did Legion, so does the man you know as Levi."

"Legion," Owen repeated. His face turned ashen. "The river."

Jordan had stopped listening. "Who's Adam's Rib?" she asked, instantly regretting the question. *Why are you getting involved in this ridiculous discussion?*

"I should think it is obvious," Dinah said. Owen and Madison's heads swiveled in Jordan's direction.

"I need you to leave now," Jordan said. She got to her feet and approached Dinah, ready to shove her out the door if necessary.

Dinah reached behind her and pulled her sword free.

"Whoa! Hold on!" Owen said, rushing forward to pull Jordan back.

Dinah hefted the sword in both hands, lifting it high in the air before bringing it down in front of her so hard that the tip embedded into the hardwood floor. Madison made a choking sound as Dinah knelt down, her hands clasped over the pommel.

Jordan glanced at Owen, then Madison, who seemed to be just as shocked as she was. *At least you know you're not seeing things*, she thought to herself.

"I, Dinah, Guardian of Adam's Rib, vow to protect and guide her in saving the world from utter damnation."

"Uh, excuse me?" Jordan said.

"To assist her in atonement for the First Sin," Dinah continued. "For if she should fail, the Apocalypse will fall upon the earth and all its inhabitants."

"That doesn't sound good," Owen said.

"She shall seek the *Book of Eve*. She shall seek redemption. She shall send Satan back to the depths from which he came."

"Oh my," Madison said. She had produced a pen and pad of paper from somewhere and was scribbling furiously.

"I shall not rest. I shall not bend the rigorous laws binding me to this task. I shall be hers until my life is taken from me." Dinah got to her feet, yanked the sword free from the floor, and slid the sword back into its scabbard. "Amen."

Jordan wanted to wrap her hands around Dinah's neck. The whole situation was absurd. Owen and Madison were stupid enough to buy into it. *I don't have time to play pretend to keep this fanatic happy*, she thought to herself. *I need to find Parker.*

"I'm going up to the loft," she said, keeping her voice quiet even though she wanted to scream. Her head was pounding. "When I come down tomorrow morning, you"—she pointed at Dinah—"will be gone, and you two"—she gestured to Owen and Madison—"will stop acting like idiots and help me find Parker!"

"You're going to get yourself killed," Dinah said.

"Well," Jordan called over her shoulder. "With you as my guardian, I won't have to worry about that, will I?"

Chapter 14

Decisions

Jordan heard Dinah leave shortly after. She spent the rest of the night staring at the ceiling. At one point she considered calling Tully, but decided against it. She was tired of relying on other people. They had a tendency to do nothing but let her down.

And just as Owen and I are starting to get along, he starts believing in warrior angels and demons, she thought to herself. *Madison sees a few creatures and all of a sudden she's packing a suitcase and boarding the crazy train.* Jordan flipped over onto her stomach and pressed her cheek into the pillow. *I was attacked, that much is true*, she forced herself to admit, *but I could have been attacked by anything, or anyone. It still doesn't prove that God exists...*

Early the next morning, Jordan got up and went over to the window. The Mustang was still sitting in the driveway, useless in her current condition. Jordan ran a hand through her hair.

You've got to get out of here, she told herself. *You need money, so it's time to suck it up and ask Dad...*

The thought died as the weight of the words made it impossible to lift her head.

They're gone, she told herself. *They aren't going to appear and save you from any of this.* A new weight pressed down on her chest. *You should have asked Mom and Dad for help when you had the chance. Maybe you could have helped them out yourself, but you were nothing but selfish. So they turned to Parker instead. A man they shunned because he refused to share anything from his life with you.*

She blinked to clear her eyes, then crossed her arms over her chest and turned to look at the bedroom door.

Owen has more money than he knows what to do with, she thought. *Chances are he won't miss any if you take some. If he does, you'll be miles away.*

She frowned when she thought about all the damage taking money from him would do to their recent truce.

Is it worth it?

Jordan blinked again and saw that she was already downstairs, standing in the middle of the living room. It was hard to see, but she could still make out the dark shape of Owen's wallet on the fireplace ledge.

He won't even notice it's missing, she thought as her stomach turned.

She pulled out the bills. Shoved them into her back pocket.

The light beside the sofa flicked on.

Jordan took one look at the furious green eyes staring her down and cringed. "You've decided to start spying on me?" she asked. Her face burned.

"Please don't insult me by getting offended," Owen said.

"Easy for you to say. You've always had everything," Jordan snapped. Her skin was starting to itch. She scratched at her arm. It only made her feel worse. "I'm tired of struggling all the time."

"You could have just asked," he said. "I would have gladly given you whatever you need."

The heat she felt slipped down a few degrees. "Would have?" Jordan asked in a small voice. She pictured Tully's face in her mind, yelling at her. Telling her to get out of his house.

"Do you know what I was doing, sitting here?" Owen asked. Jordan started to shake her head, then stopped. Her skin felt so *tight*. It almost hurt to move. "I was trying to figure out how I was going to help you," he continued. "With so much going on, I figured, heck, my Jo's bound to be feeling pretty confused. Maybe even a little sad."

"When will you get it through your thick skull that I can take care of myself?"

He stared her down until she was too embarrassed to even look at him. "Why won't you admit that something is going on?" he asked. "Something's happening to you. I don't like it."

She threw the bills down on the coffee table. "Parker was sending my parents money." She let herself fall back into the couch. "I don't know what came over me. I thought maybe I deserved some of yours."

"That's pretty shitty of you, Jo."

"Yeah. I know."

Owen was silent for a moment. "Here's the deal," he said. "The way I see it, you have two choices. Take the money and run from this, or, you can stay. Let me help you, and we can figure out what's going on together."

"You're giving me an ultimatum?" she asked with a laugh.

Owen didn't seem amused. "I'm trying to make you see what you're doing to yourself," he said.

"Why?" Jordan said. "If you want me to apologize——"

"Actually, you haven't."

"What?"

"You've yet to apologize for anything," Owen said, furrowing his brow. "Since you've shown up here, you've been surly, uncooperative, and let's not forget downright rude. I don't see sorry anywhere in that list."

"If you can't stand who I've become since you used me, then that's your problem."

Jesus." Owen tugged at his hair. "I feel like all we do is have the same conversation over and over. Why can't you get over it?" he asked. "Is it because you need an excuse to start running again? Haven't you realized by now that it isn't going to solve anything?"

"Fuck off, Owen."

"You know what? Take the money," he said, his voice cold. "I think it would be better if you left."

It took Jordan a moment to register what he had said. When she did, her entire body felt like it was engulfed in flames.

"Finally," she said, shooting to her feet and snatching up the bills. "We agree on something."

It took Jordan twenty minutes to walk to the nearest gas station. The fresh air cooled her down, but not enough. She tugged at the collar of her shirt as she waited to pay for a can of gas, wishing the line would move a hell of a lot faster.

When it was her turn, Jordan handed over the cash. *Good riddance*, she thought, and hauled the gas out the door.

A hand came down over hers. Expecting to see Owen, she was startled when she looked up to find Levi's face tilted toward hers. His touch made her think of the vision she saw at the River Six, which only reminded her that a few moments later, she had been barely able to make it out of the place in one piece.

"Do you need some help with that?" Levi asked.

"No," she told him in a strained voice.

His fingers tightened, but he released her when she started walking away. "I'm sorry about last night," he called after her. When she didn't stop, she heard his footsteps chase after hers. "I tried looking for you later on in the evening, but you had already left."

"I'll bet that surprised you, didn't it?" Jordan asked. "I admit. You almost had me. The charm, the way you've been trying to seduce me. You're nothing but a sick bastard, aren't you?"

"I don't understand." He grabbed her arm, and pulled her around to face him. Jordan cried out, not because he hurt her, but because she could see him, feel him, in her mind. His perfect face, his kiss, his caress. The sensations overwhelmed her.

"Don't touch me," she hissed.

Levi's hand lingered, then dropped to his side. "I don't know what you're talking about," he told her.

"Oh, you need me to remind you about the drinks you roofied?" Jordan said. *Why are you still talking?* she asked herself. *You shouldn't be alone with him.*

"You think I drugged you?" The expression on Levi's face held her rooted to the spot. *He looks like he's just been told he has a terminal illness...*

Jordan realized she was staring and cleared her throat to try and make it appear as though she hadn't been. "I *know* you did," Jordan said. She turned away from him and got her legs moving again.

"Wait. Wait a minute." He caught up to her, and grabbed her arm. "What makes you think I'm responsible?" he asked. "Why would I do something like that?"

"I thought I told you not to touch me," Jordan said, pulling her arm away. She continued walking. "Your waitress gave us the drinks. On the house."

Levi's pace matched hers. "I didn't send them to you, or your friend."

"Then who did?" Jordan turned to face him and had to take a step away. "Is this payback for Owen and my brother trashing your club?"

"I have a strong...dislike for those two," Levi said, his voice tight. "But I would never do anything to hurt you."

Jordan wasn't listening. "I actually started to feel something for you," she told him. "Although I'm not sure why I'm surprised. I tend to trust the wrong people."

"You felt something?" Levi asked, cutting her off from what she was going to say next. His lips began to curve, and she knew she didn't have a lot of time to stop what would inevitably happen next.

"*Felt*," Jordan repeated. "Past tense."

She was too late. Levi grabbed the back of her head and crushed his mouth against hers.

*****

She had been standing in the middle of a lush garden. Flowers were her favorite, and they certainly were everywhere here. They made her feel vibrant and alive. She wanted to fall to her knees, press her face to them, and inhale their fragrance.

"Their scent reminds me of you," a man said. A pair of arms slid around her.

She turned around to look up into Levi's face. His arms moved to accommodate her, his hands cupping her naked bottom to pull her against him. Her face felt like it would split in two, she was so happy to see him. "I didn't expect to see you here," she said.

"You make it difficult to stay away," he said, bending his head to press his lips against hers.

She let him lower her to the thick grass, too absorbed in the trail of kisses he left across her cheek to think about much else. He made his way down the column of her throat, and made her hiss with anticipation when he gently moved her long hair away from her breasts.

When his mouth didn't follow, her eyelids flickered open to find Levi staring down at her. *He looks at me with such tenderness*, she thought. *The way a husband should look at his wife.*

"Why won't you share an apple with me?"

The question brought her up short. "Why must you ruin the moment by bringing that up?" she asked.

"Don't you love me?"

"Of course I do," she replied, kissing him on the cheek. "The guilt I carry for what happens between us is enough of a burden. I dare not add to it." She sat up, her hair spilling over her breasts, covering them. "Why can't you take me from this place? Why must I eat the apple?"

"It is the way things must be," Levi told her. "We can be together forever, away from here." His eyes were so intense when they were focused on her. It sent little shivers shooting up her spine. "But we must share an apple first."

She bit her lower lip, then rested her cheek on her knees. "Give me seven days," she said.

"Until you will see me again?"

"No," she said, lifting her head. "Until I make my decision."

*****

Jordan stiffened, breaking the kiss, and pushed from Levi's embrace. He only held her tighter.

"Eve," he murmured into her hair, then sighed. "You remember."

"No." Her voice came out in a whisper. "Not you too."

"Who have you been talking to?" he asked. He cupped her face in his hands. "Who has been giving you these ideas about me?" He caught her eyes, narrowed his, then swore. "She's here, isn't she?"

"Are you and Dinah good friends, then?" Jordan asked. "Do you both have memberships to the same crazy club?"

"But you saw," Levi said, furrowing his brow. "You saw what we had."

"I'm not who you think I am," Jordan said, "and you only want me because you think I'm someone else."

"That's not true."

A great splintering sound shattered Jordan's focus. She looked down the street, startled to see how close to the warehouse they were.

The can fell from her hands. The front door was hanging from its hinges. The wood was engraved with long slashes.

"What the hell?" Jordan said.

"He will never love you," Levi said. "If you go to him, he still will never love you."

Her heart ached at the sadness she saw in his eyes.

A piercing scream from inside the house made her forget all about him.

She ran inside, down the hall, and into the living room, frantic to find either Owen or Madison. When she spotted them, she almost fainted from relief. Owen was huddled down with Madison on the couch. They were clinging to each other, and when Owen's dresser shot through the wall as if it were flying through the air on its own, they cringed, cowering. Jordan wanted to do the same except a very large, scaled head appeared through the hole.

He had a pair of golden eyes, which narrowed as the length of his neck entered the living room. In the dying light of the chandelier, he flicked a forked tongue out.

"He's still alive," Jordan whispered. She thought back to the image on the paper Owen had printed. "Apophis."

His great head swung in her direction. When she tried to swallow, she discovered her throat had gone dry.

"Get out of here!" Owen called out.

In that moment Jordan realized what a fool she was for wanting to leave. *He doesn't hate me*, she thought. *He only wants to see me safe.*

"What are you doing, you idiot?" Owen's voice cut through her thoughts. "Run!"

"Right," she said before ducking and dashing toward the couch.

Apophis let out one of his piercing screams before shoving a limb through the wall.

Chunks of plaster hit Jordan in between her shoulder blades. Apophis didn't give her any time to recover. She was hit again with something that felt like a blast of hot coals. It sent her soaring across the room, over the couch, and into the fireplace. Her hands stopped her from smashing her face into the mantel, but the wind was knocked from her lungs. She landed on her hip and rolled onto her back. She desperately tried to catch her breath, while a ball of heat formed in her stomach.

Apophis's tail whipped past her, embedding itself in the fireplace. Twisting onto her front, Jordan managed to crawl forward on her hands and knees, and finally pulled herself behind the safety of the chair.

"What are you doing back here?" someone asked. Still gasping for air, Jordan managed to make out Dinah's face.

"Damn it," Jordan wheezed. "Never mind what I'm doing. What are *you* doing here?"

"I came here ten minutes ago looking for you. Now. *You* must face this demon," Dinah said, her lack of expression a stark contrast to her heated words. "You are the only one who can defeat it."

Are you crazy?" Jordan asked. She shifted and winced as her shirt made contact with the gashes on her back. "Never mind. I already know the answer to that question."

"You *will* face Apophis."

There it was; confirmation of the demon's name, and existence.

A crash of glass followed by a shout from Owen caused the burning sensation to rise from Jordan's stomach to her chest. "I—I can't," she cried. "You do it. You're the one with a sword."

"If you don't do as I say," Dinah shouted over the piercing cry of Apophis, "your friends are going to die, and then you are going to die. Trust in me."

Jordan didn't want to. The concept felt so foreign.

"Stop holding on to your anger," Dinah was saying. "It does not belong to you. You are Adam's Rib, you can use Apophis's anger against him. Release it."

"I don't know how!"

The chair was ripped out from in front of them. Apophis raised his claws.

"Now, girl," Dinah cried. "*Now.*"

Jordan let go of the little ball of heat she had been trying to smother and turned her shoulder into the blow. *I'm going to lose my arm*, she thought, squeezing her eyelids shut. Apophis was strangely quiet. The strike never came.

She opened her eyes. Her gaze shifted to Owen. He was crouched down in front of Madison, who was holding her leg. Blood seeped between her fingers and onto the floor. It seemed Apophis was much more interested in going after them.

Without thinking Jordan ran and leapt onto his back, pulling him off course by rolling to the side. He landed on top of her with a force that should have broken most of her bones. *You're still breathing*, she told herself. *You're still alive.* She wrapped both arms around his neck and squeezed.

Apophis thrashed about with his limbs, trying to reach for her, but they were too short to do any damage. Jordan heard his tail whip out from his body and embed in the wall on the opposite side of the room. They started sliding forward as he started reeling himself in. *You can't let him reach that wall*, she told herself. *Don't give him the advantage.* She increased pressure on his neck, until his movements began to slow. She didn't let up until she felt his throat crunch.

"I'm stuck," Jordan said, feeling the weight of his body increase painfully. The second time she tried to heave his limp body from her, she collapsed to the ground feeling too weak to move. "Anyone? Help?"

The body vanished as if it had never been there. The only indication was a thin layer of black slime, which coated Jordan from neck to toe. Disgusted, she tried to get to her feet, only to realize she didn't have the strength to do it. About to give up, Owen's hand appeared in front of her.

137

"My intention is not to be rude," Dinah said as Jordan was helped back to her feet, "but I must be allowed to speak to you." She pointed to Jordan. "Alone."

"I'm sorry," Jordan told Owen, ignoring Dinah. "Something's happening to me, and I need you to help me figure it out." Owen opened his mouth, but she turned to Madison. "You're hurt. You need to tell him how to patch you up, unless you prefer we call for help?"

"Yes. I mean, no," Madison said. She shook her head, and the dazed look in her eyes faded. She gripped Jordan's arm in return. "It's just a minor flesh wound. Owen's more scared of me than he is of a little blood." She sounded like herself, yet the wild look in her eyes told Jordan she was barely holding it together. "They're real, Jo. Demons are real."

"Yeah. They definitely are."

"Come on, little one," Owen said, putting Madison's arm over his shoulder. "Let's get you patched up." Jordan wanted to help him. She took a step forward, and was quickly reminded of the lashing she had taken. "I've got her," he said. "Your things are still in the loft. Couldn't bring myself to carry them all the way down the stairs when I knew you'd be back."

Owen assisted Madison out of the room. *He's forgiven you*, she thought to herself. It helped to lessen the churning in her gut, but not by much. *If anything had happened to either of them, especially after you were so horrible*...She didn't even want to finish the thought.

When they disappeared behind the wall and Jordan could still see them, it took her a moment to take in what was left of the room. All the furniture would need to be replaced, half of the floor had chunks of wood missing, and the bricks surrounding the fireplace were cracked or crumbling.

"You shouldn't have come back," Dinah said in a low voice. "You have made it known who is dear to you."

"I don't understand," Jordan said. It took everything she had to remain standing.

"You wouldn't, since you have refused to listen to a word I've said," Dinah said. "Now you must deal with the consequences of your actions."

"I'm listening now," Jordan said. She wanted to bury her face in her hands, but felt like it would be a show of cowardice. "I can't let anything happen to them."

"Ah. And what happens when you discover that protecting your friends will not be enough to protect your heart from the truth?" Dinah asked.

138

"About what?"

Dinah hooked her thumbs through her belt loops. "Who murdered your mother and father," she said with a shrug. "Or the real reason your brother left Rolling River."

If Dinah was trying to get Jordan's attention, she truly had it now. "Tell me. Who murdered my parents?" She grew impatient when Dinah set her lips in a firm line. "If you know anything you need to at least tell—"

"Mortal law does not bind me in any way." Her voice was piercing. "The question I asked was, are you prepared to hear the truth? The answer is a simple yes or no. What have you decided?"

Jordan took a breath through clenched teeth. "Yes," she said.

"Excellent," Dinah said. "I shall see you tomorrow morning just as the sun peeks above the horizon." She leaned toward Jordan and breathed in.

"What are you doing?"

Dinah's upper lip twitched. "You smell like you've been kissing someone I knew a long time ago," she said. She adjusted her sword strap over her shoulder and walked toward the door. "Don't make the same mistake twice."

Chapter 15
The Lesson

"I've been doing some research," Madison said.

Jordan looked up at her from beneath the arm she had laid across her face. She had been trying to figure out if she was ill. Her skin still felt unbearably tight. Madison towered over her like a beautiful giant. She had to look away. It hurt her eyes to look at Madison for too long.

The fluorescent lights of the hotel suite Owen had rented for them were too bright. It wasn't the first time she mentally cursed Apophis. The damage he had done to the warehouse was so severe, the contractor Owen had hired to fix up the building declared it structurally unsound. Luckily, the crew had been completely blasé about the job and hadn't asked many questions.

The hotel room was nice enough; it had two queen-size beds, a pull-out sofa, and a bathroom the size of a small car.

Books littered every available surface. Jordan wasn't sure where Madison had managed to find them, but there they were; books on demons, the occult, Egyptian history, and even a few editions of the Bible. It took a lot of effort for Jordan not to feel irritated by the latter.

Madison nudged Jordan's thigh with her foot. "I did some research," she repeated.

Jordan sighed. "Of course you did," she said. "When did you have the time?"

Madison grimaced at Jordan's remark, and joined her on the floor. "I couldn't sleep after Dinah left yesterday." She kept her injured leg stretched out in front of her. Her toes were painted bubble-gum pink.

Guilt welled up in Jordan's chest. "How does the hospital feel about you missing a few shifts?" she asked, needing the distraction.

Madison shrugged and became very interested in a loose thread on her shirt. Her nails were a dark purple today. "I've actually decided to take a leave from my residency."

"They let you do that?" Jordan peeked up at Madison, and then sat up. "You quit. Why?"

Madison rolled her eyes. "Because there's a little too much going on in my personal life for me to focus on making sure someone doesn't die on my watch. Family comes first."

"I'm not family."

The door opened. Jordan tensed, and jumped to her feet, stepping out in front of Madison.

"I thought we all could use a little caffeine," Owen said. He held a tray with three cups in one hand and a brown paper bag in the other. He took a step back. "Everything all right?"

Madison rose, favoring her left side. "Everything's fine," she said. "Jordan was just demonstrating how she doesn't consider us family is all." She grabbed a cup and snagged the bag. "Chocolate croissants?" she exclaimed. "You sure know how to brighten a girl's day at the expense of her hips."

"Those aren't for you," Owen said, snatching the bag back. He put the tray down on the coffee table and stuffed half a croissant into his mouth. "Did you tell her?"

"Not yet," Madison said. She gingerly got onto one of the beds and leaned her back against the headboard. "I was working up the courage. She tends to get a little snippy when we talk about this kind of thing."

"Because we are grown adults talking about fiction as if it is real," Jordan said, taking the cup Owen forced into her hand.

"See?" Madison said, eyes sparkling.

"How about we play a game?" Owen asked Jordan. "You sit." He took her by the arm and led her toward the love seat. "Now, you listen."

"But—"

"Here." Owen dropped something heavy into her hand. "The old girl's got a full tank again. Still drives like a dream."

Jordan's fingers wrapped around the Mustang's key. He must have taken it while she slept. "You've got five minutes."

"Let me start then, by saying that I was right from the beginning," Owen said.

"Based on my research," Madison said in a loud voice, frowning at her brother, "Apophis is indeed a demon from ancient Egypt. A deity of darkness and chaos; its true form is that of a snake."

Jordan kept her mouth shut. She watched Owen and Madison exchange glances.

"I also had Maddie do some research on Mr. Murphy," Owen said.

Jordan raised a brow, but managed to stay silent.

"There was something about the name Levi that seemed familiar," Madison explained.

"Leviathan," Owen supplied. "An epic sea monster. You can find him in the Bible if you care to take a look."

Jordan furrowed her brow, then shook her head.

"No? Too bad." Owen picked up a Bible resting on the coffee table and flipped through it until he found what he was looking for. "Job, chapter forty-one."

Jordan stiffened.

"Relax," he said without looking up, "I won't read the whole thing." He took a breath and started to read.

> "The folds of his flesh are tightly joined; they are firm
> and immovable.
> His chest is hard as rock, hard as a lower millstone.
> When he rises up, the mighty are terrified; they retreat
> before his thrashing.
> The sword that reaches him has no effect, nor does
> the spear or the dart or the javelin.
> Iron he treats like straw and bronze like rotten wood.
> Arrows do not make him flee, sling stones are like chaff
> to him.
> A club seems to him but a piece of straw, he laughs at
> the rattling of the lance.
> His undersides are jagged potsherds, leaving a trail in the
> mud like a threshing-sledge.
> He makes the depths churn like a boiling cauldron and
> stirs up the sea like a pot of ointment.
> Behind him he leaves a glistening wake; one would think
> the deep had white hair.

Nothing on earth is his equal—a creature without fear.
He looks down on all that are haughty; he is king over
all that are proud."

Owen looked up at Jordan and closed the book. "He's creepy *and* indestructible!"

"There's something else, hon," Madison continued. "Leviathan is also a prince of hell. He embodies envy, one of the seven deadly sins, but that's beside the point." She waved her hand around as if she were erasing the fact from an invisible whiteboard. "If he's a prince, we think it could mean that he has some control over demons. Especially those that are like him."

Serpents. Jordan felt herself pale. *I didn't tell them what happened with him this morning. What I saw when he kissed me.*

"There's more," Madison said. It was clear she was taking the five-minute timeline seriously. "My friend at the hospital lab called me about the black substance we found the morning after Owen was injured." She took a breath. "The tests came back negative, no positive match with any DNA. The closest it comes to is canine, but even that is inconclusive."

"Canine." Jordan wanted to throw up.

"Will you at least consider what I've told you for now?" Madison asked.

Jordan released the breath she held. "Tully told me that the DNA they found on my parents was canine."

"Shut. Up," Madison shouted.

Owen lowered the pastry he was about to stuff into his mouth. "It's too strange to be a coincidence."

"We need to go back home," Madison said, getting off the bed. "Tully needs to know."

"I'm not sure if he'll believe us," Jordan said.

"No, no. This is perfect," Owen said. "We can get the yearbook at the same time."

"I still think Tully should know what we think," Madison added.

Jordan closed her eyes against the noise Owen and Madison were making. *I can't go back into that house. Not yet.*

"I think we need to stay here. At least for a little while longer," she said, raising a hand when Owen opened his mouth. "Look. I believe most of what you've told me."

"You do?" Owen asked.

"Sherlock Holmes," Jordan said, sharing a grin with Madison before continuing. "At this point we have more than enough evidence that demons exist."

Owen furrowed his brow. "Then why do we need to stay here?"

"I think Dinah knows what happened to Parker." Jordan pressed a hand to her stomach. "I think she knows who killed my parents."

"Oh," Madison said, in a voice that was overly casual. "Did she mention any names?"

"I hope to get it out of her tomorrow morning."

"Let's hear Dinah out, then," Owen said. "What time do we need to be ready?"

Jordan looked at Owen and Madison, their faces turned expectantly toward her, waiting for her answer. It felt strange to be looked to for a decision. *Something tells me Dinah isn't going to be a fan of them tagging along*, she thought. *But I can't leave them alone...*

"Tomorrow morning, just as the sun peeks over the horizon," she told them.

"Okay-yyyy," Madison said, drawing out the word until it was three syllables long.

"What time is that?" Owen asked.

"Hell if I know," Jordan said.

*****

Early the next morning, the three of them stumbled into the Mustang, still rubbing the sleep from their eyes. Jordan drove and parked in front of the warehouse. The entrance was blocked off with bright-yellow caution tape. A construction crew would be in later to continue salvaging what they could.

A thin strip of gold broke above the horizon, blinding Jordan through the rearview mirror. "It better be the right friggin' time," she muttered to herself. A tap on the window caused her to jolt in her seat, then she rolled down her window.

Dinah seemed intrigued by the mechanics, and watched the window until it had disappeared into the door. She wasn't wearing her sword.

"Well?" Jordan asked. "I'm here."

Dinah gave her a bland stare before speaking. "It pleases me to know that you are capable of following instructions to some extent." Her gaze slid to the backseat, where Owen and Madison slept.

"You said they're targets now," Jordan told her. "I won't leave them behind."

Dinah was silent for a moment. "Follow me," she finally said.

It took a few minutes to wake and get everyone out of the Mustang. Jordan knew she really shouldn't, but she did feel a little pleased to see Dinah's eyelid twitch just once.

When Dinah started walking, Jordan almost had to run to keep up with her. It limited her ability to make conversation. She wished someone would at least say *something*. The morning stillness made her thoughts loud and clear. She desperately did not want to think about anything Madison and Owen had told her the day before. Especially the part about going back to the house.

Dinah turned onto Main and headed toward the town limit. All the stores were closed, not another soul in sight. *I should have convinced her to let me drive us there*, Jordan thought. *Who knows how far she's going to make us walk?*

The church bells began to ring. The sound startled Jordan and had her picking up her pace to catch up with the others.

Dinah slowed as they approached the steps of the church. "We are here," she said, not waiting to see if anyone would follow her up the stairs and through one of the two giant wooden doors.

Jordan pressed her fingertips against the foundation. The church was made entirely of white brick. She tilted her head back to look at the steeple. The last note of the bells rang out into the morning. "I should have known," she murmured. This was the last place she wanted to be. She held her emotions in check and forced herself to walk up the stairs behind Owen and Madison. It was difficult to keep memories of her parents' funeral at bay.

Expecting to enter the sanctuary, Jordan was taken aback when Dinah headed for a steep, narrow staircase leading down to a basement. She followed, once again behind Owen and Madison. Her nose twitched when she reached the bottom. The scent of mildew was sharp in the air. A single lamp provided light for the entire room. It was large and carpeted, with a few foldable metal chairs arranged in a semicircle around a weathered lectern.

In the middle of the wall directly across the stairs was a short wooden door with a wide brass knocker.

"Is this okay?" Madison asked as Dinah approached the door. "I mean, does anyone know we're here?" The only response Madison received was a blank look from Dinah before she gripped the knocker and pulled. When the door opened, she ducked and slipped through.

Jordan gave Madison and Owen a shrug and hunched over before walking inside. She immediately had to shield her eyes when she entered the bright white room. It wasn't very big, but it was very empty.

"Reminds me of a padded cell," Owen said, letting Jordan know that both he and Madison had followed. "Where are we?"

Dinah inhaled sharply. "They stay here," she said pointing to the ground. "This is not negotiable."

"You know I can't do that," Jordan argued.

"This is a church. They will be safe if they stay here. You have my word."

Is your word worth their lives? Jordan thought, and worried her bottom lip between her teeth. *Damn it, I don't think she's going to budge on this one.*

"Go on. We won't move from this spot," Madison said. "Don't worry."

"Satisfied?" Dinah asked. She didn't give Jordan time to respond. She turned to face one of the walls and placed her hand against it. A draft breezed across Jordan's cheek. Its strength increased until gusts of wind whipped her hair across her face. When it stopped, Dinah's sword was strapped across her back, and part of the wall had disappeared. In its place was a dark, narrow corridor. Jordan could just make out a tiny dot of light in the distance.

Dinah took a step forward, placing a hand on either side of the wall. Flares went off, one after the other, bathing the floor in a yellow glow.

Jordan heard Owen's sharp intake of breath. "Stay here," she reminded him, before following Dinah forward.

"Be careful, hon," Madison said.

The air around her felt heavier as she walked into the mouth of the tunnel. There was a faint humming sound, which grew louder, drowning out their footsteps. Jordan's eyes began to water. She plugged her ears, which did little good. She could still feel the vibrations in her chest, as if she were standing next to speakers at a concert.

The humming stopped when Dinah reached the end of the corridor. From behind her shoulder, Jordan caught a glimpse of a room the size of a movie theater with vaulted ceilings.

"This is amazing," Jordan said, her voice echoing across what appeared to be a black marble floor. She arched her neck, trying to take in every detail. There wasn't much to see. Only the center of the room was visible. The rest was dark. "Is this some sort of old hidden passageway for people to hide in?"

"Mortals' minds tend to break in this place." Dinah said. "Therefore, the true appearance of this space has been masked."

Jordan completed a small circle. "Where are we, then?"

"Would you believe me if I told you?"

"Probably not," Jordan said. "Call me curious."

"I don't understand why you want me to call you that."

Jordan caught her tongue between her teeth and waited a beat before answering. "It's just an expression. Never mind."

Dinah had disappeared. Jordan went still, afraid that she had been left to figure a way out on her own. *The woman would drag me out here just to leave me behind*, she thought.

A light flared.

Dinah's pale face appeared. "Welcome to hell," she said before touching the torch to the wall.

The flame traveled along a line in the bricks, until the entire room glowed from the ring of fire. Jordan took a step back to admire the architecture, then froze. She realized that the wall wasn't made of brick. Square metal cages lined the perimeter of the room. Thousands of pairs of bulging eyes stared at her. Arms and legs hung limply though the spaces between the metal bars, which glistened like ice from the number of mouths producing yellow slime.

Holy shit.

"You have nothing to fear from these imps," Dinah said, walking toward Jordan. "They will not harm you unless they are released."

Instead of voicing her concerns about that, Jordan asked, "Should we really be here? What if someone catches us?"

"Ah, but I thought you didn't believe in demons. Why would you be worried about being disturbed?"

"Will you tell me what we're doing here, then?" Jordan ground out between clenched teeth. *Please don't say we're going to release any of these things.*

"Imps breed like rabbits," Dinah told her. "You are going to help me with a little population control."

"I think they look very happy right where they are," Jordan said. "In fact, if I tilt my head to the side a little, that one almost looks cute with its face smushed up against the bars."

"Foolish girl," Dinah hissed, dragging Jordan by the arm toward the cages. "In that alley, while you cowered, they would have torn your limbs from your body and peeled the flesh from your skin while you were still alive to watch."

Jordan really didn't want to get any closer. She pulled away from Dinah. "These ones aren't a threat to me. They're barely moving."

"Do you *want* to die?" Dinah asked. Her eyes seemed depthless as she stared down at Jordan.

"Of course not."

"Then you need to learn how to protect yourself. You also need to start using this a little more." Dinah rapped Jordan on the head with her knuckles.

"Ow! Cut that out," Jordan complained.

"Courage. Get some," Dinah snapped. "A few bumps on the head are the least of your concerns. A few imps are the least of your concerns. You will need to save Earth from demons far more powerful than you dare to imagine."

"I can't be responsible for saving the world," Jordan said, clenching her fists. "That's impossible."

"Fine," Dinah said in a tight voice. "Leave now, but one day these imps will be released. All of them." She swept her arm around the room. "They will kill your friends. They will kill everyone you love and will feel no remorse for their actions." She pulled her sword free and swung it toward one of the cages. "I can teach you how to protect your loved ones. I can teach you how to stay alive." She lowered the sword when Jordan didn't respond. "Your parents are looking down on you from heaven—"

"No," Jordan interrupted, her voice sharp. "They aren't. They're dead, and that's all there is to it." She clenched her jaw. "Listen. I didn't come here for a lesson. I came because you said you could give me information on who murdered them—"

"What would they think of you then, were they still alive?" Dinah said in a calm voice, ignoring the question. "Would they be proud of their daughter? A daughter who refuses to learn how she can help save those she loves the most in this world?" She raised a brow.

I never got to tell them... Jordan licked her lips as she choked down some saliva. She warily faced the imp. "Let it out," she said in a weak voice.

148

Dinah pointed the tip of her blade toward the metal bars. The cage door swung open on rusty hinges. The imp rushed forward, not seeming to notice the four-foot drop to the floor. It landed with a squeak, rolled to its feet, then stared at Jordan.

"It's not doing anything," she said.

"Can you feel it?" Dinah asked.

Jordan licked her lips, and switched balance from one foot to the other like a boxer. She hoped it would make her look as though she knew how to defend herself at least a little bit. "It's hungry," she said.

"They always are."

Jordan turned her head to look at Dinah. *Was that amusement I heard?* she thought.

Then she was on the floor, with slime smeared across her face. She could hear the imp wheezing from its position right beside her head.

"You're lucky imps aren't very smart," she heard Dinah say. "You would be dead otherwise. Focus."

I'm so hungry. I want to rip, rip, rip your heart right out.

Jordan rolled to the side. The imp crashed into the empty space, scoring the floor with its claws. Its eyes bulged farther out of its sockets. *Where is it? It was here, now it's gone?* She started looking around, even though the imp was right in front of her.

"Do not listen to its inner dialogue," Dinah called out. "You are a sponge. What the creature is *thinking* is of no importance to you. It's how the imp *feels* that fuels you."

Hungry, Jordan thought to herself. *I already told you that, you stupid bitch.* The thought brought her up short, and she narrowly avoided getting her gut spilled all over the floor. *Anger*, she thought. *Use it.*

Like she had done before when facing Apophis, Jordan released the tightness in her gut. It felt easier now, more fluid, the rush of rage heating her veins. It was different this time too. Her left hand felt like a thousand tiny ants were biting her. She screamed. Bones cracked; she could *feel* them lengthen. Her hand felt heavy, as if she had a five-pound dumbbell glued to it.

The imp jumped at her again. Reflexively, Jordan lifted her arm to block it. When she saw the two-inch claws extending from where her fingers should have been, she pulled back in terror. The imp landed on her, its feet caught in her shirt. Jordan was still trying to recover when it began to climb all over her, kicking her in the ribs, digging its toes into her skin. It wasn't until she saw the imp open its mouth to bite her that she gripped its folds of skin and pulled.

The imp soared across the room, and bounced across the floor a few times before sliding to a stop on its face.

Jordan was enraged. *That's not me*, she thought. *The imp is enraged. I feel awesome.* She watched it pull itself to its feet. Yellow slime and black goo covered its body in splotches. *My hand*, she thought. *I sliced him right open.*

She rushed forward, swinging. Her claw caught the imp across the face. She darted away as it leapt blindly at her. Jordan hit it again, then again when it fell to the ground.

"You're still connected. Pull away." Dinah's voice barely scratched the surface of her consciousness.

This hurts. I am dying.

Jordan fell to her knees then, clutching at her own stomach. Fear whipped through her body; there was nothing she could do. She was going to die.

"Cut yourself off!" Dinah sounded very far away.

Closing her eyes, Jordan tried to distinguish the imp's pain from her own. She discovered she wasn't the one who was dying. The imp was. When Jordan opened her eyes, she felt fantastic. The room was bright, colors were vivid. She tentatively raised her left hand, which now had five fingers, and five regular, albeit slightly broken, nails.

"How do you feel?" Dinah asked.

Jordan took a deep breath, testing her sense of smell. Her euphoria slipped away, leaving her buckled over. The sharp pain in her abdomen made it impossible to straighten.

"Let this be a lesson," Dinah said. Jordan couldn't see her, but it sounded like she was standing next to her. "Power can be a strange beast when you lose control over it."

Jordan nodded her head to show that she understood.

"Lately, you feel emotions that seem extreme." Dinah appeared suddenly. She made a fist and jabbed it toward Jordan's belly. "Your gut feels like someone is building a fire pit within it. It burns and never really extinguishes."

Jordan straightened and wrapped her arms around herself. "How did you know?" she asked.

"It is your gift," Dinah told her, her voice soft. "Your power. You have the ability to absorb and take on characteristics of beings that are either from heaven or hell. What you have been experiencing is the effects of *not* using

150

characteristics you have absorbed. If you don't use it, that power will slowly poison you from the inside out." Her boot heels echoed across the smooth floor as she moved to stand in front of the cages. "You need to learn how to turn yourself off so that you are not soaking up everything and anything that moves." Jordan stared at Dinah's back as she spread her arms wide to encompass all the imps. "You also need to learn how to embrace and use the power when you need it. To protect those you love." She turned, lowering her arms and fixing her gray eyes on Jordan. "To save the world."

"I would only make a mess of things," Jordan said. *It's the honest truth*, she thought. *I haven't done anything useful since... well, since Parker and Owen left.*

"You want to see him again. Don't you?"

What's the woman going on about now? Jordan winced. "I don't follow."

"You like the way he makes you feel," Dinah said, coming closer. Jordan was in too much pain to really see the iron mask her features had become.

"Who are you talking about?" She said the first name that came to mind. "Parker?"

"Guess again."

"Levi?"

"Well done," Dinah said in a voice dripping with sarcasm.

"That's it. We're finished here," Jordan said. The pain had decreased enough that she was able to shuffle forward. "I'm a grown woman, and can make my own decisions. If I choose to see him again, I will."

"You need to stay away from him," she said.

"I can do whatever I damn well please."

Dinah drew her sword and advanced on Jordan. "How dare you. You know nothing!" she spat. "I wish I could leave you. Everyone else in your life is smart enough to do so."

The words hit their mark hard. Jordan did her best to keep her features impassive.

Dinah's lips twisted into a sneer. "You're just like *her*."

"I don't care."

"Eve was weak too. She wanted a man who offered her nothing in return. She betrayed her husband. She betrayed mankind." The tip of Dinah's sword made contact with Jordan's flesh. "Tell me. What kind of woman are you?"

"Whoa, hold on. This isn't funny," Jordan managed to say. "I—I don't know!" She took a step back but the sword followed.

"Tell me," Dinah roared. "Who *are* you?"

"Nobody!" Jordan yelled. "I'm nobody."

The sword dropped away from her throat. Sweat broke out along Jordan's back and she pitched forward in her relief.

Expecting to hit the ground, she was startled when Dinah was there to steady her.

"Isn't it time you changed that?" Dinah asked in a soft voice.

Tears welled in Jordan's eyes. She swallowed them back. "Yes," she whispered.

A smile broke across Dinah's face, dazzling Jordan with how striking she really was. "It takes strength to admit something like that," Dinah said, "and it takes a brave soul to do something about it." She helped Jordan regain her balance before moving toward another cage. "Are you ready?" she asked.

"I am," Jordan replied.

Chapter 16

A Friend, A Love, A Knight in Shining Armor

Standing in line at a coffee shop felt a hell of a lot different to Jordan than it ever had before.

"Can I help you?" the barista asked.

Jordan knew that she needed to answer quickly, as the patrons waiting behind her would start to get antsy. "I..." she began. *I just killed a bunch of imps with claws I grew out of my hand.* She bit down on the inside of her cheek and hoped the thought had remained in her head.

"What would you like?" the barista prompted. The slight roll of her eyes told Jordan that she was just impatient, not freaked out.

"Three coffees, please," she mumbled.

"What size?"

Jordan couldn't help it. She took a moment to stare at the woman behind the counter. After everything she had done a few hours before, making a decision about the size of a cup suddenly seemed pretty damn trivial.

After doing away with the first imp, Dinah had her practice on at least a dozen more. Jordan had lost count after her eighth kill. She still felt uneasy about the whole training session; the creatures really didn't seem that dangerous until they were set free. Shivering, Jordan remembered the look on Owen's and Madison's faces as she reentered the white room in the church, covered in blood and slime. Disgust didn't quite sum it up.

When they had reached the hotel, Madison steered Jordan in the direction of the shower. When she was finished washing, Owen shoved a few bills into her hand and suggested she go and get them some caffeinated beverages. That the fresh air would likely do her some good.

No one waiting in this line for a drink has any idea what I've faced today, she thought.

"*Excuse me*," the barista's voice pierced through Jordan's inner dialogue. "Do you want the coffee or not, lady?"

Jordan finished ordering and paying without any further incidents. She was handed a tray, which she carried in both hands toward the door, which she opened by pushing against it with her back. It hit her then, looking at all the patrons.

What happens if all those imps freed themselves, or what if Apophis comes back a third time? she thought. *Who here would be able to help?* She froze in place, clutching the tray closer to her chest. *I would*, she told herself. *I'd be able to help.*

It took only a few minutes to walk back to the hotel. When she entered their room she noticed that both beds had been made. Madison was hunched over the desk, taking notes from a thick book.

"Where's Owen?" Jordan asked.

Madison looked up and dropped her pen onto the paper. "He's meeting with his manager," she said. "And just as a heads-up, he didn't sound happy about it." She closed the book she had been taking notes from. "How are you feeling?"

"Better. A bit stiff, but it's my mind that's been working overtime." Jordan handed Madison a cup of coffee and walked over to the sofa by the window. "Are you sure there's no way your program will let you come back?"

"I totally appreciate the vote of confidence," Madison said, turning the chair so that she faced Jordan. She tucked her feet up onto it before she continued. "But I'm sure. It's not going to happen." She flipped her hair behind her and cleared her throat. "When are you going to tell me what happened with Dinah this morning?"

"I'm working my way up to it," Jordan said. She took a large gulp of coffee and scalded the inside of her mouth. "I, uh…" she started when she could speak again. "Damn, I have no idea where to start."

Madison took the lid off her cup and blew on the hot liquid a few times. Steam curled from the lip of the Styrofoam and disappeared. She continued to watch Jordan, her eyes calm as her fingers coiled and twirled hair from her ponytail.

"You know how when you get to know someone, you start to pick up on their little habits and what they mean?" Jordan began. "You, for example, like to play with the ends of your hair when you're anxious."

Madison's hand stilled and she looked as though she wanted to deny it. "Guilty," she ended up saying with a gleam in her eyes.

"It's similar to what happened with the imps in the alley of the River

154

Six, even with Legion or Apophis," Jordan told her. "At first, I only picked up little things about them. The next thing I knew, I started to think and feel what they were *actually* thinking and feeling." She licked her lips, and took another sip of coffee to wet her throat. "It's scary, at first. It feels like being sucked under a crushing wave, but then you reach the surface and when you catch your breath, you know you have the advantage against the next wave because you know how and when it's going to come at you."

"You have the power to read minds?" Madison asked in a soft voice.

"Sort of," Jordan said, shaking her head at how it all sounded. "This morning Dinah made me practice using my...ability on imps. Damn, this is hard to explain. I'm not sure that I'm doing it right." She pursed her lips and put the cup down on the coffee table. She rested her elbows on her thighs and leaned forward. "I know there's a Supernatural nearby when I can feel a little ball of heat, like a hot coal, right here." She pressed a fist against her stomach.

"A Supernatural?" Madison asked.

"Dinah said it's what we puny mortals call creatures that are not of this world. She may have left the puny part out." Jordan shrugged before she continued. "Apparently, I can absorb any Supernatural's power and use it. When I do, it feels like tiny needles poking into my pores." Jordan looked at her hands. *And then I'm supposed to kill them*, she thought, but couldn't bring herself to say the words out loud.

"I wonder how it works." Madison's perfectly groomed brow creased. She picked up her pen and absently began to roll it between her fingers.

"You aren't going to get all scientific on me, are you?"

"I'm thinking," Madison said. She clasped her hand around one knee, and held the pen between two fingers.

"Here we go..."

Madison grinned and ignored Jordan. "Genetics!" she said and got up from her chair. A few pieces of paper fluttered to the ground from the desk as she began to pace. "What if Eve also had the same power? You could be a direct descendant."

Jordan nodded. "There could be a kernel of truth to that," she said. "Or"—she leaned back into the sofa and crossed one leg over the other—"I could be a direct descendent of anyone who had the absorbing powers of a sponge." Even as she said the words, she knew she didn't believe them. *When are you going to tell her about what you see when Levi touches you?* she asked herself.

Madison took a moment before speaking again. "The research speaks for itself," she said. She stopped pacing, and held out a hand in front of her. "Apophis." She held out her thumb. "Legion." Her index finger went up. "Dinah, and let's not forget the temptingly gorgeous Leviathan." Two more fingers. "We can't ignore that we're being faced with characters from biblical literature or historical mythology.

"What if we stopped thinking of Eve as this imaginary woman?" Madison continued. "What if she was real, as real as you and me? What if, regardless of what either of us believes, she was a human being who disobeyed the law and was punished for it?"

"I don't know," Jordan said. "I feel like we're grasping at straws here."

"Can you talk to Dinah?" Madison asked.

"I can try," Jordan said.

"Great." Madison pursed her lips and tapped a finger against them. "How do you feel about all of this?"

"Wonderful," Jordan said in one breath, then added, "Terrified," in the next. She glanced at the hotel room door. "You know how close Parker and I were," she said in a hushed voice. "We did everything together, and I thought we always would. Pretty stupid thing to think." She wrapped her hands around the coffee cup and took comfort from its warmth. "When Owen dumped me, it broke my heart. When I couldn't even talk to Parker about it, when he just left for his tour without so much as a good-bye, it felt like a part of me died."

Jordan could still feel it, the sadness that lingered even now. "Ever since, I've been trying to figure out what the hell to do with the half I have left. Why do you think I left the country?" she asked, not expecting an answer, wishing she could explain to her parents. "Parker made everything he did look so easy, including knowing what he wanted to do with his life. Now *I* have this power. I haven't decided if it's a gift or not, but the more I think about it, the more I know I can help people. I can protect them." She finally looked at Madison. "I think I've finally found what I was meant to do."

"Are you saying you believe in destiny?" Madison pressed on, "In God?"

Jordan snorted. "My parents were murdered in their bed." She looked at Madison and saw her lips part. Jordan held up her hand. "When I was traveling I saw people who were more than willing to help the elderly cross the street," she continued. "I also came across people who would rather set fire to buildings. Bad things happen all the time. Good things happen too. It's called life, not divine intervention."

"A day ago I didn't believe in demons, or even think it was possible for anyone to have superhuman strength," Madison said.

"Oh, I forgot to mention. I can also grow a claw out of my hand." Jordan held up her hand and wiggled her fingers.

Madison's eyes widened. "Sure. Okay." She ran a hand across her forehead. "As I was saying, if all of those things are possible, then shouldn't God be as well?"

"Sherlock Holmes," Jordan said, her lips quirking upward. "If he exists, and I'm so damn important, why hasn't he introduced himself?"

"Well, would you look at that. I'm rubbing off on you!" Madison said. "Which can only mean that you're right." She reached out and gave Jordan's knee an absent pat. "However, there's a piece of the puzzle that's missing. It's been nagging at me like a bad itch I just can't reach..."

"You know when I said I was terrified?" Jordan said. She wasn't sure she should say the rest, but she plucked up the courage to say it anyway before she changed her mind. "I wasn't kidding. Feeling responsible for another life, it scares me shitless."

Madison gestured for Jordan to make room for her on the sofa. When she sat down, she snuggled up against Jordan's side. "But you'll do it anyway," she murmured. "Regardless of what you believe, but because of what you can do. I've always known that about you. Even when you didn't."

"Really?"

"The day Parker left, I don't think a part of you died. I think that part of you has always been there, just waiting to be found," Madison said. "Congratulations, my friend. Today's the day."

*****

It was dark when Jordan woke. She lifted her head to squint at the alarm clock. It was just after three in the morning. Testing her limbs, she was a little surprised to find that she felt fine. Aside from a slight ache in her ribs, she was able to move quite gracefully.

A roaring snore almost startled a scream from Jordan's lips. She sat up to look over at Owen, who was making all the noise from the other bed. Wide awake and restless, Jordan slipped out into the hallway.

Not feeling like wandering the streets half-naked, Jordan headed for the roof. There was some patio furniture, and a few barbeques, but at such an early hour it was empty. The cool breeze felt wonderfully fresh against her skin. She walked over to the edge of the building, and looked over the cement wall. Its width seemed like a rather thin barrier against her and the street below.

Jordan didn't know how, but she knew Levi was behind her even before he spoke.

"Are you waiting for someone?"

His words were reminiscent of what she had seen the last time they were together. One look at him told her he was thinking the same thing. He put his hands in his pockets and sauntered toward her.

"I came here to be alone," Jordan told him, crossing her arms over her chest. What she really wanted to do was wrap them around him. It irked her. "I'm beginning to think you're stalking me, Leviathan." She didn't know why she said the name. *It's not as if Madison's research was accurate...*

"I don't need to stalk you, darling," Levi drawled. "Not when you've been broadcasting your emotions all over town. I'm glad you're feeling better."

"Impossible," Jordan muttered.

"I wanted to see you," he said. "I can't stand having you think I tried to hurt you."

"Then why did you?" she asked. "You couldn't wait until I said yes to get me into bed?"

Levi cocked a brow. His eyes shone. Jordan couldn't tell if it was with humor or anger. "Are you suggesting that *I* have any problem finding a *willing* woman?" he asked.

No sound came out of Jordan's open mouth. She thought about the horde of women who were fawning over him at the River Six.

"It's a serious accusation," he continued. "Make sure you know where you stand before you start throwing it around," he said. He took a breath. "I'm pleased you've finally remembered who I am." The impish grin that spread across his face was almost childlike. He kept his hands in his pockets, but moved to stand beside her.

"I *don't* remember you," Jordan snarled, angry that he was confirming what he should have denied. "I read about you in a book. Should I start addressing you as a prince of hell? Or is that only reserved for weekends?"

"If you want to know more about me, you just need to ask," he said. His gaze never faltered. "I know many ways for a man and a woman to get reacquainted."

"I bet you do," Jordan said weakly. She refused to look at him now, knowing that he was trying to distract her, and it was working. "It's too late," she forced herself to say. "I've heard enough about you to ask that you stay away from me."

"I find that disappointing," he said. "The woman I knew made up her own mind. She refused to be a pawn."

"I know my own mind," Jordan snapped. He was getting under her skin. So much so, it was starting to feel tight again.

"Then discover the truth." Levi extended his hand.

Jordan straightened. Curiosity won out over caution. *What's the harm?* she thought.

She slapped her hand against his before she could talk herself out of it.

*****

"It's been seven days," Leviathan had said.

"He left again," she said in a soft voice. "He didn't tell me why, but he didn't have to. I know it's because of *her*."

"Lilith?" he said with a loud snort. "The woman's a nuisance. He's welcome to her, don't you think?"

She didn't reply.

"Do you love him?"

She blinked at Leviathan, the question catching her off guard. He had never asked her before. "I used to," she answered honestly.

Leviathan dropped his mouth to hers, dragging out a kiss that was deliriously possessive. When he released her, there was a dark gleam in his eyes. "Do you love me?" he asked.

"Yes," she said. Her heart swelled just looking at him. In that moment she knew. "I will come with you," she said, and laughed when she saw the expression of joy dance across his features.

"I will make you happy, Eve," he said, taking both of her hands in his and kissing each in turn. "I vow it here and now." He tugged her to her feet. "Share the apple with me. You have nothing to fear now."

Together they walked to the apple tree. She had never been this close to it before, and tried to ignore the knots of fear twisting in her stomach. Spots of red had colored the foliage like polka dots. Leviathan reached up and plucked one from the lowest branch. He took a big bite; the meaty flesh crunched loudly between his teeth.

He handed the apple to her. "I love you, Eve," Leviathan said. The words were everything she had ever wanted to hear.

She held the fruit in both hands, brought it to her lips, and took a bite.

*****

"Leave this place," Levi said. The words were said in such a soft voice, Jordan doubted for a moment she heard them. "I can make all your nightmares disappear with the snap of my fingers. Let me protect you. Come with me."

Jordan put her hand against his chest. She could feel the rapid beating of his heart. The warmth of him. To all appearances, he was a man, one who was offering her the very thing she yearned for.

The only difference was, she could feel it now. The one thing that made him different. She closed her eyes and let her mind wander. Levi wrapped his arms around her, and she let him. The closeness helped her to focus in on his power. She found that it was very different from the imps. Instead of being something external that was easy to touch, it was more intricate, as if it were wrapped around each vein in Levi's body as opposed to sitting on the surface like a layer of film.

With a gentle touch, she pulled at a strand, soaking it in. She felt weak in the knees from the heady rush. It was so much more than she had experienced with the imps. Their power was simple. Pure anger, and hatred. Levi's was so much more complex. And he had been using it against her the entire time.

Two can play at this game...

"Why don't you tell me why you drugged me?" she asked. "What do you really want from me?"

It was incredible. She could feel his power laced around each word. Confidence rushed through her like fuel, and she leaned forward, letting her gaze fall on his lips before settling on his eyes.

"I..." Levi began, "I never..." His hand went to his head before his eyes sharpened on her face.

A barrier went up, severing Jordan's link with Levi as cleanly as a guillotine's blade.

"Where did you learn how to do that?" he snapped.

It took Jordan a moment to realize he had pushed her away from him. His stance had completely changed. His hands formed fists, which he held in front of his body.

"I don't know what you're talking about..."

"Don't," he shouted at her. Jordan flinched, and felt a trickle of fear, knowing that she was alone with him. "I suppose that's fair," he continued in a more neutral tone. "I'm not playing fair myself, but I can't risk losing you again."

"I don't know you," Jordan said. His actions reminded her of that. *How stupid of you to forget.*

"Can't you see? I'm not giving you an ultimatum this time," Levi said, grabbing her by the shoulders. "I'm just a man who wants to spend the rest of eternity with you. And don't ask me if I'm sure. I've spent too many centuries without you to know that I won't change my mind."

There was no power in his words this time, and the man who said them moved her. She wanted to take everything he promised. She wanted to be loved, truly loved in the way that she knew he was offering her. In the way she always wanted Owen to love her.

Is it because you need an excuse to start running again? She heard his voice in her head, clear as day. *Haven't you realized by now that it isn't going to solve anything?*

"I—I can't," she heard herself say. "I have to stay."

Levi's eyes were sharp in his face as he moved his hands to cup both her cheeks. "There will come a time when I won't be able to ask again..."

"I hope I'm not interrupting anything." Owen's voice sliced through Levi's last word. Jordan's breath hitched in her throat and her heart began to race as he walked toward her.

He frowned, and Jordan realized she was holding her own hand up to her cheek. "I thought I heard you talking to someone," he said.

Jordan dropped her hand to her side, hoping it looked casual. "Just myself," she told him. "It helps when I need to work out my thoughts." Together they turned to the building ledge. She rested her elbows on it and studied Owen as he studied the ground below.

"Madison filled me in on what you two talked about earlier today," he said. "Is that what's bothering you?"

"She should still be in medical school," Jordan told him, ignoring the question. "Why did you let her quit? She would have been the only one of us to have an actual profession."

Owen shifted his attention to her face. "What are you talking about?" he asked with a slight frown. "She flunked out at the beginning of this year."

"What?" She clamped her jaw shut to stop it from hanging open.

"I thought you knew." Owen crossed his arms in front of his chest. "She flunked out, and was looking for a change. She asked if she could move into the warehouse until she decided what to do next."

Jordan didn't know what to say. *Why would she lie to me? Doesn't she trust me?* she thought, trying to mask her reaction from Owen. *She's had plenty of time to tell me the truth.*

"Is something wrong?" Owen asked.

What else has Madison lied about? Jordan thought. "No," she said aloud. She gave her head a quick shake. "No. I'm fine." The air on the roof felt much too cold now.

"Cool," Owen said. He threw an arm around her shoulders. "So I didn't want to ask earlier since you seemed pretty spaced-out and covered in goo," he began, "but did you get the information we need about Parker and your parents from Dinah?"

Jordan tilted her head back and closed her eyes. "I tried to bring it up but never got an answer," she said. "Although..." She bit down on her bottom lip and eyed Owen before continuing. "With everything that's been happening to me, do you really think we should focus on trying to find him?"

"Of course," Owen said. Jordan wondered if it were possible for his brows to raise any higher. "We can't give up on him."

"He's the one who gave up on us," she murmured, then said in a louder voice, "I'll ask again the next time I see Dinah."

"Okay," Owen said. He dropped his arm from her shoulder and let the fingers of that hand bounce against the top of the roof's ledge. *Tap, tap, tap.*

She didn't think he sounded convinced. "We'll get the information from her. Don't worry."

Owen didn't say anything for almost a minute. "I found out today that the band is finished," he said, his voice flat. "Management is tired of dealing with unreliable artists. Our label will be dropping us in a few weeks."

"Damn," Jordan said. She reached out and gave his hand a squeeze before letting go. "I'm sorry, Owen."

"The worst part is, that's not even what's bothering me. I miss Parker *so* much." He fixed his gaze somewhere over her shoulder. "I don't even know if he's okay. It hurts to think about it too much."

"I know. Same here," Jordan told him, and tried to mean it.

"He left me, and I can't help but feel broken," he said in a soft voice. *Tap, tap, tap.* His fingers rapped against the wall. He turned away from her and stared down at the ground below. *Tap, tap, tap.* "I can't take it anymore, Jo."

Owen leaned forward and toppled over the edge.

Jordan's arm shot out faster than she thought possible. She grabbed at Owen's ankle and caught it, bashing her chest against the wall, almost flipping over herself from the momentum.

There was a moment when all Jordan could hear was the rush of blood through her ears before Owen cried, "Oh, God. Please, don't let go!"

"I won't," Jordan snapped. She reached out and secured her grip with her other hand. "Stop wriggling around, you moron. I've got you." She gritted her teeth and braced her toes against the wall. She yanked, and didn't stop pulling, even when she heard Owen's body smack against the side of the building.

When most of his weight was back on the right side of the wall, Jordan fell backward, barely avoiding getting hit in the face with his foot.

"What the hell!" She wanted to scream the words, but she was too busy catching her breath. She pushed him off her instead. "Don't you *ever* do that to me again, do you understand?"

"I don't know what happened," Owen said. He was shaking so hard he couldn't stand. Although her one arm felt like it had been ripped from its socket, Jordan offered him her shoulder. "That wasn't me. I would never...I mean, you know me. Suicide? It's never crossed my mind but, shit. Right then I felt I had to."

"I believe you," Jordan told him, feeling less angry now that he wasn't splattered on the sidewalk below. She blanched, and swallowed.

"I'm starting to think there's a target on my back," he said. "But who would want me dead? And why?"

"I have an idea," Jordan muttered, and then in a louder voice said, "We need to get inside."

Owen let her lead him. "I've had it wrong this entire time," he said. "You're not the one who needs looking out for."

"Everyone needs someone to look out for them," Jordan told him, her voice thick with emotion. *You really scared me this time, you handsome bastard.* "I'll always look out for you. You know that."

Owen bent his head to hers and pressed a kiss into her hair.

Chapter 17
The Book of Eve

The next morning, Jordan didn't want to get up. Every muscle in her body ached, and she was supposed to meet Dinah in less than an hour.

I wonder if she takes bribes, Jordan thought, rubbing the sleep from her eyes. *Like coffee. I could use about a gallon myself.* She made her way over to the bathroom, which was currently occupied. Jordan had just convinced herself to spend the time waiting back under the covers on the sofa when the door opened.

"Good morning," Madison whispered. "How was your sleep?"

Jordan started smiling, and then stopped. *Liar*, she thought to herself. She glanced over at Owen, who was still asleep. Now wasn't the time to confront Madison. Instead, Jordan brushed past her and shut the door.

When she reentered the room, Madison was making the bed Jordan had slept in.

"Are you all right?" she asked in a hushed voice.

Jordan kept her mouth shut as she ran her hand through her damp hair. She reached the sofa and found her pants from the previous day on the floor.

"Looking for the key to the Mustang?" Madison whispered. "It's over here. You were in a bit of a daze last night. I had to take it from you." She paused to toss some hair over her shoulder. "Don't you remember?"

Jordan remembered well enough. Fresh emotion had the corners of her mouth tug downward as her temper flared. "Why should I believe you?" she asked.

"Excuse me?" Madison hissed. "Well?" she demanded when Jordan didn't answer. "Are you going to tell me what's got you all out bent out of shape, or are you going to be all passive-aggressive about it?"

"You didn't drop out of medical school," Jordan spat out. She hated how petty she sounded, but it was too late to stop now. "You flunked out."

Madison's lips thinned as she grimaced. "You're right," she finally said. "I did."

"Are you going to tell me why you lied?" Jordan demanded.

"Ladies." Owen's groggy voice interrupted Madison's response. "A rooster's crow would be easier on the ears. What's with all the screeching?"

"You sister was just about to tell me why she's been lying to me," Jordan told him without hesitation.

"You're acting like I've committed a crime," Madison said to Jordan. "I was embarrassed. How's that for an answer?"

Jordan was speechless.

Madison's hands went to her hips. "Try and think about it from my perspective. Here you were, back from traveling the world. I didn't know how to tell you that my plans had failed spectacularly."

"Let's not forget that she needed to convince you not to take me to the hospital," Owen piped up. He was propped up on an elbow, watching.

"I knew you'd take her side," Jordan said.

"Stay out of this," Madison snapped over her shoulder. "Why does there have to be a side?" she asked Jordan. "I'm so sorry. I wanted to tell you, but I didn't know how."

She was bound to break my trust at some point, Jordan thought. *Isn't that what everyone does?*

"You told me that you've finally found out who you are, what you were meant to do," Madison told her. "I'm still searching for myself. You of all people should understand what that's like. It's the only reason why I would lie to you for so long…"

The words hit too close to home. *Don't think about Mom and Dad*, Jordan commanded herself. *Don't think about them now.* It took her a minute to feel composed enough to say, "I'm heading out to see Dinah." She clutched the Mustang's key tightly in her fist. "You guys will be safe here. I won't be long."

"Are you sure you don't want us to go with you?" Owen asked. Madison sat down beside him and leaned her head against his shoulder.

"I'm sure," Jordan said. She waited at the door for a moment. She wasn't quite sure what for. If it was because she had expected Madison to try to apologize again, she was mistaken.

"We'll see you when you get back, then," Madison said instead. "Be careful!"

Jordan left the room; guilt lay heavy on her heart.

*****

Jordan's mood had worked itself into a fine temper by the time she reached the church. When she opened the door to the white room, she told herself that she didn't care that Dinah was pacing the length of the floor.

"I'm here," she said. "Save the lecture for another time. I'm not willing to listen today. What happened to my parents? Where's Parker?"

Dinah wasn't dressed for battle. She wore a pair of white, loose-fitting slacks and a tank top. It was odd to see her without the hilt of her sword peeking out from behind her shoulder.

Instead of responding, she asked, "Where are your mortals?"

Jordan sighed before she hooked her thumbs in her belt loops. "I decided to let them sleep in today." *No need to mention Owen's condition, the cause, or the argument Madison and I just had*, she thought. "Who killed my parents?"

Dinah ignored her again, but stopped pacing. "Aren't you worried about their safety?" she asked.

"Owen and Madison's? Yes. Of course I am."

"Then I won't take much of your time."

"Oh," Jordan said, surprised. "Thank you."

Dinah stared at her. "You're welcome."

The words sounded forced, but considering it was the first time Jordan had ever heard her say this, she didn't mind.

"You have proven yourself to me in these last few weeks," Dinah continued. "I am pleased that you are taking ownership of your abilities, but we must now move on."

"Are you sure?" Jordan asked, parents forgotten. She could barely think; her heart was pounding a furious beat in her chest. "I mean you mentioned I needed to prepare for something big, you've just never mentioned what that meant."

"I'm sure," Dinah told her. "But you are getting ahead of yourself. We still have time. Not much, but we must gain an advantage where we can."

"How?"

Dinah's face glowed as she spoke the words. "The *Book of Eve*."

Jordan half expected trumpets to sound. "Never heard of it."

"I mentioned it to you, when you were not willing to listen," Dinah said, "but I'm not surprised. After what she did, many have tried to bury her words. To silence her forever."

"Her?" Jordan worried her bottom lip through her teeth. Took a breath. "You're telling me Eve wrote a book?"

"She didn't, no," Dinah said with a shake of her head. "Her words were passed down through her children, and her children's children, until one of her descendants was able to write it down."

"And what am I supposed to do with it?"

Dinah's lips formed a thin line before she said, "Read it."

Jordan couldn't help but laugh. "You expect me to save the world by reading a *book?*" she said. "Why didn't you tell me it was going to be this easy?"

Please," Dinah said, bringing her hands to her temples. "You need to read the book to find out what you must do."

"I already know the answer to that," Jordan said. "I need to take down Levi."

"Absolutely not. You aren't ready yet."

"Then let me fight you," Jordan said. "You're the strongest Supernatural I know. It'll be good practice for the real deal."

Dinah placed her hands on her hips and tilted her head to the side. "Tell me. When have you sensed my power? Am I using it now?"

Jordan pursed her lips. "Yes," she said, and then paused. "No?" She decided to ignore Dinah's triumphant gaze. "That's beside the point. I was able to feel Levi using his, *and* I was able to absorb some of it, just like you taught me."

"You did *what?*" Dinah roared.

Jordan shied back, half-afraid that she was about to have a sword pointed in her direction again. Instead, Dinah pinched the bridge of her nose with her forefinger and thumb and closed her eyes.

"I thought we resolved this little problem," Dinah snapped. "There are leagues of distance between soaking up an imp's power, and even touching the power of a prince of hell."

"For the record, *he* followed *me*," Jordan said. She ran a hand through her hair. "I've done everything I can to make it clear that I want nothing to do with him or his damn promises."

"Are you sure?" Dinah asked. She took hold of Jordan's chin, but was gentle about it. "Has he made you want him again, Eve?"

"Don't call me that," Jordan said, then rolled her eyes. "Have you *seen* him?" she continued, her tone dry. "Of course I want him. You'd have to be blind not to." She brushed Dinah's hand aside. "But I'm not a fool. What he feels isn't real. He's in love with who he thinks I am."

"We must move quickly, then," Dinah said. Jordan watched her movements, the way she stalked back and forth across the length of the small room. "You must get that book."

Jordan's mind was elsewhere. "What's it like?" she asked.

Dinah didn't even pause. "I don't understand the question."

"You're a warrior...of some kind," Jordan elaborated. "What's it really like, fighting in a real battle?"

"I do not think that is at all relevant..."

"All right, all right," Jordan muttered, then sat down cross-legged on the ground. "It was a stupid question anyway." She didn't look up when she heard Dinah sigh, or when she sat down in front of her.

"Do you know how I became a guardian angel?" Dinah asked. Her voice was soft, yet commanding.

Jordan shook her head.

"My father was Jacob. Yes," she added when she saw the look on Jordan's face. "*That* Jacob. The man who worked for seven years to marry his beloved Rachel, only to discover on his wedding night that he was married to her sister instead. The man who then worked another seven years to eventually marry the woman he loved."

"I thought that was just a story..."

"What you mortals use today to teach lessons and values was very much a reality. Of that, I can assure you." Dinah folded her arms across her chest. "Are you familiar with the rest, then?"

"The Bible isn't exactly on my reading list," Jordan replied.

"As I suspected," Dinah said. "My father had recently purchased land, and I went with him to visit with the women of the city. It was there that I first laid eyes on him, my Shechem." Dinah's voice had gone all soft and wistful. Jordan was careful to keep her face composed.

"He was a prince, and I was enamored with him, and he with me," Dinah continued. "It wasn't long before we decided to lie together. He promised me the moon, the stars, and the one thing I truly cared about. His heart."

"You were in love," Jordan said, and cringed at how surprised she sounded.

"Yes." Dinah hadn't seemed to notice. She was staring off into the distance. "Shechem's father offered to pay whatever bridal price my father wanted."

"I'm guessing he wasn't impressed?"

"It was my brothers who were not appeased. They felt my virtue had been stolen from me, and so they told Shechem's father that the men of the city needed to be circumcised before we could be married."

"That sounds rather...painful."

"It was meant to be," Dinah said, rising to her feet, her voice whipping around the room like a windstorm. "They waited until all of the men were recovering from their wounds. Then, they entered the city, and killed them." She dropped her arms to her sides and clenched her fists. "I was with Shechem when they came. I managed to injure one brother, but together they overpowered me. I watched them kill the man I loved. Then they killed me."

Jordan didn't know what to say, so she said nothing at all.

"When I awoke," Dinah said, moving closer, "I was given my sword, and the power to protect those who are unable to protect themselves." Her gray eyes shone as she looked down at Jordan. "I know what it's like to be betrayed. I know what it's like to be helpless. I know what it's like to be scared." Her gaze never wavered as she finished. "And because I have the ability to stop it, I would rather die than let anyone else feel what I felt that day." She seemed hesitant, but she sat down and put her hand on Jordan's knee. "I will not let anything happen to you," she said. "I need you to change the world."

"To fix someone else's so-called mistake," Jordan said. "Why can't you convince someone else to do it so I don't have to be terrified all the time?"

"Do you know anyone else who can grow claws out of their hand?"

Jordan shook her head, then grinned despite herself. "At least that part is pretty fun."

"You are unique and special. You are precious. You must not forget that," Dinah told her. "Now. We need to discuss how you are going to get the *Book of Eve*."

Jordan tried to shake off the glow she felt from Dinah's words. No one had ever called her precious before. "Right," she said. "Where can I find it?"

"In the Rolling River Museum's private collection."

"You aren't ever going to give me an easy answer, are you?" she asked.

*****

Back at the hotel, Jordan found Owen stretched out on the bed, watching television.

"Where's Madison?" she asked.

He turned off the TV and shifted so that he was angled toward her. "At the library. She mentioned something about gathering all the facts before coming to any conclusions."

"So she can lie to me again?" Jordan mumbled under her breath.

"Give it a rest." Owen ran a hand over his jaw, but the gesture didn't mask the twinkle in his eye. "Actually, scratch that. Cut Maddie some slack. Even you're aware that you're acting weird."

"I'm not even going to pretend to know what you're talking about," Jordan said, lying back on the bed.

"You didn't finish college," he said. "You gave everything up when Parker and I left. Are you telling me you don't feel the least bit ashamed about it?"

Jordan laid her hands across her stomach and debated giving him an equally glib answer. "I was so lost without him," she said instead. "At first I blamed you. Then I realized that no matter how much I missed you, it was only a fraction of the loss I felt without Parker."

"Yeah. Well, we're both stuck loving him, aren't we?"

"Against our better judgement." Jordan let a smile flutter across her face as she brought Parker's to mind.

"Speaking of love, who were you talking to up on the roof?" he asked. "He sounded dreamy."

Sly subject change, Jordan thought as she squirmed; she was glad that he couldn't see her face. "Levi," she finally said. "You're getting ready to give me a piece of your mind. I can feel it. Please don't. I already got an earful from Dinah."

Owen let out the breath she had felt him hold. "Do you have feelings for him? I can't say I approve."

"I think he's responsible for your fall," Jordan told him in a stern voice. "So no. I'm not in love with him. I think being around him makes me *think* I want him." She paused. "But every time I consider what could have happened, it breaks

170

me a little."

"It's made me reconsider a lot of things," Owen said. Jordan didn't have to look at him to see the wistful look on his face. "I want to find Parker."

Jordan rolled onto her belly to look at him. "Now?" she asked.

"The summer's almost over," Owen said. Worry was etched in the lines on his face.

Jordan sighed. He tugged her hair. "All right, all right," she said. "I've avoided thinking about him because I'm horrified something terrible has happened."

Owen closed his eyes. A lock of hair fell in front of his face. "I hope to God he's okay."

Jordan bit her lip. "He was seen leaving the house, our parents' house, a few days before I got back." She was ashamed that she had forgotten the information until now. "Tully called to tell me a while ago. Parker is the lead suspect in the murder of our parents."

"Jesus, when did you plan on telling me this?" Owen lifted his head and stared at her with wide eyes. "You don't believe he did it, do you?"

"Of course not. I happened to be a mess at the time of the call. You know how I was when I got here," Jordan said. "I really should have said something earlier, but I was so busy trying to figure out how to get the hell out of town. Then we were attacked and you were more concerned about monsters than you were about Parker."

"It's my fault too," Owen said in a softer voice. "I was so mad at him for leaving, I didn't want to find him."

"What do you want to do?"

"We need to go back to your parents'…to your house," Owen said. "You need to show me that yearbook."

"Uh, right. Sure," Jordan forced herself to say. "But I've got to tell you something else…"

"I'm back!" Madison's voice preceded her through the hotel room door. "I've had such a productive day."

"Wait." Jordan held up a hand. "Before you tell us, there's something I need to say. I might as well take advantage and tell you both at the same time."

"Oh! I'm glad we're on speaking terms again," Madison said, her voice bubbly as she dropped her oversized purse on the other bed.

Jordan ignored her, and continued, "Dinah told me I need to find a book. The *Book of Eve*. The only problem is, it's in the museum's private

171

collection."

"Well, I don't think it's such a big deal," Madison told her. "I'm sure if we called and explained that we're doing a research project, they would at least let us get a good look at it."

"If there's a fee, money won't be a problem," Owen added.

"Well, if you don't mind," Jordan said, feeling a little more than stupid that Madison was still so eager to help. "I can't tell you how relieved I am right now. I thought we were going to have to break in or something."

"Don't be silly," Madison said, waving her hand as she walked over to the phone.

"The curator is a Bill Wilson," she told them a few minutes later with a smug smile. "I booked an appointment with him this afternoon."

Jordan turned her head to look at Owen. "It's your call," she said.

He frowned before letting out a sigh. "Let's go see him," he said. "We'll head back home tomorrow."

*****

The Rolling River Museum surprised Jordan. She was expecting a tiny building with little rooms you had to squeeze through in order to see anything behind layers of glass. Instead, she walked into a sprawling mansion, which had been restored to showcase the town's history in open exhibits. It was nothing compared to the Louvre, but it was fascinating in its own way.

I wonder how the book ended up here, she thought as they approached the front desk. *It seems rather strange that it wouldn't be in a bigger city...*

"Hi there." Madison's hundred-watt smile illuminated her face as she leaned forward on the counter. "Greg, is it?" she asked, reading his name tag.

Jordan couldn't help but snicker when Greg's mouth fell open. *I wonder how many more shades of red he's going to turn...*

"We have an appointment with your curator, Bill Wilson," Madison continued.

A few seconds later, Greg still hadn't moved. Owen cleared his throat. "We don't want to keep him waiting."

Greg shook himself, and picked up the phone.

"Keep it up, Maddie," Owen whispered. "Bill will be shoving the book into your hands with only your promise to bring it back."

"Er, excuse me," Greg said. "Mr. Wilson is ready for you in his office."

He pointed to a door on their left.

"Thank you." Madison gave him a wink, and the three of them walked through the door.

"Good God," a man said when they entered. His voice was sharp and authoritative. "Do you people not believe in knocking?" Bill Wilson leaned forward on his desk and rose to his feet. He glared at them above the rims of a pair of round spectacles.

"My apologies, Bill," Madison said. "You're right. We weren't thinking."

Jordan watched his frown deepen. *Uh-oh*, she thought.

"My sister, Madison, booked an appointment with you," Owen continued. "We're interested in an artifact you're holding here."

"First of all, I ask that you call me *Mister* Wilson," the man said. "Bill is reserved for close friends and family. I see neither here."

Why do I feel like this situation is slowly spinning out of control? Jordan thought.

"Secondly, you did not make this appointment with me, you made it with my receptionist. I neither know who you are nor what you want from me."

"Mr. Wilson," Jordan said. "I hope you'll accept my apologies. My name is Miss Andrews, and my colleagues are Mr. and Miss Neilson."

"It's a pleasure to be formally introduced." Mr. Wilson sat back down, but didn't offer them a seat. He picked up a pen and began to mark some papers.

Jordan let out a soft hiss when Owen moved to sit down. When he straightened, she clasped her hands in front of her and hoped that he couldn't see how hard her jaw clenched.

"We've come to see you because we happen to know you have a relic," she said. "The *Book of Eve*, to be specific." She put on a smile that hurt her cheeks. "We were hoping to be able to get a closer look at it."

"Are you under the impression that you are in a library, Miss Andrews?"

"No."

"Then what makes you think I would allow you to see that particular piece?" The pen hit the desk. *Tap. Tap. Tap.* "Or any artifact for that matter? Are you under the assumption that we allow anyone to poke their nose through priceless items?"

Jordan didn't say anything for a moment. She waited until the pen hit the desk again.

Tap. Tap. Tap.

"I have another meeting now," he continued. "We're finished here."

"Are you kidding me?" Owen exploded. "If it's money you need, it's not a problem. Name your price."

Mr. Wilson's eyebrows shot up towards his hairline. "Are you attempting to bribe me, Mr. Neilson?"

"What?" Owen shouted. "How dare—"

"Don't," Jordan said. It startled her, how calm she sounded. "We wouldn't want Mr. Wilson to be late for his meeting. We've already taken up too much of his time."

"But, Jo..." Madison whispered.

Jordan ignored her. "Thank you for your time," she ground out. "Have a great day." She turned on her heel and strode out of the office.

"I can't believe this." Madison tossed her hands in the air as they passed the front desk. "That self-absorbed prick was totally lying to us! The book is supposed to be on display for at least a few more weeks."

"There's nothing we can do about it," Owen said.

He looks tired, Jordan thought, then she corrected herself. *He looks defeated.* The thought made her link her arm through his. "What if we borrowed it?" she whispered.

"Weren't you listening?" Owen asked. "If that man doesn't already have a stick up his ass, I'm willing to volunteer to put one there for him."

Madison giggled. "Such a crude little rock star you are," she said linking her arm with Jordan's free one. "I think you're the one who needs to listen. She isn't talking about getting *permission*. Am I right?"

Jordan looked up at Madison out of the corner of her eye. *Why are you acting like we didn't have an argument?* she thought. She forced herself to wait until they were outside before continuing the conversation. "No," she said. "I'm not talking about getting permission."

Creases appeared in Owen's forehead. "If we get caught, I'm the one who's going to jail."

"That's why you're not going to be involved," Jordan said. "None of us are." She waited a beat to make sure she had their full attention. "We're going to get Mr. Wilson to hand it to us himself."

Chapter 18

Letters on the Wall

$\mathcal{J}$ ordan refused to say anything else until they were back at the hotel, which only annoyed Owen further.

"If we're just going to borrow the damn book, why'd we leave the museum?" he asked.

"It's Levi," she explained. "Damn it, I don't know if he can hear me right now...he said something about being able feel my emotions or some bullshit like that..."

"Slow down," Owen said. "You're not making any sense."

It's not safe to talk here, Jordan thought. An idea struck. "Let's go find the yearbook," she said.

"Right now?" Madison asked.

"Yes. Now." Jordan started shoving them toward the door.

Once they were in the Mustang and on the road, Owen proclaimed, "You're really going to need to tell us what's going on. You're jumping all over the place. You're starting to scare me."

"Give her a minute," Madison said from the backseat. Jordan glanced at the rearview mirror. Madison was looking into a compact and swiping on some lip gloss. "If you were listening, you'd know that she can't talk until we're out of town."

At that moment, they passed a sign: THANK YOU FOR VISITING ROLLING RIVER! Owen swung his head in Jordan's direction. "We're out of town."

She glanced at him before turning her attention back to the road. "Last night, before you dramatically threw yourself off of the building, you started tapping the wall."

"I did?" Owen asked.

"Yes. Several times in a row, in fact," Jordan told him. "I don't know if either of you noticed, but *Mister* Wilson did the exact same thing."

"Now that you mention it…" Madison said.

"People tap on things all the time," Owen interrupted. "What makes you think it's anything other than a natural tic?"

"I'm telling you, it's Levi," Jordan insisted, pressing her foot down a little harder on the gas. "He's powerful. Even Dinah doesn't want me around him. What if he has the ability to make people *do* things?"

"Like Legion?" Owen asked. He shuddered. "You think he was being controlled by Levi? But then why didn't he just try and possess me himself?"

"Maybe he didn't want Jordan to suspect him," Madison chimed in.

"Thank you, Madison. Speaking of Legion," Jordan said with a smirk, "if I have the ability to absorb power, then I should be able to absorb his. I can then use it to make Mr. Wilson hand me the book himself."

"That sounds like a terrible plan," Owen muttered loud enough for her to hear.

Before Jordan could respond, Madison leaned forward. "So what's stopping us?" she asked. "I thought you were only *saying* we were going home so Levi wouldn't catch on." She sighed. "I mean, realistically, if he's powerful enough to take over a person's body without being nearby, then isn't it highly likely that he could do it right now?"

Jordan turned her head to look at Owen, and saw that Madison was doing the same thing.

"Whoa. Why are you guys looking at me?" he exclaimed.

"Oh, my darling brother," Madison said, leaning back against her seat. "So far you're two for two on being possessed."

Owen crossed his arms. "Why is it that I can't help but feel like I'm being picked on?"

"I think you are," Jordan said. "Levi's jealous of you."

Owen snorted. "Are you joking?" he asked. "Does he know my interests lie with the other team?"

"I've told him," she said. A slight flush warmed Jordan's cheeks. *Don't tell Owen it's because you still have feelings for him. Don't tell Owen it's because you still have feelings for him.*

"I don't understand what his problem with you is. Anyway," she continued, running a hand through her hair to cool the back of her neck, "we're going home because we are going to get the yearbook." She put her hand on Owen's knee and gave it a gentle squeeze. "Then the both of you are going to look for Parker, while I handle getting the *Book of Eve*."

She could feel both sets of eyes boring into her. She put her hand back on the steering wheel, and gripped it tightly. "This isn't something we're going to negotiate. If something goes wrong, the blame all falls on me."

"Shit, Jo," Owen complained. "We're in this together, remember?"

"I'm not discussing it," Jordan said, her tone harsh. She took a deep breath and tried to ignore how soon they would be arriving at her parents' house.

*****

"Did you guys want to call Tully while I get the yearbook?" Jordan asked, staring at the front door. "He'll probably want to talk to me. To us."

She continued to stare at the door.

Owen draped an arm around her shoulder. "Tully can wait," he said.

He knows, she thought. *He knows how I feel coming back here.* Jordan wanted to smooth away the crease in his brow. She denied herself the pleasure by bending down and retrieving the key she had left under the mat.

"The entire time I was traveling, I never told them that I loved them," she said in a soft voice. She didn't dare look at Madison or Owen. Her gaze remained steady on the key resting in the palm of her hand. "When I didn't come home, they wanted to know why. When I didn't respond, they wanted to know why." She felt Madison slide an arm around her waist.

"I told them what I thought of their overbearing parenting," Jordan continued. "I told them I might be home in six months if I felt the need to see them again. I never told them the truth. That I was hiding from everything that reminded me of Parker." She wrapped her fingers around the key. "I never told them that I loved them."

Jordan felt Owen rest his hand on her shoulder. "Are you ready?" he quietly asked.

She was thankful he had known not to say anything else. "No," she told him, but unlocked and opened the door anyway.

The house was exactly as she had left it, except everything was coated with a thin layer of dust. She was drawn to the urn, still standing on the table by the door. She ran her hands over it, wiping the dust away. Owen was drawn to the picture frame. He turned it upright, and ran his thumb along the side of Parker's face.

"Where's the yearbook?" he asked, his voice soft.

"It's upstairs," Jordan told him, swallowing the bile threatening to choke her. "In my room."

The three of them moved to stand at the foot of the stairs. Madison shifted forward, but Owen caught her arm and gave her a slight shake of his head. Jordan held her breath and tried not to think about corpses. She took one step, and then a second before she felt a wall go up against her back.

"Jordan!" Owen shouted.

She spun around, slapping her hands up against the invisible barrier. Madison and Owen banged their fists against it. *They're afraid*, Jordan thought, taking in their panicked expressions. *They're afraid for me.*

"Stop," she said, her voice oddly calm despite the way her legs were shaking. Their hands stilled. "I'll be all right. I'm going to get the yearbook. I'll find a way out. I need you to get back to the car."

Madison shook her head, her eyes filling.

"Both of you listen to me," Jordan pleaded. "I can't think a way out of this if you both aren't somewhere safe."

Jordan waited until the door closed behind them before she turned to run up the stairs. She caught Levi's scent before she felt him beside her.

He grabbed her hand. "I don't think you should go up there."

"I have to," she told him, and walked up a few steps.

"You're shaking," he said, following her, his hand still holding hers.

Jordan paused at the top of the stairs. She just had to walk down the hallway. She took a breath, but only inhaled his scent. She bit down on the side of her cheek, fought against the desire to curl up against him. It didn't help.

I can't do it," she cried. The words tumbled heedlessly from her mouth. She didn't want to share her pain, especially with him, but despite her true feelings, he meant everything to her in that moment. "It hurts too much. I never see them as they were. I only see them bleeding. Dead.

Levi leaned his head against hers. "It wasn't a painful death," he told her. "It was only meant to look painful. To hurt you, you see."

Jordan thought she was going to black out, and wrenched her body away from him. "*You*," she hissed venomously. "I should have known. I can't believe I let you touch me." Disgusted with herself, she gagged. "You killed them, didn't you?" she asked, rounding on him with clenched fists. "Didn't you."

"I *didn't* kill them," he said. His eyes narrowed slightly. "But you've already made your mind up about me, haven't you?"

"You're a monster," Jordan hissed, and swung a fist at him. Levi neatly

178

dodged it in one move, and had her pressed up against the wall in the next.

"Tell me, then," he said in a low voice. "How did I do it?"

"You possess people," she replied, hating how breathless she sounded. "You make them do things they would never do."

"You're wrong, darling," Levi sneered. "I'm *Envy*. I make people long for what someone else has."

*****

"Tell me again," she had said, "about the place you are taking me."

"Well, to start, it's stunningly beautiful," Leviathan told her.

"More so than here?"

He laughed, pausing to pick a flower as they walked toward the gates, hand in hand. "Yes, my love. I know it's hard to imagine, but such a place does exist."

"I want to see it now," she told him, licking her lips. She brought her free hand to her mouth. "Will there be apples there? Ones that I can eat freely?"

Levi paused, and turned her toward him. "You will have whatever your heart desires. There are no rules where we are going."

In her joy, she leaned forward and kissed him.

"Eve?"

She pushed Leviathan from her, as if he were made of the sun. A man stood before them, his face contorted as if he were in great pain.

Her husband had returned.

*****

Jordan found herself on the floor in the hallway with Levi on top of her. He cupped her face with both hands as he finished the kiss. The air around them smelled fragrant, like flowers.

It was in complete contrast to how she felt about what she had just seen.

"Do you see now?" he asked. "I have waited for you, for centuries. I have loved you just as fiercely, every minute of every day." He kissed her brow, her lashes, her cheek. "Who else in your life can say the same? Certainly not Owen, who spurned you, or your brother, who manipulated you. What about your parents, who felt they couldn't trust you anymore?"

"They loved me less for it?" Jordan murmured. It was the first time she had voiced the fear out loud.

"Oh, lovely," Levi said, lowering her head to give her a quick kiss. "I don't say these things to hurt you. I say them to help you understand." His eyes were so dark. "I have watched, and despite everything, my love for you has grown."

"Then tell me the *truth*," she said, pushing at him until he rolled off her. "Have you been involved in any of the attacks on me and my friends?"

"Attack you? Of course not," he said, helping her to her feet. "Although, I did send Apophis to watch after you."

"Why would you—"

"Let me finish." Levi quirked an eyebrow at her until it seemed he was satisfied she wasn't going to continue. "I sent him because of that fool you were with. He hurt you. I wanted to make sure he wouldn't do it again."

"Owen is harmless," Jordan said in a low voice.

"How was I supposed to know that? I sent my pet to be sure—"

"Your *pet* almost killed Owen. *Twice*," Jordan ground out.

"Apophis was only sent to frighten your mortal away," Levi said. "If I recall correctly, you ended up killing him."

She pursed her lips, not wanting to admit that perhaps two wrongs didn't make a right. "Anything else?" she asked instead.

"No." Levi frowned. "Well, yes, now that I think about it. I had Legion possess your mortal as well."

"What?"

"He was about to tell you the truth, *again* I might add, and you were being stubborn." Levi reached out and brushed the dust from the front of her shirt. "I was trying to help you move on."

"Legion almost had Owen kill me!"

"Yes, I know." Levi's frown deepened. "I had a very intense conversation with him about it afterwards. He's a difficult creature at the best of times, but he's paying for it now, I assure you."

"Did you murder my parents?" she asked in a quiet voice.

"No." Levi sighed and brought her hands to his lips. He kissed them both, keeping his dark eyes on her. Mesmerized, Jordan tried to focus on his mouth, which only tempted her weakening resolve. "All I've done is try to keep that bumbling dolt away from you," he said. "I would never..." He straightened sharply, and dropped her hands.

The house began to shake. "What's happening?" Jordan asked, trying to keep her balance. "What are you doing?"

180

"I'm not doing anything." Levi looked past her shoulder. When Jordan followed his gaze she stumbled into the wall.

"Watch out!" she heard him call out. It was too late.

The butterfly plates fell off the walls and smashed into the floor. Judging by the sound, it seemed all the plates in the house broke at the same time. The butterflies themselves fluttered into the air, as if they had been trapped within the ceramic, waiting to be released. They swirled together in the air, gaining speed until Jordan was surrounded. More and more butterflies joined the attack until their blurring forms looked like a solid wall.

There was no power that Jordan could absorb. All she felt was helpless. She dropped to the ground, unable to answer or respond to Levi's muffled shouts. The butterflies' wings were like knives, slicing at her arms as they beat through the air. Scrambling forward on arms and legs, Jordan kept her head down until she made it to her room. She opened the door, slammed it closed, and reached for the baseball bat she kept in her closet.

The butterflies had disappeared.

She checked twice to make sure that she wasn't just imagining things before sliding down to the floor. It took several moments for her to realize that nothing was coming after her. Exhausted, Jordan struggled not to fall asleep. She concentrated on the details of her room. What she saw had her rising to her feet.

The words WELCOME HOME! were spread out across the wall. Several deflated balloons lay on the floor beside her desk and bed. Jordan stretched up on her tiptoes to reach the letters. *You keep lying to me, Levi. My parents still loved me*, she thought. *They never stopped.* Pressing her face against the cool wall, she barely felt the heat from the tears coursing down her cheeks.

The loud *honk* of a car horn made Jordan jump. She wiped her eyes with the back of her hand and went over to her bedroom window. She gritted her teeth, expecting the window to resist, but it slid open smoothly. Both Madison and Owen were hanging out of the Mustang's windows. Twin smiles bloomed across their faces as she waved.

Jordan rushed to her bed, and pulled out a box from beneath it. Rummaging through it she pulled out the yearbook she had come for. Clutching it to her chest, she took a good look around the room. After a quiet moment, she reached out and carefully pulled the Welcome Home sign down, folding the letters one over the other. She slipped them in between the pages of the yearbook.

A loud bang at the door had Jordan scrambling back toward the window. She let the yearbook fall out onto the roof of the porch and heard something splinter behind her. She swung one leg over the ledge, and then the other. It was hard to contain her nervous laughter when she could hear Owen cursing from across the street. Ignoring him, she scooped up the yearbook with one hand and slid down toward the eaves trough.

A low rumble made the shingles vibrate beneath her feet before a roar shattered the window above her head. Jordan threw herself off the roof, and into the bushes below. She was on her feet a second later, ignoring the pain of having rolled over the corner of the yearbook as she fell. She didn't look back. Not even when one of her bookcases crashed into the lawn inches away from where she ran.

Owen was starting the Mustang as Jordan's feet pounded against the pavement.

The blood had drained from Madison's face. "Hurry!"

Jordan wrenched open the passenger-side door and was barely into her seat when Owen peeled away from the curb. She peeked into the yearbook, glanced at the letters tucked inside, then concentrated on catching her breath.

"What was that?" Madison asked. "Is it coming after us?"

"I don't think so," Owen said, his eyes shifting to look up at the rearview mirror. He didn't take his foot off the gas.

"It was Levi," Jordan said.

This time, Owen didn't argue with her. "You got the yearbook," he said. "Let's find out what's on that missing page, shall we? The suspense is killing me."

Jordan was thankful for his suggestion. It gave her trembling hands something to concentrate on. She flipped open the book, but her hopes were dashed when she reached page fifteen. "Damn it. There's nothing here," she said, letting the book fall into her lap. "It's a picture of me, you, and Parker standing outside at lunch."

"Here." Madison's hand appeared. "Let me take a look."

Jordan let her head fall back against the headrest. "Sure," she said. *What was I thinking?* she thought. *Why would Parker leave a clue?*

"Don't worry about it," Owen murmured. "We'll go to the station to talk to Tully. I also haven't spoken to the PI in a few days. Either of them might have a lead."

"I think *we* have a lead," Madison said. She thrust the yearbook and a magnifying glass between Jordan and Owen.

"Where did that come from?" Owen asked. "Don't tell me you just carry it around in your purse like a tube of lipstick."

"As a matter of fact, I do," Madison replied.

Jordan repressed a sigh. "Where am I supposed to look?" she asked, taking both items.

"Right corner, just behind Parker's left shoulder."

Jordan placed the magnifying glass over the page. "Someone's holding out a piece of paper with some numbers on it. Three, eight, point four, five, double zero…"

"Exactly!" Madison said.

Jordan held up the yearbook so Owen could take a quick look. He wore a frown to match hers. "I don't get it."

"Longitude and latitude, guys." Madison squealed in excitement. "They're coordinates!"

"You think we can find Parker using them?" Jordan asked.

"I think it's a good place to start," Madison said. "By the way, take another look. You didn't notice who's *holding* the paper."

Jordan hunched over the book again, and gave a start when she recognized the figure. "Holy shit," she said. "It's Dinah."

Chapter 19

Is It Love?

Despite having rattled nerves, they all decided it would be best to pay Tully a visit at his office before the sun went down. Owen would inquire as to whether any new information was available on Parker, while Madison would sneak onto the front desk and use her cell phone to search for the coordinates from the yearbook.

At least that had been the plan, until they arrived, and Tully requested that Jordan sit down. He didn't look happy.

"It's nice to see you again," she said, trying not to squirm.

"It's nice of *you* to drop by," he replied. His tone wasn't quite frigid, but it wasn't exactly welcoming either. "I wish you had called. I've got a busy afternoon ahead of me."

"Don't be silly," Madison called from outside the office. "You love having visitors!"

"What's going on?" Owen said.

"The last time we saw each other, he kicked me out of his house," Jordan muttered.

"Now, Tully, why would you go and do a thing like that?" Owen asked. Jordan wanted to smack the twinkle out of his eyes.

"For the love of…Is that what she's still upset about?" Tully demanded of Owen. Without waiting for an answer, he turned to Jordan. "Is that what you're still upset about? Even after I called you?"

Jordan crossed her arms over her chest and looked away.

"I don't know what to tell you, except to maintain that I have no recollection of it. None," he said. "All I know is that I woke up, you were gone, and I've been worrying myself sick ever since."

He was tapping, she realized. *When he kicked me out, he was tapping...*

"This isn't going very well. Listen. I *am* glad to see you." Tully was suddenly very interested in organizing the papers on his desk into neater piles. "I didn't like the way things were left between us."

"It's all right," Jordan told him. *How do I tell him I think he was possessed by a prince of hell? I guess what he doesn't know won't hurt him.* She went over to him and put her hand on his arm. "I'm sorry. I've been going through some...changes. I've got myself sorted out now. The last thing I wanted was to make you worry."

Tully bent down and gave her a great bear hug. Jordan was tactful enough to pretend she hadn't seen his watery eyes.

He pushed her back until he held her at arm's distance. "So. What brings you back home?" he asked in a gruff voice.

"We were wondering if you had any leads on the case," Jordan said.

"Or if you've heard from Parker," Owen added, lifting his feet up onto the desk and crossing them at the ankles.

"I was gearing up to ask you the same thing." Tully shooed Owen's feet from the desk so that he could sit down in his chair and prop his own up. "I hate to tell you, but I would have found a way to reach you if I had any news," he said. "We've run into two dead ends, and it pisses me off. I've been reviewing the evidence, my colleagues have been reviewing the damn evidence, but there's just *nothing* to go on."

"That's hard to hear," Owen said.

"You sure don't sound like it is," Tully said. His eyes narrowed. "Do you know something I don't?"

Jordan licked her lips. "No," she said. "We don't."

"Nope," Owen added.

"Nothing!" Madison chimed in, appearing in the doorway. "By the way, do you have a couple of shovels we could borrow?"

"Bunch of liars." Tully grunted. "What do you need them for?"

"Research," Owen told him with a straight face.

Tully stared them down before giving in with a sigh. "Sure, I've got two. They're in my shed, and the wife's at home. She can help you if you can't find them." He rose to his feet. "Well, go on, get out of here. Get on with the *nothing* you have to do. If anyone asks, I didn't see you. If you need help, you know where to find me." He used his wide arms to usher them out the door.

"Oh. Jordan."

"Yeah?" She turned back.

"If you find him, you bring him to me. Understood?"

Jordan could only nod. The sound of Tully tapping his finger against the face of his watch followed her from the room. *Tap, tap, tap.*

*****

When Madison revealed the location of the coordinates, Jordan's first reaction was to take them all home. The look on Owen's face convinced her otherwise, but the drive was made in silence.

To Jordan's relief, the grounds were deserted as she parked the Mustang in the groove marks from a hundred other cars. *Lucky for us, field parties aren't scheduled on school nights*, she thought as she got out of the car.

She followed Owen and Madison, walking slowly through the trampled grass. Everywhere she looked triggered a memory. The fire pit Parker had tried to jump over. The spot just to the left where he and Owen had performed. The tree under which she had kissed Owen, and he had kissed her back.

As she got closer to it, Jordan felt her skin prickle, and her stomach clench. Her tree. The spot that once held special meaning for her now held the words OWEN + PARKER.

Owen lifted a hand and pressed a finger into the groove that made Parker's *P*. Jordan felt unbearably warm as she clenched her fists by her side.

"We did this before we left for the summer," Owen said. There was no need to specify which summer he was talking about. "We left out the forever bit, and the heart. He told me we didn't need it. That we knew what we had."

Jordan was barely listening. She was too busy trying to see any other color but red.

Just below the names, a phrase had been carved into the bark: **JORDAN, YOU'LL ALWAYS BE ALONE. P**

"What a prick," she muttered under her breath.

"Poor tree," Madison said.

Jordan felt Madison's hand rest on her shoulder. Jordan stepped forward so she wouldn't have to brush it away, sparing her a dirty look. She gave it instead to Owen, who was still tracing the engraved letters with a finger.

"What's this?" she asked in a louder voice, hoping to distract him. Much farther down the trunk, the word DIG was carved in.

"I hope he's okay," Owen whispered.

"Whatever," Jordan said. "Looks like Madison was right about the shovels. Let's get to work before Levi or one of his demons show up."

Ramming the blade of her shovel into the earth below the tree did little to release her anger. Thoughts like *I would have let Owen carve a heart around our names* and *I would have* never *left Owen* were punctuated by random flashes of brightness. Madison wasn't doing a great job of holding the flashlight where she was supposed to.

"I wonder how Dinah managed to get into this picture," she was saying. "Why didn't she tell you about it?"

"Maddie, please," Jordan said. "You can have another look at the yearbook later. Right now I need you to keep the light steady so I don't accidentally take your brother's foot off with the shovel."

"Oops," Madison said. A moment later the light was pointing toward the ground. "By the way, I looked her up."

"Who?" Owen asked, pausing in his work.

"Dinah," Madison replied. "Her name means 'justified.'"

"That's nice," Jordan said. She placed the tip of the shovel's blade on the ground and leaned against the handle. "Why are you mentioning this now?"

"I wanted to tell you earlier, but what you had going on was more interesting at the time," Madison said. "In any case, I thought it was curious that a warrior angel should carry the same name as Jacob's daughter."

"She *is* Jacob's daughter," Jordan replied. "Or at least she was before her brothers murdered her, and she got her wings..." She shook her head and lifted the shovel. "It doesn't matter right now. Can we save the information sharing until we finish digging?"

"Totally," Madison said, redirecting the light so that it was focused on the ground.

Jordan and Owen resumed their work.

"Quick question, though," Madison said. The light shifted as she pulled her hair back over her shoulder. "Dinah was murdered by her brothers?"

"Yes," Jordan replied, hoping the word would convince her to let it go.

"That's odd." Madison crossed one leg in front of the other. "In all the material I read, her brothers murdered all the men of Shechem, but they didn't harm their sister."

"They got the story wrong," Jordan replied.

"We can't just discount academic research—"

"Yes, we can," Jordan snapped back. "How do they know what really happened? Were they there?"

"Ladies." Owen was ignored as the two woman faced off.

"It bears consideration," Madison said, placing a hand on her hip. "I know you've been spending a lot of time with Dinah, but we still need to review all the facts!"

"The Bible isn't full of facts," Jordan countered. "The people may have actually existed, but their story, what really happened to them, is up for thousands of years of interpretation."

"How do you know she isn't lying?"

Jordan thought about what she saw when Levi touched her. "How do you know she isn't telling the truth?" she asked.

"Can it, both of you," Owen said in a loud voice. "I found something."

Madison moved closer and pointed the flashlight at Owen's shovel blade. "I think you're right."

Jordan crouched down and dug with her hands, moving the dirt to the side. There was something wrapped in a burlap sack. She pulled it out, letting it land on the grass. Owen got down beside her, and Madison shone the light onto the bag. It didn't look as if it had been buried long.

Reaching inside, Jordan gave a surprised grunt. "It's a binder," she said. Her fingers tightened around the cover as she recognized the handwriting in black marker.

She opened it. The first page had a sketch of an imp. It wasn't very good, but Parker never really had a hand for art. Surrounding the image was text.

- *Size: small – medium*
- *Avoid: claws & slime (if you can, it's a bitch to get the stains out of your clothes).*
- *Strength: tenacity. The little fuckers won't stop until either you or they are dead.*
- *Weakness: they're stupid as all hell.*

"What is this?" Jordan asked, even though it was an unnecessary question. It was clearly a binder full of demons; some she had seen, most she had not. "Why would he bury this?"

"Hey, there's our buddy Legion," Owen said, pointing to the page as

Jordan flipped through. Sure enough, there was a page with a drawing of a tall, faceless figure.

"The bag," she said after staring at the image for a moment. "Is there anything else inside?"

The flashlight bobbed as Madison picked up the burlap sack and took a look. "Nope. Nothing."

Jordan closed the binder, hoping the muscles in her shoulders wouldn't snap as she rolled them back. After a moment, she got to her feet and turned away from the tree.

"Is she okay?" Jordan heard Madison ask Owen, then, louder, "Where are you going?"

"We're heading back to Rolling River," Jordan said.

"Aren't you going to tell us why?" Owen said.

Jordan stopped, but didn't turn around. "No," she said, and continued to walk back to the car.

*****

"You've been awfully quiet," Owen said. He fiddled with the seat belt, readjusting it over his lap.

When he reached out to touch her hair, Jordan said, "Don't do that." She wanted to scream at him, but a glance in the rearview mirror told her that Madison was sleeping.

Owen gave a loud sigh, and shifted in his seat. "You've been surly since we left Tully's office."

Jordan pursed her lips at the word *surly*. "I'm pissed," she told him. "There's a difference."

"So tell me about it. Maybe I can help."

Jordan let out a choked laugh. "You can't," she told him, very careful to keep her eyes on the road.

"Jo, I..." There was heartache in his voice, which only made her feel more pathetic.

"Fine," she said in a low voice. "Help me to understand. Explain why my brother is such a *dick*." The steering wheel creaked as she tightened her grip. Owen went still. "Oh, don't look so shocked. I've only said aloud what we've both known for a *very* long time." Jordan didn't wait for him to respond before continuing. "Instead of trusting me with his secret, he pushed me away. He made

189

damn sure I had nothing to do with you either."

"He was jealous of us," Owen said quietly.

The breath Jordan had taken whooshed out of her. She had to take another before she could speak. "Hell if I know why I'm even feeling sorry for you right now."

"I love him," Owen said. "I know he loves me, and you. He has a hard time showing it is all."

"Is it love? Really?" Jordan countered. "The words are too damn easy to say. What has he done lately to *show* it?" She waited for him to respond. When he didn't, she glanced over to find him staring out the window. She cleared her throat. "I'm sorry, Owen." *Change the subject. Now.* "I...I can't tell you what my plan to get the *Book of Eve* is," she said.

"Now you don't trust *me*?" The hurt was evident in his tone. "Listen, I can't help the fact that I'm gay, any more than you can't help the fact that you're straight..."

"No, no!" Jordan hissed. "Moron." She rolled her eyes. "I don't care that you're gay. Well, I do, but for reasons that are purely selfish."

The corner of Owen's mouth quirked upward. "Then why the sudden need for secrecy?"

"Tully was tapping," Jordan told him. She took a deep breath. The tightness in her chest was loosening. "When we left, he was tapping, and when he kicked me out of his house, he was tapping."

"That happened weeks ago. Are you sure?"

"Dead sure," Jordan said with a frown. "It means that Levi has been interfering with my life for longer than I thought. It means that anything I discuss with you or Madison could be something he uses against us."

"So what do we do?"

Jordan bit her lower lip. "I have no idea."

"What about Dinah?" Owen asked.

"She and I are going to have a nice chat about Parker," she said. "She's avoided the question long enough."

"I..." Owen started, then stopped.

"What?" Jordan asked.

"I want to thank you. For looking out for me and Madison," he finished.

"It shouldn't come as a surprise." Jordan finally allowed herself to look at him. "How else do you expect me to show you how I feel?"

Chapter 20

Sweet Promises

Jordan drove Owen and Madison straight to the hotel when they arrived back in Rolling River.

"You need to get some sleep," Owen told her. He was standing outside the Mustang, with one arm around a bleary-eyed Madison.

"I will when I get back," Jordan promised from behind the wheel. "Do you have the binder?"

Owen held it up with his other hand. "Won't let it out of my sight," he said.

Jordan nodded, glancing down at the yearbook taking his place in the passenger seat. "Great," she said, and watched them enter the building. When the door closed behind them, she waited, craning her neck upward until she saw the light flick on in the window. For good measure, she waited a few minutes more, then drove to the church.

The doors were unlocked, but she made sure to tread carefully, as she wasn't sure anyone would be pleased to find her lurking around the basement. She slipped past the door leading to the white room. It was empty.

"I need to talk to you," Jordan said, in a loud voice. She held the yearbook in both hands to try to steady herself. "I don't have time to wait until morning," she said, addressing another wall. "I know you're there."

Dinah appeared barely an inch in front of her face. "Are you all right?" she asked, grabbing Jordan's shoulders and studying her face. "Are you hurt?"

"I'm fine. Really." Jordan wanted to erase the look of panic on Dinah's face. *Stay objective*, she told herself, but she couldn't help but be touched by Dinah's concern. "I need to ask you something."

"Proceed."

Jordan opened the yearbook and shoved it at Dinah. "Why are you in this picture?" she asked, her voice cracking. She swallowed. "How could you know that Parker would bury something at that exact location months after this photo was taken?"

Dinah took the book. "There are things I cannot yet explain..." she began.

"Answer the question." Jordan's voice echoed hard against the walls. "Please. Tell me the truth, or you can find someone else to help you."

"It was never my intention to withhold this information from you," Dinah said, closing the book and handing it back. "I should have anticipated that you would find it, that your brother would be selfish enough to try and distract you. Jealous enough."

"When we met, you told me you knew where he was," Jordan said. "Why can't I find him?"

"I'm getting to that." Dinah gave Jordan a tentative smile. "I didn't reveal myself to you until recently. However, I have been watching you for a very long time."

"Why?"

"Finding you wasn't as easy as sticking a pin in a map," Dinah said. "It was more like examining every pin in the box before finding the right one." She wrung her hands. The gesture felt odd and out of place on someone whose emotions were typically impossible to read. "I approached Parker first," she said.

Jordan frowned. "What do you mean?"

"I thought he was Adam."

Jordan pressed a hand to her stomach as her thoughts tumbled over themselves.

"I thought my job was done, that I had found both of you," Dinah continued. "I made the mistake of telling him who I thought he was."

"When?" Jordan asked.

"At the beginning of what you called your graduating year," Dinah said. "I wanted to tell you as well, but he convinced me it would be better to wait, to give you a chance to finish your studies, and have a normal year."

"*He* convinced *you?*" Jordan raised a brow.

"Partially."

"You should have just talked to me," Jordan said. "It would have saved us a lot of time and trouble."

Dinah waited until Jordan was looking at her before she spoke again. "You always followed your brother's lead. I needed you to come to a decision on

192

your own. You should understand that it was for this reason that I did not want to make myself known."

"You were wrong."

"I did what I thought was best," Dinah said. "When Parker changed, I could only thank God that you weren't under his influence."

"What changed him?"

"Levi's promises were sweeter than mine."

"You still haven't explained why you're in this picture," Jordan said in a weak voice. She could barely keep her grip on the yearbook.

"In the beginning, Parker was very protective of you," Dinah said. "He wanted me in this picture as a favor to him. He wanted a way to communicate with you in case something went wrong."

"So you don't know where he is?"

"No." Dinah shook her head. "I don't. I lost him when your mortal did."

"Owen's not my mortal," Jordan said, "and I need to sit down."

"You didn't go to the coordinates, did you?" Dinah asked, helping her to the floor. "Your focus should be on getting the *Book of Eve*."

"We went," Jordan said. She took a deep breath and followed the words with a lie: "We found nothing."

Dinah pressed her lips together. "You should have spoken to me about it," she said, putting a hand on her shoulder. "I am relieved it wasn't a trap, and that you are well…What's this?" The letters for the Welcome Home sign had slipped out of the book.

"Nothing," Jordan whispered.

It wasn't a painful death, Levi had told her. *It was only meant to look painful. To hurt you, you see.*

"Levi needs to pay," she told Dinah. "I know he killed my parents."

"You need the book," Dinah said, giving her a level gaze.

"I'll get the damned thing," Jordan said, "but when I do, you tell me where to find him. Deal?"

Dinah stroked her chin with her free hand. "I don't like it."

Jordan got to her feet, shoving the sign back into the yearbook. "Good luck, then," she said.

"Stop." Dinah's hand remained on her shoulder. "You misunderstand me. I have come to…" She took a breath. "I have come to care for you, Jordan. More than I should. You are right. When you get the book, we will divert our attention to defeating Leviathan."

All the tension went out of Jordan's shoulders. "Thank you," she said. "Then I'll let you know, that in order to get the *Book of Eve*, I need Legion."

Dinah's fingers tightened. "Why?"

"I'm unable to get the book on my own," Jordan said, running a hand through her hair. "I can use my power against Legion. Use him to possess someone to get the book." She caught Dinah's eye and gave what she hoped was a plaintive stare. "If I can get someone to hand it to me, then I avoid stealing it. Technically."

"That seems rather…manipulative," Dinah said.

"I know," Jordan replied. "But I can't think of any other way."

The corner of Dinah's lips quirked up. "It will take great strength to control him," she said. "It will be a challenge, but I think it will help you to prepare to face Leviathan. Listen carefully…"

*****

Jordan was ready to throw in the towel when she got back to the hotel. After Dinah had explained how exactly she needed to use Legion, Jordan wasn't going to go through with it. It was far too dangerous.

Owen and Madison were waiting for her on the couch when she walked through the door. The binder was on the coffee table in front of them.

"Why do I get the feeling that I'm getting ambushed?" Jordan asked, eying both of them warily. "Again?"

"Because you are," Madison told her in a cheery voice. She pushed the binder toward Jordan with a finger. "Have a seat."

Jordan did as she was asked, eying the binder even more warily than her friends. "Doing some reading on Legion, I see," she said.

"You said you wanted to use Legion to get the book," Owen piped in. "Well, according to this fact sheet, you need a host, someone you can use to get Legion to use his power, so you can use his."

"Uh-huh," Jordan said absently. Her thoughts immediately turned to what Dinah had told her earlier:

Legion is a tricky beast. While you have the ability to attack the imps directly, the same cannot be said of Legion. You must trigger his power in order to use it, and the only way to achieve that task is to use a mortal.

Jordan caught Madison and Owen looking at each other before Madison covered Owen's hands with hers.

"You're going to use me," Owen said.

Fear grabbed hold of Jordan's heart and yanked it until it was racing. "I can't do that," she said. "And we shouldn't be talking about this." She pointed to the air around them. "He could be listening."

"So let him listen," Owen said, taking one of his hands out from under Madison's. "We're just talking about getting a book. I don't see how this affects him."

"That's all well and good, but—"

"The way I see it, we've got one problem," Madison interrupted, leaning forward to point to the page. "Parker's written here that we need something of Mr. Wilson's in order for you to find and successfully possess him." She tossed her hair over her shoulder.

Owen was digging in his pocket for his wallet. "That isn't a problem. I swiped one of his business cards," he said, tossing it down on the table. "I'll tell what you our real problem is: How the hell are we going to *get* Legion here? And how are we going to keep him from killing us all while some of us are being possessed, and some of us are doing the possessing?"

"Dinah's going to deliver him to us," Jordan said in a soft voice. "We need three circles of salt. One for Legion, one for the mortal he possesses, and one for me." Her eyes moved to look at Madison. "And we need someone to close the circle to contain all three parties."

Madison licked her lips. "I can do that," she said. Her lips trembled as she pulled them into a smile. "Looks like we're all set, then!"

"No, we still have a problem." Jordan ran her hands over her face. "Damn it. I can't do it. I can't use you, Owen; I can't use anyone. It's too risky."

"Why?" Owen asked.

"We have an hour," Jordan said. "Sixty minutes. No more. If I don't break the possession for all of us within that time, we all get to live in some sort of limbo. Forever."

"Did Dinah tell you that?" he asked. "Did she also explain what she was doing in that yearbook photo?"

"Can we talk about this later?" she whispered. "It's been a trying day."

Madison blushed. "We shouldn't have confronted you like this," she said.

"Maddie's right. It was a terrible idea. Get some sleep okay?" Owen told Jordan. "It'll all look better in the morning."

Jordan nodded sharply, and got ready for bed. She was asleep before her head touched the pillow.

*****

"I don't know what you hope to accomplish by speaking to me alone," Levi had said. He took pleasure in watching the mortal rein in the urge to smash one of his fists into Levi's face, but the acrid scent of flowers almost had him rubbing his nose. "She has made up her mind. She no longer needs you."

Adam stood in front of him, fists clenched and half-poised in front of his body. "How dare you bring darkness to this place." He hissed the words through clenched teeth, sounding like the breath had been squeezed out of him.

"*I* didn't do a thing," Levi said, turning his back on Adam to look at his nails. "She was lonely. We became friends." He gave a careless shrug. "Then we became more."

Adam's body trembled. His jaw clenched. To Levi, he smelled like rage. It brought a smile to his lips.

"Who are you?" Adam asked.

"I feel for you, mortal," Levi told him, his tone belying his words. "I will tell you the truth. I am Leviathan, a prince of the Seven Gates of Hell."

Adam shied away, and took a half step before he regained his composure and ground. "A demon." Adam paused. "Does she know who you are?" His eyes narrowed. "Who you *truly* are?"

"She does not need to know." Levi took another menacing step forward, but Adam held his ground.

"Then your love is built on nothing but lies. Tell me, *prince*," Adam sneered, "how long do you think you can keep her from finding out the truth? From shunning you?"

"Longer than you were able to keep her in your bed, boy," Levi snapped. He was immediately disappointed in himself for losing control so easily.

"Do you love her?"

The question took Levi by surprise. "Yes," he replied solemnly. Truthfully. "I do."

"I will not allow this!"

"You don't have a choice."

"She is my *wife*," Adam said. "She will do as she is bid."

Levi crossed his arms over his chest. "She is my *lover*," he said. "And I think we both know that she'll do as she pleases."

Chapter 21

You Before Me

*J*ordan woke with a start. The dream was already fading from memory, but her skin felt warm. It was as if Levi's arms had actually been wrapped around her. Shivering, she threw the covers off, grabbed Parker's binder, and stumbled into the bathroom.

Sitting on the floor, she leaned her back up against the door and slowly flipped through the pages. There were so many demons, creatures she had never even heard of before. She barely registered their names, their powers. She didn't care.

"Of course you didn't include any information on Levi," she muttered when she reached the end. Burying her face in her hands, Jordan stifled a groan. Also missing was any alternative to using Owen as demon bait. *Looks like I don't have a choice. I have to use him*, she thought. *Damn it.*

She flung the binder across the floor. A piece of paper fluttered free, and landed beside her foot, while the rest of the binder crashed against the wall.

"What the...?" Jordan said, reaching out to pick up the loose sheet.

"'Tips,'" she read aloud. Her eyes scanned the page, until she almost reached the end. Her breath caught in her throat. "'Discovered: if complete possession occurs, knock the demon out via extremely hard hit or impact.'"

Jordan got to her feet and picked up the binder. There were no secret pockets in the cover, nor could she remember seeing the paper before. She tucked it between two pages, and decided that it was time to try and get some sleep.

"Jordan," Madison asked. "Is everything all right?"

Jordan's head snapped up. "I'm fine," she said, bending to lift the coffee table. "I'm just running through the details of the plan." *More like mulling over that tip you found last night*, she thought to herself.

Madison was already holding her end of the table; her eyes sparkled, then dulled. "Don't worry," she said, drawing in a breath. "The plan's pretty much all I can think about too."

Together, they flipped the table upside down and put it down on the sofa. Hands on her hips, Jordan surveyed the room. Every piece of furniture had been moved as far toward the walls as they would go.

"So I was thinking," Madison said, putting her hands into the back pockets of her skintight jeans. "Owen's kinda putting himself on the line here. I mean, not that I think anything's going to happen, but if something does go wrong, I want..." She paused. "No, I *need* you to do whatever it takes to make sure he makes it through."

"Maddie, I..."

"Whatever it takes, Jo," Madison said. She paused to play with the end of her ponytail. "Even if that means you have to save him instead of me. Promise?"

Jordan didn't have the chance to respond. The door opened, which had the two women moving away from each other as if they had been caught with their hands in the cookie jar.

"The room's looking good, kids," Owen announced from the doorway. He handed Madison a brown paper bag. "The salt," he told her, before taking Jordan's hand. "You ready, champ?" he asked, pulling her toward him.

"Uh, yes," she told him with a sharp nod of her head. *Don't look at Madison. Don't!* she warned herself.

Owen's eyes sharpened on her face.

"I just need a moment," Jordan told him before he could say anything else. She slipped into the bathroom and closed the door behind her. Leaning forward onto the sink, Jordan lowered her head and refused to look at herself in the mirror. She was positive the expression on her face would convince her to call the whole thing off.

"You have more courage than that."

Jordan's fist clenched, ready to strike. As she turned she realized she was about to clock Dinah right in the face.

"Shit," Jordan cried, pulling in her arms to clutch at her chest. "What are you doing here?"

"I wanted to speak to you," Dinah said.

"Fine. Sure," Jordan said, sitting down on the toilet seat lid. Her heartbeat was still going crazy. "You aren't the only one."

Dinah held up a finger. "First, I want you to tell me the order in which the circles must be closed."

Jordan let out a breath. Took a deep one and closed her eyes. "You will bring Legion into one of the circles of salt," she said. "Owen will be ready in another. Madison and I need to close the circles, to contain both of them."

"Good. What's next?"

Jordan licked her lips. "I get into the third circle," she said. "Madison will close it. Then she needs to draw a line of salt between Legion and Owen's circle. Legion will possess Owen."

"After that?"

"Madison will draw a line between Legion and myself," Jordan said, opening her eyes. "While Legion is using his power to possess Owen, I will absorb Legion's power, to possess Mr. Wilson." *Theoretically, of course, considering I've never actually done it before.*

"Destroying those imps gave you all the practice you need," Dinah said. She sat down on the bathtub ledge. "Using Legion's power is no different. You already know what to do."

Jordan reached out and grabbed Dinah's hand. "Can you be there with me?" she asked. "Can you make sure that if anything goes wrong, you help Madison and Owen?"

Dinah lowered her gaze and gently pulled her hand away. "I'm afraid I cannot," she said. "I am already breaking many rules by bringing Legion to you. He is not mine to control."

"Right," Jordan said, clenching her hands together in her lap.

"Despite this," Dinah continued, "you must get that book."

"And then we bring down Levi," Jordan said.

"That has already been agreed upon," Dinah snapped. "Your constant need to remind me is grating. I have given you my word."

Jordan's muscles screeched in protest as she forced herself to remain seated upright on the toilet instead of falling to the floor and cowering. *What the hell's gotten into her?* she thought.

"Let us focus on completing your current task." Dinah took a deep breath through her nose, then exhaled slowly. "I understand you have strong emotional ties to your mortals," she said, "but if your time runs out, you must keep your mind focused on your goal."

Jordan's mouth worked until she knew she had the volume of her voice under control. She didn't want Madison or Owen to overhear. "Let me see if I understand you correctly," she said. "If something happens and I run out of time, you want me to forget about Owen and let his mind be destroyed?"

"Yes."

"I can't do that," Jordan said. "I can't believe you'd even ask."

"I wasn't asking," Dinah told her.

"The only reason I'm getting the stupid book is because I need you to help me kill Leviathan," Jordan replied. "If it comes down to choosing between saving my friends and stealing a book, I'm going to save my friends."

The look on Dinah's face made her desperately wish she could shrink and crawl into a crack in the floor.

"Besides, I—I have a backup plan," Jordan stuttered. "I read somewhere that if I don't release Legion on time, and Owen gets fully possessed, that I can fix it by hitting him...or something."

Dinah tilted her head to the side. "It would have to be a hard, solid blow," she said. "One that would kill your mortal if Legion does not. You *must* be prepared to lose him."

"No. If it comes down to it, I'll find another way to get the book."

"We don't have time for you to find another way," Dinah said.

"What is this timeline you keep referring to?" Jordan hissed. "You've never told me what it is, and yet it keeps changing every time I see you."

Dinah hooked a thumb through the sword strap crossing her chest. "I am...disappointed in you," she said quietly. "Do what you will, then. The fate of the world is in your hands."

"Listen, I'm sorry. I'm stressed out and—" Jordan began, but Dinah held up a hand to stop her.

"I will return shortly with Legion," she said. Then she was gone.

Jordan immediately left the washroom, half expecting to find Legion already standing in the middle of the room. Instead, she found Madison had almost finished making three open circles with the salt Owen had bought.

He approached her immediately. "Can I talk to you?"

"Legion will be here soon," Jordan announced. "You better get into

201

position."

"I'm getting there, but I need you to promise me something."

Jordan tried to brush past him. "I really don't think we have time…"

"If anything goes wrong," he continued, moving with her, "I want you to get Madison someplace safe. Forget about me."

"Christ," Jordan muttered, rubbing her hands over her face.

"I'm serious," Owen said. "If something happens and you feel like you have to choose between saving me and saving Madison, you save her." He grabbed her face between his hands and forced her to look at him. "Promise me."

Jordan leaned her cheek into his palm. "I can only do my best," she told him.

Madison shrieked. Jordan shoved Owen out in front of her. "Get into your circle," she shouted, reaching for a box of salt from the brown paper bag.

Legion had appeared in his circle, floating several feet above the ground. Madison remained frozen in front of him, the box of salt slipping from her fingers.

"Don't just stand there," Jordan cried as she ripped the top of the box open. "Close the circle. Close it now!"

"Something's wrong," Owen said, his arms tensed as if he were ready to leap from his circle. "He's possessing her."

"No." Jordan shook her head. "I'm not absorbing anything yet." She dumped the salt out, completing Owen's circle with one swing of her arm. "Stay here." She pivoted, snatched the box Madison held in her hand, and knocked her aside. *Now* she could feel Legion reaching out with his power. She rushed to close his circle.

When Jordan was done, giddy with relief, she started laughing. "You all right?" she asked, helping Madison to her feet.

She brought a hand to her head. "I think so," she said. "I don't feel anyone else in here with me."

"Good," Jordan said, pulling her into an embrace. "Damn, I can't believe the salt actually worked." She held Madison out at arm's length and grinned.

"You didn't know if it would?" she asked in a small voice.

"Well, no," Jordan said, scrunching up her face. "I mean all we had to go on was what Parker wrote in the binder, and the instructions Dinah gave me."

"But you didn't believe?"

"I figured there was enough faith between you and Owen to go for it."

Jordan frowned. "You were the ones who convinced me the plan was solid."

"Jo," Madison said, her eyes dark and serious. "Eventually, you're going to have to believe in something."

"Hey, ladies," Owen called. "I think it might be best for this conversation to take place after we deal with the demon in our hotel room."

Both Jordan and Madison turned around.

Legion was up against the line of salt. Jordan knew if he had eyes, they would be locked on Owen.

"He's right," she told Madison. She handed her the box of salt, and got into her circle. She pulled Mr. Wilson's business card from her pocket, and sat down cross-legged in the middle.

"Be safe, Jo," Owen said. The look on his face told her, *Remember what I said.*

"Damn you," she muttered under her breath.

"What's that?" Madison asked.

Jordan rubbed at her closed eyelids. "Nothing," she said. "Just trying to clear my thoughts."

"Of course," Madison said. She paused, then leaned forward. "Before you do this, I just want to make sure you remembered what I said," she whispered.

Jordan gave her a blank look. "How could I forget?" she asked.

Madison gave her a half smile before taking a step back. "You can do this," she said. "Bring us back that book." She paused. "Are you ready?"

"Yes," Jordan said, even though her mind was screaming *NO!*

Madison sealed her circle with the salt.

Chapter 22

Sixty Minutes

Jordan could feel the exact moment when the line of salt was drawn between her circle and Legion's. Through Legion, she was able to feel Owen as well.

Jordan left that link alone. If she dwelled on it, she would end up breaking the connection, and they'd end up without the book. She could feel Legion all around her, his power like tentacles, reaching and searching for another host to possess. To set him free.

It took her a moment to gather enough courage to even attempt to establish her link and use his power. The moment she did, the countdown would begin. Sixty minutes.

It's now or never, she thought, focusing her energy on one of the tendrils of power she felt was the easiest to catch hold of. The sensation of leaving her body was something she hadn't expected. Dinah had told her it would happen, but it was another thing to actually experience it firsthand.

When fighting the imps, Jordan remained whole. She simply felt what they were feeling and could use their power against them. In order to take on Legion's power, the physical part of her was required to remain behind, while the rest could venture forth and make use of the ability to possess someone.

That's why I have no face, Jordan thought. *I don't need it to get my work done.* In that moment, she realized she was thinking Legion's thoughts. In the next, she felt a sharp sense of desperation. She needed to possess someone. She needed help. *I'm trapped. I need to get out! The damn woman tricked me. She always tricks me...*

Jordan's grip on his power tightened as she tried to smother the thoughts that were clearly not her own. At the same time, she could see her body still within her circle. She could also see Madison, sitting between everyone, the box of salt still clutched in her hands. Her watch read two thirty.

I need to possess someone who can help…NO! Jordan pushed Legion's thoughts from her mind and tugged sharply at the power she held. *Get moving,* she told herself. *Focus.*

Jordan dragged Legion's power along with her as she floated through the door and out into the hallway. It was frustrating to keep moving in a straight line in her ethereal state, especially since she could sense the heat from several bodies through the walls. All she could think of was getting herself inside one before she became trapped forever. She forced herself onward. *Stop wasting time.*

She drifted down Main, which was an even stronger test of will. The people here were unpredictable. They would dart into stores, in front of each other, and even weave back and forth on the sidewalk. Mentally holding her breath through most of it, Jordan made it to the correct street and arrived at the museum without any incidents. In fact, she caught up with Mr. Wilson just as he was walking through the front door of the museum.

Feeling a little smug about how well she was doing, Jordan pushed herself forward, and braced for the connection. Mr. Wilson turned, and his receptionist, Greg, who held the door open, moved to close it. Jordan careened straight into, and then inside of, him.

At first there was chaos. Jordan couldn't tell the difference between herself, Legion's power, and Greg. After a brief tug-of-war, she came out the victor, holding the power firmly to her, and Greg at arm's length. It was uncomfortable. She could see through his eyes, but held the most intimate part of him, his essence, his life force.

"Shit, shit, shit!"

"Excuse me?" Mr. Wilson had turned around, and was looking at Jordan with his hand hovering over his mouth. "What has gotten into you this afternoon?"

I'm possessing the wrong person, Jordan thought as Mr. Wilson continued to stare.   "Uh, I'm really sorry?" she said through Greg. It was no small shock to hear her words spoken in a man's voice. "What I meant to say," she continued when Mr. Wilson raised a brow, "is that you have my sincere apologies. It won't happen again."

"It had better not," he said, turning on his heel. He strode toward his office, leaving Jordan to trail after him. "Oh, one more thing."

She didn't quite have control over Greg's body as Mr. Wilson turned back around. They crashed right into him.

"I fell earlier this morning," Jordan made him say. "It looks like I haven't completely recovered."

Mr. Wilson didn't look impressed. "Mr. Murphy will be by later this afternoon to take a look at our private collection," he told her. Jordan pushed at Greg until she had his body under control again. "He's interested in purchasing the *Book of Eve*, so I do hope you can get this"—he waved his hand up and down—"*situation* resolved by then?"

"Of course," Jordan said, then thought, *That bastard! Not if I get to it first.*

Mr. Wilson was looking at his watch. "It's already two forty-five. Where's my afternoon latte?"

"I was just about to make it when you arrived," Jordan said. "Do you think I could get the keys to the private collection now? I'd rather not disturb you later. I know how busy you are."

"I don't think that's wise," he replied, pushing his glasses up his nose. "My latte, Greg. Sooner rather than later, please." Without another word, he strode into his office. The door shut behind him with a soft click.

How am I going to get the damn keys? Jordan thought. She got Greg to stomp over to his desk. The noise echoed through the first floor. *Calm down. Think!* She made him turn around in a slow circle. *There. The coffee machine. Make the latte, steal the keys.* She tried not to think about how hard it would be to actually execute each step.

Controlling Greg's hands was about as easy as learning to use chopsticks for the first time. She almost broke the mug by slamming it down onto the machine too hard. When she finally got the machine working, half of the latte dripped into the saucer instead of the cup. Eventually she decided that she didn't care how *Mister Wilson* liked his stupid coffee, she just needed the key before her hour was up.

Jordan almost spilled the rest of the latte onto the floor as she navigated Greg into Mr. Wilson's office. A key rested on his desk. It was large and old, threaded through a thick brass ring. She didn't know if it was *the* key, but the only way to find out was to take it.

"Thank you," he said as she put the cup down on his desk. As she brought her hands back toward herself, she swept it up. Mr. Wilson's gaze flicked to Greg. She made him lean forward, trapping the key ring between her hand and the desk.

"Do you need anything else, Mr. Wilson?" she asked, thankful that Greg's smooth voice masked how shaken she felt.

Mr. Wilson pursed his lips. "That will be all for now."

Closing her fingers around the ring, she walked out of the office. She waited for Mr. Wilson to stop her, but all she heard was the sound of Greg's blood rushing through his ears.

Jordan rushed over to the map of the museum. *Private collection. Third floor*, she thought to herself. *Elevator?* She found it, and got Greg toward the back of the building. It only took two attempts to get him to press the call button, and only one to press the button for the correct floor.

Inside the elevator, she looked at Greg's wrist. 2:50.

He lurched to the side. Jordan almost lost her hold on Legion's thread of power.

Legion's voice resonated in Greg's mind like a gong. *Let go, little girl.* The doors slid open. Jordan forced Greg forward. *Give me my power back.*

Not yet. She could see the door at the end of the hallway. The key would fit. She would get the book...

Greg crumpled to the floor. Jordan screamed through him as a great pressure began to build. It felt like someone was gradually putting their weight on her head.

When I am free, I will make you pay. I will destroy you.

Jordan clung to Legion's power with everything she had. The pressure grew sharper. Instead of a heavy weight, it now felt as though her essence was being jabbed repeatedly with a searing hot knife. Forcing herself to move past the pain, she discovered that Legion was using some of his other tentacles of power to try and force her to release the one she was using.

Instead of fighting back, Jordan grabbed at one of them and added it to the initial thread she held on to. Then another. She felt stronger, and the pain wasn't as sharp.

Legion's voice boomed like a thunderclap. *I will never forgive you for this!*

When Jordan took her next breath, Legion was gone, and she had increased her grip on his power. Greg was on the floor. She could feel the sweat dripping down his forehead. Pulling his wrist up to his face, Jordan took note of the time. 3:05.

Even with the additional power, he was difficult to get moving. Jordan could feel his muscles shaking from the effort. She felt terrible. Never during any of the planning had she given any thought to how the person she possessed would fare. She managed to get him to his feet, and to the door. She got his trembling arm to reach for the lock.

The bell of the elevator rang behind her.

"What do you think you're doing?" Mr. Wilson shouted from the other end of the hall.

"Come on. Come on!" Jordan muttered through Greg. The key found the lock and she wanted to weep in relief when it opened with a *click*.

Mr. Wilson's voice was getting louder, and closer. "Don't you even *think* about it."

Jordan pushed Greg's body forward and, when he slipped through, swung his arm around and slammed it shut behind her. The knob turned as Jordan made Greg's other hand slide the dead bolt home.

"Consider this a warning," Mr. Wilson shouted through the door. "If this is your idea of a practical joke, I'm not amused."

Greg's body lunged to the right. Jordan tried to stop him from smashing into a large vase resting on the floor, but Legion chose that exact moment to try and get his power back again. The sound of shattering clay echoed in the room. She gave Legion a shove, using the extra power she held. He disappeared.

"I'm getting the extra set of keys," Mr. Wilson called. Jordan could almost see the righteous indignation on his face. "It's in your best interest not to touch anything else."

Listening to his footsteps recede, Jordan waited for Greg's vision to adjust before she was able to look around the room they were in. It was an archaeologist's dream, and her worst nightmare. The entire upper floor had been remodeled to accommodate the enormous private collection. There were several long tables, each surrounded by shelves that held a combination of books, items in protective glass, and locked cases.

How the hell am I going to find the book? she thought. *It would take me all day to even figure out where to start looking.*

Greg's arm twitched. Jordan's inner dialogue stilled. She hadn't been trying to move him. *When Owen was possessed, he said he was trying to stop Legion from hurting me,* she thought. *He's always aware when someone's possessing his body...*

Greg's watch read 3:10. It was worth a shot.

With Legion's power trailing behind her like a kite string, Jordan went hunting for the part of Greg that she had put aside when she possessed him. He wasn't too hard to find, and he wasn't exactly pleased with her. She could feel the anger rolling off his essence in waves. When he realized she was reaching out to him, he pushed her.

For a split second, Jordan wanted to laugh. He had used all his strength to try and kick her out, and yet it had felt like a light tap.

I need some help, Jordan told him. *I'm looking for the* Book of Eve.

She felt Greg give her the equivalent of a cold shoulder.

The faster I find it, the sooner you get your body back.

Greg's essence tensed, then released like a sigh.

Take me to it. Please, she asked him.

Greg walked with considerable effort. Jordan did everything she could to give him full access to his limbs, but it seemed she couldn't do so without leaving his body. She couldn't do that. Not yet. He continued to take one slow step in front of the other until they were in the middle of the room. He turned so that they were standing in front of a bookshelf. He bent down.

3:15.

His arm twitched, and then moved to the lowest shelf. He carefully pulled a few books from it, turning to put them on the table behind them. He returned to the shelf, and reached into it. Half his arm disappeared, and then reappeared with a thick book that was longer in length than width. The words *Book of Eve* adorned the cover in a scrawling script.

Thank you, Jordan told him, and meant it. She felt bad when she nudged him away again, and promised herself she would do her best to get him out in one piece. This whole plan affected another person, one who had no knowledge of what she was doing, and this thought left a bad taste in her mouth. *Get the book, get Levi*, she reminded herself.

Holding the book in one arm, Jordan turned Greg in the direction of the door. Then she heard footsteps.

I'm screwed, she thought.

Back. Stairs. Greg's voice was faint, but it was definitely him.

Jordan reversed his direction and loped toward the back of the room. True to Greg's word, there was an emergency exit. She awkwardly navigated him down the stairs and out into the street.

3:20.

The hotel was at least ten minutes away.

Making Greg run took most of her concentration. The smacking of his shoes against the pavement turned heads in her direction. She didn't care. She couldn't get him to move fast enough.

Sweat dripped from Greg's forehead, blurring her vision. *There's got to be an easier way*, she thought. She cut down a side street, but didn't shift Greg's weight fast enough and ended up smashing into a brick wall. She overcompensated, and sent him spinning into the wall on the other side.

When she had him steady, Jordan clutched the book to his chest. *I don't have time to get this back to the hotel*, she thought. *I've got to hide it somewhere.* She turned Greg to the left, and then to the right. *Why does this alley seem so familiar?*

Levi's voice felt as though it was wrapped around her. It stopped her cold. "I was hoping you'd stop by." It took her another moment to realize he was behind her, running a hand along Greg's shoulders until he was facing her. He licked his lips. "I prefer your other body, but we can make this work."

It clicked. *The River Six*, Jordan thought. *This is the alley where Dinah saved me.* "I—I don't know you," she said.

"Come now, darling," Levi said. His eyes seemed unusually dark. "You think *you* can hide from *me?*"

"I really wish I had time for this," Jordan snapped. "Find me again later, damn it. I'll be ready for you then."

"I'm tired of playing this game," Levi said, moving so that he towered over Greg. "I have no other choice but to force you to face the truth."

Unsure as to what Levi would do next, Jordan loosened her grip on the book and took a step back.

"Thank you," he said, and plucked it from her.

"I need that!" Jordan tried to get Greg to reach out for it, but she was too clumsy. Levi danced away. His erratic laughter bounced against the alley walls as he bent down over a sewer grate. "No," she whispered.
"Consider this a test." Levi lifted the grate and tossed it aside. "What will you decide to do? Get the book so you can have sweet, sweet revenge? Or save your mortal friends? By the way," he said, giving her a saucy wink. "Time's up."

Chapter 23

Double Take

Jordan immediately let go of Legion's power. It sent her essence away from Greg like a shot. The world around her blurred, as she rushed back toward her body. She couldn't feel anything, couldn't see anything. She couldn't breathe. *I still have a few seconds*, she thought. *I'm not too late. I can't be too late!*

She reached the hotel room, slammed into her body, and opened her eyes.

Legion wasn't where he was supposed to be. Jordan glanced down at the floor. Salt from his circle looked as though it had been kicked aside. She quickly spotted him. He was hovering in the air above the coffee table. His faceless body turned in her direction.

She tried to let go of his power, but the thread stuck like glue. Trying to mentally shake it off did nothing either. No matter what she did, it wouldn't release.

"Take it back," Jordan told Legion. Her attention shifted when she saw Owen's circle was empty as well. *Shit. Where is he?* she thought.

You know I can't take my power back. It's too late. The deep grating sound of Legion's voice had Jordan whirling back to face him. *I will make you pay.*

"Where are they?" Jordan asked. "If you've hurt either Owen or Madison, I'll…" Jordan trailed off to glance down at the salt surrounding her. She was relieved to see that it wasn't broken, but debated breaking through to find them.

"You'll what?" Owen said from behind her. Laughter that sounded nothing like his own bubbled from his lips. It gave Jordan the shivers and had her shrinking away from the edges of the circle. Madison stood beside him. Her beautiful features held a matching sneer.

"You will pay," they said in unison. "You will pay."

211

Together, they lifted their hands and placed them out in front of their bodies at chest height, as if they were participating in some sort of mime routine. Jordan watched the muscles in their forearms tense, their torsos tilt forward.

Owen and Madison took a step forward and started screaming. The screams were their own, which pulled a gasping sob from Jordan. Tiny red welts began to pop along the skin lining the palms of their hands as they continued to try and push their way through the invisible salt wall.

"Stop!" Jordan put her hands against Madison's. She started to push back, but hissed and cradled them against her body when the burning sensation became too much to bear. "Please stop. Don't do this to them!" She couldn't stand listening to their cries, or watching the blisters spread down the back of their hands...

Without thinking, Jordan turned and ran. She almost knocked herself out when she hit the salt border. Ignoring the spinning room, Jordan kicked out at the salt on the ground, thankful for her shoes. She could feel the heat through them, and by the time she had made a wide enough gap to scoot through, they were smoking.

The room was silent. Jordan didn't notice. She was busy trying to get the burning shoes off her feet. Her efforts were cut short when Owen's hands closed around her throat. They struggled on the floor, Jordan scratching at his hands and kicking him wildly. Through it all, Madison stood watching. Her arms were bright red, covered in welts that oozed.

Jordan's vision went fuzzy. Through sheer determination, she slipped the palm of her hand beneath some of Owen's fingers and pried them backward. His bones cracked, but his only reaction was to increase the pressure on her throat with his other hand. Her lungs pulsed with the urge to take a breath.

Madison's arm looked distorted, her blisters bleeding into each other until all Jordan could see was a wash of red. Her eyelids drooped. A shot of fear pierced through her consciousness. It had her bringing her leg up as hard as she could toward Owen's face. Her knee connected with his nose. Blood exploded from his face as a sharp jolt of pain shot up her leg. Owen's head snapped back, forcing him to loosen his hold on her. Slick with blood, Jordan was able to twist around and slide out of his grasp.

She sprinted toward the bathroom and swung the door closed. Madison was tight on her heels. Her arm snaked through, but the action was followed by a scream as the weight of Jordan and the door slammed against it. Madison's arm retreated back the way it had come, and the door closed.

Cursing, Jordan locked it. She clenched her teeth, and took a few paces before reaching inside herself for the thread of power that belonged to Legion.

Are you unhappy to see your friends? His voice echoed uncomfortably in her mind. *Don't worry too much about their behavior. You will be dead soon.*

Through their existing connection, Jordan reached for another tendril of power. *Maybe, just maybe, I can take more of his power, and gain the upper hand*, she thought.

Laughter rang through her head, and was echoed by Owen and Madison outside the door. *Fool. You have no idea what you are doing, do you?*

The door rattled on its hinges as it seemed like Owen and Madison renewed their efforts to get through.

Jordan wiped her sweaty hands onto the back of her pants and closed her eyes. She mentally found the tendril of Legion's power that belonged to her, and without knowing what else to do, she began to follow it like a rope. Her essence left her body again, floating through the bathroom door, past Owen and Madison and straight into Legion's hovering form.

Get out. Legion's presence overwhelmed Jordan. It was strange, feeling him all around her, giving her no room to move, trapping her within him.

Jordan was distracted by a tingling sensation. It was hot and poked at her, causing her temper to flare. *No!* She threw the word at him like a gauntlet. His essence pulsed, squeezing hers from all sides like a python making its kill.

Cut off from all escape routes, Jordan did the only thing she could think of. She absorbed Legion into her. It was like sucking down a refreshing drink through a straw. Her essence swelled and her anger was replaced by a giddiness she quickly squelched. She didn't know how dangerous taking his power might be.

What are you doing? Legion's voice seemed smaller, even though he was shouting. *Stop!* It was too late; barely anything of him remained.

What was left of the thin layer of Legion's resistance shattered like thin ice. Jordan's essence whipped backward toward her body. For a terrifying moment, she thought she was dead. When she was able to open her eyes, she couldn't help but let out a joyous laugh. It caused her some pain; her feet were dangling over the ledge of the tub, while her back and head were on the bathroom floor. She cringed, putting her hands to her sides as she slowly got to her feet.

Legion was gone. She couldn't feel him inside her head anymore, yet his power remained. A burning sensation in the pit of her stomach increased until it was worse than it ever had been before. She willed herself to ignore the taste of bile rising at the back of her throat.

You've taken too much power, she thought to herself. She then realized that the banging on the other side of the door had stopped.

Ignoring the twinges in her muscles, Jordan wrenched the door open. In her rush to see Owen and Madison, she almost tripped over their bodies. They had both collapsed, and if Jordan didn't know any better, she would have thought they were taking a nap.

"Can you guys hear me?" she asked. She bent down and shook Owen, then Madison. "Are you all right?" She shook them harder.

A pair of feet appeared in Jordan's periphery. Startled, she looked up and saw Dinah staring down at her.

"They can't hear you," she said. "Where is the book?"

"What do you mean they can't hear me?" Jordan asked.

"Did you get the book or not?"

"Yes, I got it…"

"Well? Where is it?"

Jordan tried shaking Owen and Madison again. "What?"

"Where. Is. The. Book?" Dinah repeated.

"Levi took it from me," Jordan replied in a tightly controlled voice. "Please. Answer my question. What's wrong with them?"

Dinah's nostrils flared. "I should think the answer is obvious," she said. "Did you run out of time?"

Jordan leaned back on her heels as the horrible truth sunk in. *We're stuck,* she thought as Legion's power threatened to eat its way through her digestive tract. *Owen and Madison were possessed by Legion and I was linked to him.* A hand went to her head. *And now I'm stuck with what's left of him.* She wanted to lie down on the ground too, but forced herself to keep thinking. *A hard impact,* she reminded herself, thinking of the paper she had found earlier. *If I can somehow give us all a hard enough impact, maybe…*

Dinah bent down to kneel in front of Jordan. "I told you to prepare yourself for this, the idea that you might never get your friends back."

"It can't be true." Jordan could hear the panic creeping into her voice.

Dinah sighed. "The damage is done. He is gone, and because they were still linked to him, they too are no longer with us."

"That can't be right." Jordan felt her lower lip tremble. She bent over Owen and grabbed him by his shirt so she could try to lift him.

214

"What are you *doing?*" Dinah asked.

Jordan released Owen, and rounded on Dinah. "I need to make sure my friends are safe," she said. "I can help them." She paused. "I just…I ran out of time."

"Well, you're wasting it now," Dinah snapped. "There's nothing you can do for them. I told you to get that book, so get it." She left Jordan feeling cold as she disappeared.

"No." Jordan's voice sounded hollow in the empty room. *What I need is an impact*, she thought to herself. *A hard impact.*

A moment later, she was struggling to get Owen out of the room and into the elevator. She was reminded of the night she had brought him to Madison. Cursing under her breath at his weight, Jordan used all the strength she had to keep him propped up against her. The ride down to the lobby felt as though it would last forever. Her eyes remained riveted on the floor numbers as her stomach continued to churn.

Going through the lobby would attract too much attention, so Jordan slipped out the back exit and managed to drag Owen into the Mustang without meeting a soul.

"I'll be right back," Jordan told him, pulling the seat belt over his chest and making sure it held him securely in place. She smoothed his hair away from his brow before turning on her heel and running back into the hotel for Madison.

Madison was much lighter to lift, but Jordan was still sweating. "I'm going to get us out of this mess," she promised. "And when I do, I'm going to apologize for acting like an idiot. I'll even take you shopping."

They got into the elevator without much trouble, or so Jordan thought. As the doors closed, dark gray spots clouded her sight. She blinked rapidly, and leaned her back against the wall for support. The spots only grew larger.

"Oh, shit," she said. "Not now." Her vision grayed out completely. When it cleared she was no longer standing in the elevator.

Startled, Jordan realized she was looking at Mr. Wilson, who was standing over her, glasses perched on the tip of his nose. "You're lucky I know your mother."

"I'm really sorry," she heard Greg say. "I can't explain what happened, I…I'm just really not feeling well today."

"Go home," Mr. Wilson said. "Come back tomorrow. You will need to begin working off the cost of that priceless vase you broke."

Jordan felt a pang of regret as Greg turned and headed out of the museum. He stopped beside a silver car and pulled out a set of keys. He rubbed an eyelid with the back of his hand, and then she was back in the elevator with Madison propped up against her. She felt stunned as she watched the doors open to the first floor. "Well, I'll be damned," she grumbled, bending her knees to get a better grip on Madison. *My link with Greg isn't broken either.*

There wasn't any time for Jordan to think. She was desperate to get Madison into the Mustang without anyone noticing. She took the same route as before, through the back exit of the hotel and across the parking lot. Her hands trembled in relief as she carefully lowered Madison into the backseat.

Dinah appeared behind her. "Trying to help them is pointless," she said.

Startled, Jordan bashed her head on the roof of the old girl. "I told you," she said when she could speak again, "I'm saving my friends." Head throbbing, she managed to get Madison into a seated position.

Jordan reached for the seat belt, but Dinah grabbed her shoulder and pulled her around until they were face-to-face. "It will *not* work!" she hissed.

The heat in Jordan's stomach boiled, stealing what was left of her attention. She slammed the Mustang's door shut. "You don't know that," she snapped as she stalked away from Dinah, around the front of the old girl and over to the driver's side.

"You will only end up killing yourself," Dinah said, resting her hands on the roof.

Jordan paused with her hand hovering over the door handle. "I have to try." Not waiting for a reply, she got into the Mustang, ignoring Dinah's shouts of protest, and drove out of the parking lot.

"So. Big impact," she said out loud, then glanced over at Owen and back at Madison. "Right, then. Speed. I need more speed." She made a U-turn and headed for the highway. A quick glance in the rearview mirror revealed the wildness she felt reflected in her eyes.

Jordan blinked and found herself looking into Greg's rearview mirror. He was parking his car in front of the bakery, making sure he had no food in his teeth before he went inside. He had one hand on the door release when Jordan made him stop.

You're going to hate me for doing this, she told him, hoping he could hear the sympathy in her voice. *But it's our only chance.* She could feel his confusion as she gently nudged him aside. He grew upset with her then, and fought her to get his body to do what he wanted.

Jordan was at her wit's end. *Greg, listen to me.* Her voice resonated in a pitch that was borderline hysterical. *I don't want to be here either. The truth is, if you don't trust me, right now, we are both going to be stuck like this forever. While I get the sense that you're a hell of a guy, forever isn't something I think either of us is ready for.*

…Okay. He released Jordan from his mental wrestling hold.

Jordan didn't waste time. She made Greg buckle himself in, start the car, and head toward the highway.

"Oh, shit." Her view switched in an instant. She was now looking through the Mustang's windshield, and was rapidly approaching a ditch. There wasn't enough time to turn. Jordan slammed on the breakes. The old girl's tires screeched until the car came to a hard stop.

"Did it work?" she asked in a small voice. Neither Owen nor Madison responded. Jordan reached for Owen and saw that his eyes were still closed, his body limp. "Damn. Damn, damn, damn!" She rested her elbows on the steering wheel and buried her face in her hands. *Greg's still out there*, she reminded herself. *You've got one more chance, so make it count.*

Jordan pushed her hair away from her face, and set her jaw. There was a silver glint in the distance. She reversed the Mustang, and then headed toward it.

Now there was a green speck in the distance. It took Jordan a moment to settle into Greg's body again. She had him grip the steering wheel firmly in both hands, and slowly apply more pressure on the gas pedal.

A second later she was back in the Mustang, pressing her own foot down on the gas. Her heart jumped as the old girl leapt forward, but it was in fear, not excitement.

Jordan took a deep breath. As she exhaled, she could see the Mustang coming toward her. Someone gave her a shove, which jerked the car out of its lane. Greg was resisting her now. She didn't blame him.

I don't want to control you. I never wanted to control you, she told him. *This is the only way to save us all.*

Jordan gasped for air. Her palms were slick as she gripped the Mustang's steering wheel. Greg's car was bearing down on the old girl. Jordan could make out the shape of his body in the driver's seat.

Her instincts told her to get out of the way, to avoid the inevitable. She heard Dinah's voice in her head: *You will only end up killing yourself.*

If I don't do this, she thought, *we're all going to be better off dead.*

A split second before the crash, Jordan was looking out of Greg's eyes again. She felt his confusion and panic and matched it with her own. She could see herself, her body braced for impact. She could see Owen, his eyes closed, blissfully unaware.

A second later, Jordan didn't know if she was screaming or if it was everyone else around her. She couldn't tell the difference between the shriek of a voice, the screeching of metal on metal, or the shearing of broken glass. She couldn't tell the difference between her and Greg.

But they both saw the Mustang eject Madison like a shot from a cannon.

*****

Jordan woke to the sound of her own groans. Her head felt funny, and heavy. It was as if it had suddenly grown too big for her neck. *Open your eyes*, she told herself. It was difficult at first, but she managed to get her lids to flutter apart.

The inside of the Mustang was a disaster. There was broken glass everywhere, and now that she thought about it, her entire body ached. "I'm sorry, Dad," she mumbled. She looked down at herself and saw that her arms were bleeding. She lifted them and was glad to know she still could.

In that moment, her memory of the crash came flooding back. *Owen,* she thought.

"You all right?" She let her head loll in his direction.

Owen's face was turned toward the window on the door. He didn't respond.

"Come on. Answer me." Fear sent a shot of adrenaline through her veins. *It didn't work*, she thought to herself. *Damn it, it didn't work.* She raised herself so that she could shake him. "Can you hear me? Are you all right?"

Owen didn't respond.

Jordan was about to shake him again, harder, when he stuck his tongue out of his mouth. He licked his lips before saying, "That really hurts."

Jordan released him and collapsed back against her seat. She was so tired and so relieved. She just wanted to go to sleep.

"Where's Maddie?" Owen asked.

"She's here," Jordan told him. "In the back."

"Madison," Owen called. He turned slowly. "No. She's not. Why isn't she there?"

"I don't..." Jordan didn't finish the thought. Her gaze locked onto the gaping hole in the windshield.

Words tumbled frantically from Owen's mouth. "Where is she? Why can't I find her?"

Jordan could only manage to point.

"No." Owen's lower jaw quivered. "No!" His fingers were clumsy, but he managed to unbuckle himself and open the door. Jordan remained where she was. *Seat belt*, she thought in horror. *I forgot Madison's seat belt.*

It took Owen's cry of alarm to get her moving. She stumbled from the car on wobbling legs. Her head ached like a sore tooth, doubling her vision. "Is she all right?" Jordan choked the words out and walked in front of the hood. Her next question got lodged in her throat.

Blood pooled out from beneath Madison's head, drenching her golden hair. Her eyes were open, but vacant. Owen was down on his knees beside her. His hands hovered over her body for a moment before his fingers went to the pulse that should have been beating at her neck.

It's my fault, was all Jordan could think.

"What did you do?" A man's voice broke through Owen's wailing shouts.

Jordan's stomach clutched, watching Greg fist his hands in his hair. Her hand slammed down on the hood of the Mustang as she lost the ability to stand on her own.

"Oh my God. Jesus…Jesus!" Greg took a few limping steps back toward his car. "I'll call the police. Don't move her. Don't move her!"

Owen wasn't listening. He tugged Madison into his arms, and pressed his ear up against her heart. He closed his eyes before his features crumbled. Madison's body shook as his sobs punctured Jordan's soul.

It's my fault. She slumped down onto the ground and rocked herself as the blare of sirens sounded in the distance.

*****

Jordan stood in Owen's hospital room, looking down at him.

"You're doing very well, considering the force of the impact," the nurse said. "You must be glad that the police are arresting that man. Driving on the wrong side of the road like that." He made a *tsking* sound with his teeth. "Don't worry. They'll have him behind bars as soon as we release him."

Jordan cringed. Owen stared silently at the wall. He had done so for most of the twenty-four hours they had been in the hospital.

"He's *very* lucky you know," the nurse said, gesturing to Owen. He turned to Jordan. "And so are you. Not many people get released as quickly as you did after getting into a crash like that."

Jordan's hand went to her forehead. *I don't feel lucky*, she thought. The bump had almost disappeared. All that remained was a dark purple bruise. Her arms were spattered with tiny red cuts that stung anytime her skin rubbed against her shirtsleeves. The red strip left across her chest by the seat belt ached fiercely every time she breathed.

But the burning sensation in her stomach was gone.

It should be me lying in the morgue.

The nurse moved over to the side of Owen's bed, adjusted the IV drip, and then made a few notes on his chart. "There. All done," he said in a cheerful voice. "If the pain gets to be too much, you call me."

Owen didn't move.

Jordan continued to study Owen as the nurse left the room. The right side of his face was a blend of colors; his left was eye swollen shut, and bandages covered his nose. A sheet covered him, but beneath it she knew his ribs were tightly bound. She wanted to reach out and comfort him, but kept her hands tucked inside her pockets.

He would heal. He was whole. He was alive.

But Greg had been arrested, and Madison was *dead*.

You know whose fault this is, Jordan told herself. She stared down at Owen. She wanted to see his chest rise and fall. Rise and fall. *If Levi hadn't taken the book, I would have made it back on time. I would have made it.*

"How are you feeling?" she asked, not knowing what else to do. "Do you need me to…"

Owen turned his face away from her to stare at the opposite wall.

Jordan's fists clenched.

Levi killed my parents.

He's the reason Owen's lying here.

He's the reason Madison is dead.

"I'll be back soon," she told his back. She hoped he was listening. "There's something I need to do."

Chapter 24

Revelations

*J*ordan went back to the alley behind the River Six, and lowered herself down through the open sewer hole. Water seeped through her shoes as she touched the ground. The smell of excrement overwhelmed her. Standing beneath the beam of sunlight streaming down from the surface, she covered her mouth with the back of her arm. Beyond the light's edges was darkness; a dense, pitch-black darkness.

"Levi," Jordan shouted. "Where are you?"

After the echo died away, all she could hear was the sound of her breathing, hitching like sobs. She didn't have time to participate in this foolish hunt. He was definitely toying with the few remaining threads of her patience.

She wanted that book. She needed him to pay.

In the distance, a splash rebounded against the tunnel walls. Jordan squinted, trying to see. She took a hesitant step in the direction of the sound, and placed her palm flat against the wall. It slid forward through a slime coating the cement. Feeling her throat constrict, she focused on lifting her other hand. It trembled, sweeping the air in front of her body as she slowly moved forward.

That's it, keep moving, she told herself. *One foot in front of the other.*

Despite the encouragement, she couldn't force herself to move any faster. The air felt solid, like it was pushing against her shoulders, pressing down against her limbs. Jordan had to take a few deep breaths to fight against the tightness building in her chest. It was like swimming through mud.

The wall ended abruptly, and Jordan wasn't prepared. Her hand slipped, sending her off balance, and she stumbled forward. Her heel crushed down onto something solid. She let out a shriek as it pierced through the sole of her shoe and into her flesh. She toppled forward. The putrid-smelling water drenched her clothes as her hands broke her fall.

Get up, Jordan commanded herself. *You have to keep moving.* When she got to her feet, she paused. *Is that a pinprick of light in the distance?* Her hands throbbed, her foot felt numb, and it was probably already infected. She continued to limp toward the light.

It grew in size with every step she took. It flickered like candlelight, and when she finally reached it, she realized what it was. She had entered a cavernous space, a room that didn't look as though it belonged in a sewer. It was large, lit by what looked to be several thousand candles.

In the middle of the room, there was a metal ladder. It rose out of the ground and reached the ceiling. Jordan moved toward it, placed a hand on one of the rungs, and looked up. A wooden door covered a small square hole. Light shone through from the cracks around the edges.

"…no, I wish I didn't need the wretched girl. I wish I could kill her and be done with it…" Although faint, the voice was familiar. It seemed to be coming from above her.

"…always had a tender spot in my heart for that woman…" was all she could hear of the response.

The second voice definitely belonged to Levi.

Jordan climbed to the top of the ladder and pushed her shoulder up against the wood. It lifted slightly, creating enough of a gap for her to peek through without being seen.

She was looking into the River Six. It was empty except for Levi and Dinah, who were standing near the dance floor. Levi was casually leaning on one of the round tables, while Dinah paced the floor in front of him like a captive tiger. They were the last two people Jordan expected to see in a room together. *Is she getting the book for me?* Jordan wondered.

"What have you done?" Dinah's voice was so sharp, Jordan almost lost her grip on the ladder. "You know she needs that book."

"Then why didn't you get it for her?"

"Because I *can't*," Dinah said. "I can't touch it; I can't even get near it!" She threw her hands in the air. "The entire museum is protected by that bloody book. I couldn't even manipulate that infuriating curator into allowing Jordan to see it."

"Well, thanks to you, she believes I killed her parents," Levi replied in a calm voice. "She thinks I drugged her so that I could send imps after her. *Your imps!* What have you been telling her about me?"

"Nothing specific," Dinah said with a shake of her head. "I can't help what the girl assumes." She walked over to another table and rapped her knuckles along the surface three times. *Tap, tap, tap.* "Tell me why you took the book. Now."

Dinah's tapping. Holy shit, she's tapping, Jordan thought with a frown. *What the hell is going on?*

"You told her to stay away from me." Levi moved away from the table, toward where Jordan was listening. Captivated by the conversation, she didn't even worry about being seen.

"Only for your own good." Dinah's voice softened. "She still won't have you."

"What about that little trail of destruction you've been leaving behind?" he asked. "That certainly hasn't left her in the mood for romance."

"Events needed to be set in motion. You know that," Dinah replied. She brought a hand to her head, and whirled back around to face Levi. "Jordan would not be here if her parents were still alive. She wouldn't be here if she hadn't seen that letter." She sighed. "You have to understand..."

Everything clicked into place. *Levi isn't the one who manipulated Tully and Owen...He told you the truth*, she thought. *You were just too stupid to listen.*

Jordan seethed with anger and guilt. She pushed back the wooden door. It landed behind her with a bang as she climbed the rest of the way into the room. "You did it?" she shouted through whatever it was that had lodged in the back of her throat. "You killed my parents?"

Dinah went very still. Her hand fisted in her hair before dropping back down to her side.

Unshed tears stuck in Jordan's eyes. "Tell me the truth," she shouted. "Answer me!"

"I will," Levi said in a quiet voice. He held out his hand. "Jordan. Let me show you."

"Don't you dare touch her," Dinah commanded.

It was too late. Jordan reached out and rested her palm in his.

*****

The wind had felt harsh and cruel. There was no foliage in this strange place to protect her from the elements. She was down on her hands and knees, gently blowing on the tiny spark she had started.

"This." The sounds of his voice sent shivers down her spine. "This is what you left me for?"

Levi had finally found her. She rose to her feet slowly, feeling suddenly ashamed of the garment she had fashioned to cover her body. Her shame.

"I waited for you," Levi said. "You were supposed to meet me, but you never came."

She wasn't able to look at him. "I thought my actions would be clear enough," she said in a soft voice. "I'm not going with you."

"Adam has filled your head with lies," he replied, taking her hand. "Come. Leave with me now."

"I am speaking the truth," she said, digging her heels into the ground. "And he is *not* the one who has been lying to me."

Levi's hand unconsciously went to his chest and clenched. "You would stay here with *him*?" he asked. "After everything we've shared?"

"He is my husband," she said. "I made an oath. I…I cannot leave him."

"Do you know what I have done for you?" he yelled. "I gave up my place in line on the throne. I gave up my family! My life!"

"You tricked me," she said with heat in her eyes. "You told me no harm would come from eating the apple."

"No harm would come to *you*," Levi said. "It was the only way we could be together. Please. Don't you see what I've done for you? For us?"

She yanked her arm away and started slowly backing away from him. "You truly are a monster," she said. "I have doomed mankind to a life outside of Eden. I have shamed myself for all of eternity, and all you care about is keeping me for yourself."

"I love you," Levi screamed at her. "I won't survive without you."

"Yes, you will," she said, shaking her head. "You are a demon. You know nothing of love." She disappeared into her cave. He was not able to follow.

Dinah appeared behind him. Levi felt her presence, but didn't turn to look at her.

You have lost," she said.

"I suppose this makes you happy," he replied. "Watching me suffer like this."

"She will be born again," Dinah told him, putting a hand on his shoulder. "Thousands and thousands of years from now she will return to Earth to redeem mankind for this sin." She paused. "You have given up much for her," she continued, "and you have always been my favorite. I will allow you to try once more to gain her love. If she will have you, then she is yours. If not, she belongs to me. Do we have a deal?"

"Yes, Mother."

*****

"You always were an ungrateful son." Dinah held Levi up in the air by his throat. She flicked her wrist. Levi's hand was ripped from Jordan's as he soared through the air. He crashed into the stage, plowing through the drum set like a rag doll.

"What have you done?" Jordan cried.

Dinah grabbed her by the arm before she could run toward him. "Only what you came here to do," she replied.

"He's your son."

"Not anymore." Dinah looked away. Jordan caught the slight tremble in her lower lip. "I tried to spare him. I *wanted* to spare him, but he has brought this upon himself." She inhaled sharply, as if she had forgotten where she was for a moment. "Listen to me. Levi is a manipulative creature. He—"

"If anyone's manipulative, it's you," Jordan interrupted. She reached out and grabbed Dinah's shirt. "You killed my parents. I heard you admit it."

Dinah grimaced. "I didn't have a choice. I needed to be able to shape and mold you. Help you to become who you need to be in order to save the world."

"I don't believe this." Jordan pushed Dinah away from her. "You're not even sorry, are you?"

"There's no sense in regretting what needed to be done."

"You're a liar," Jordan ground out between clenched teeth. Her body trembled violently. "You're a liar and a murderer."

"If you think *you* can avoid becoming the same before this war has ended, you are a fool." Dinah's eyes were as hard as granite.

Jordan shivered. "You're not really a guardian angel," she said. "Who are you?"

"I have many names," she answered with a haughty toss of her head. "Dinah, you may have guessed, is not one of them."

Many names, and mother of a prince of hell… Jordan thought. "Satan?" she

225

whispered. A giggle rose up against the back of her throat. The idea seemed so ridiculous. "You're Satan."

"Come with me," Dinah continued without breaking stride. "One day I *will* unleash my armies upon the earth. I need you on my side, to be my right hand."

"You're a psychopath," Jordan shot back. "I didn't want to leave with Levi, what makes you think I want to leave with you?"

"I will give you his birthright. You will live forever."

"I didn't really want it anyway." Levi's voice had Jordan and Dinah spinning around. He stood casually on the stage with his hands in his pockets, but something wasn't quite right with his skin. It was rippling, like something was trapped beneath it, trying to break free. Jordan gasped as she watched Levi's torso elongate and thicken, coiling around itself around the stage. A moment later, the wood splintered, crumbling beneath his weight. The drum set and other equipment were sent tumbling across the dance floor.

Levi's smooth skin began to peel, fluttering to the ground like snowflakes. He yawned, and if his arms hadn't begun to melt into his torso, Jordan would have thought he was stretching. His jaws opened wider and wider until she was staring at a gaping mouth with oversized fangs and a giant forked tongue. It took Jordan a moment to realize that his transformation was complete. Snow-white scales and yellow, glassy eyes held her frozen in place.

"Despite what you may think, I will not enjoy this," Dinah shouted at him. Jordan shied away when she looked over to find the woman had drawn her sword.

Levi charged at his mother. Jordan darted behind the bar and out of the way. The sound of metal hitting metal had her peering above the edge to see what was happening. Dinah was hacking away at Levi's underbelly, but it looked like her sword was having no effect. Levi was bringing his great head down toward Dinah, his powerful jaws snapping at her. She was too close to him; he couldn't get at her.

Jordan's knuckles turned white as she gripped the bar ledge. Levi was trying to maneuver around Dinah, so that he could get at her from a better angle. The moment his head streaked past her, the tip of her sword flicked out and nicked his giant neck. Black blood spurted from the wound. Jordan rose to her feet and looked on in horror as Levi began to shrink back into his human form.

"Stop this!" Jordan cried. She rushed around the bar, but fear prevented her from moving too close. Levi was lying on the floor, on his back. His throat oozed, but he was breathing. In fact, he was watching Jordan with eyes that glittered in pain.

If he can feel pain, then he can feel—

Jordan didn't have time to finish the thought. "Watch out," she screamed, pointing to Dinah.

The sword flared with bright-blue flames as Dinah raised it above her head with both hands. "I gave you a second chance," she told Levi. "I loved you enough to give you a second chance, and you threw it back in my face."

Levi closed his eyes and smiled as Jordan raised her hand and reached for him. She could feel the exact moment when he released his power, sending the threads shooting toward her outstretched arm.

Absorbing the threads as she ran, she could feel the skin on her chest and stomach splitting open. It felt like tiny shards of glass were growing out of her flesh. There was no time to debate what was happening to her. She threw herself in between Levi and the sword.

The tip of the blade landed on her breastbone with a resounding *clank*. Jordan fell to her knees from the weight of the blow.

Through her shock, she heard Levi laughing. "'The sword that reaches it has no effect,'" he quoted. "'Nor does the spear or the dart or the javelin. Iron it treats like straw and bronze like rotten wood.'"

"Get out of my way," Dinah's voice boomed. Jordan cowered before her as bottles of liquor and wine shattered, spraying the air with shards of glass. Through the intense fear she felt her stomach spasm, and boil.

Simultaneously, the two women realized what had happened.

Jordan immediately absorbed the thin stream of power Dinah had accidentally released. It felt thick, like molasses, and burned as it pumped through her bloodstream. One shove sent Dinah sprawling backward, sliding across the floor and into the debris from the stage.

An icy calm settled over Jordan as she flexed her hands. Both Levi's and Dinah's power flowed through her now. The scales would only protect her for so long. What she needed was something that would put them on more even ground. She scanned the debris until she found what she was looking for. As Dinah rose to her feet, Jordan pulled the hi-hat stand from beneath a large plank of wood. As she did, a ring of blue fire ignited the metal. When it was free, she held a matching sword in her hands.

Dinah faced Jordan, but her usually stoic face was expressing concern. "You don't know how to use that," she said. She licked her lips.

Jordan advanced, raising the sword to the side, just above her shoulders.

"I don't want to hurt you," Dinah said, moving her sword out in front of her.

Jordan swung her weapon down. It hissed, and sparks flew as the two blades kissed. "You *can't* hurt me because you *need* me," Jordan said through clenched teeth. "Since you lack the ability to feel any emotion, I'll let you know that there's a fundamental difference."

Dinah bared her teeth and blocked another of Jordan's blows. She pivoted, and slashed upward, across the length of Jordan's chest. The blow was excruciating, despite the scales protecting her skin. She staggered backward but saw that the momentum of Dinah's sword brought her arms upward. Her stomach was left exposed. Jordan grunted like a tennis player, using the last of her strength to change direction.

She thrust her sword into Dinah.

Dinah's mouth made an "O" shape as she looked down at the length of the blade. Blue flames licked at the white material of her shirt. "How dare you," she wailed.

Then she disappeared.

It all happened so quickly, Jordan didn't realize it was over. The stand, not a sword, hit the ground with a metallic ring, forcing reality to sink in. She grabbed her head as the last dregs of Dinah's power slipped away.

"I killed her," she said. "I fucking killed her!" She felt Levi's hands come to rest on her shoulders, and then move down the length of her arms as he turned her around.

"I hate to spoil the moment, darling, but you basically achieved the equivalent of poking an angry dog with a stick." Levi's touch lingered over her skin. "Let it go. Make sure you let it all go."

The last bit of his power slipped away from her. Pain from her car crash injuries made her tremble, but she managed to swallow a cry. She would have collapsed if Levi hadn't been holding her. Jordan looked up at him and forced herself to forget for a moment that he was a demon. She turned her head into his chest and leaned her weight against him.

"You're bleeding," she murmured, and closed her eyes against her own aches.

His response vibrated against her ear. "It's just a scratch," he said.

"I should have believed you."

"Is that an apology?" he asked.

Jordan pulled her head back to stare up at him. "Yeah," she said, with a laugh that sounded precariously close to a sob. "No." She pushed him away. "Madison died because you took the book from me. I could have saved her." She felt her eyes fill with tears. "She didn't have to die."

"She did." His voice was a mere whisper. "One day you'll understand."

Before Jordan could ask what he meant by that, Levi took a step back, and then another. "You're going to need this," he told her. He turned, and when he was facing her again, he held the *Book of Eve* in both hands.

Jordan took it from him and ran her hands over the cover. "You wanted me to know the truth. That's the reason why you took it."

"I was going to buy it for you." Levi flashed a wicked smile that didn't quite reach his eyes. "Consider it a gift," he said. "For saving my life."

Eager to see what she had risked *her* life over, Jordan cracked the book open. "I can't read this," she said in a flat voice. She flipped through a few pages, then a few more. "What the hell? It's not in English; I can't read this at all."

"You're a clever girl. You'll figure it out," Levi said, reaching out to touch the base of her throat. "I...I have to let you go now."

Jordan's pulse skittered, and her vision clouded.

"Wake up, lovely." Levi's voice was a bare whisper in her ear. "Wake up..."

Chapter 25

Epilogue

"...'ll make sure nothing ever happens to you again. But you have to wake up." Owen's hands had one of Jordan's in a death grip. She was lying on something soft, but the light seemed rather harsh for the River Six.

"Please," Owen whispered. "Wake up."

"What's going on?" Jordan said. Her throat felt like she had eaten a bucket of sand.

"Oh, thank God!" He buried his face against her hand and the bed.

Confused, Jordan started to ask another question, but all that came out was a cough. Owen had a glass of water in her hand before she could ask.

"What happened?" he asked, as she gulped the water down. "The last time I saw you, you said you had something to do." He spoke so rapidly it was hard for Jordan to follow what he was saying. "I didn't mean to shut you out, but I just…I couldn't. Anyway, the next thing I know, you're being wheeled back in here on this bed."

"I'm in the hospital?" Jordan rubbed at her eyelids with her hands. When she took a second look, it was to find Owen sitting in a wheelchair beside her. She groaned and tried to recall how she got there. "The book," she exclaimed, sitting up. "Where is it? Where's the *Book of Eve*?"

"Whoa, take it easy," Owen said. He glanced toward the door and then pulled the book out from beneath the covers by her legs and put it in her lap. "It's right here."

She stared down at the cover. "I was wrong about everything," she finally admitted.

"What happened?" Owen's voice was soft and imploring. "Tell me."

Jordan did. She told him everything. Well, almost everything. She started by explaining how Dinah had been pulling her and everyone around her along like puppets from the very beginning. She left out the part where she forgot to buckle Madison into the car.

"So Mr. Wilson was never really possessed?" Owen asked when Jordan was finished.

"Nope. I guess he's just a dick."

"So what do we do now?"

"I don't know," she said, lifting the book. She needed something to focus on instead of Owen. It felt like her mistake was written all over her face. "And the one thing that was supposed to help us, we can't read."

Owen leaned his head back against the chair. "First things first," he said. "I think we should stop looking for Parker."

"Really."

"Yeah. Really."

They sat in silence for a moment before Jordan spoke again. "Are you sure?" she asked.

Owen fiddled with the handles on his chair. "You were right." He sighed. "I've been organizing my memories of Parker into two boxes. I've got to be honest. The box of shitty things he's done to me...to us...it's pretty full."

"I need to fix what Dinah's done," Jordan told him. "What happened to Madison..." She shook her head and pressed her lips together, trying to hold on to her composure.

"She didn't deserve what happened to her." Owen folded his hands in his lap and set his jaw.

Guilt churned in Jordan's stomach like a pot full of boiling water. She cleared her throat, and changed the subject. "I think I'll stick around for a while," she said, picking at a loose thread on the blanket. "I mean, if that's all right with you."

"Like you even have to ask."

"Fixing Dinah's mess also means helping Greg," she continued, ignoring the pressure building behind her eyes. "I can't let him take the fall for Madison's death. There's got to be some way to prove his innocence."

"This isn't like you, Jo," he replied with a forced smile. "You aren't running away. People might start wondering about you."

Jordan snorted. "I've clearly lost my mind."

The sound of Owen's breath hitching sobered her in an instant. "I don't know how I'm going to get over this," he whispered.

"I don't think either of us ever will," she told him.

"I can help you," Owen said, clearing his throat. "We'll search for someone who can translate the book."

"I don't want you getting involved," Jordan said. "You're the only family I've got left."

"Together, or not at all," he said, reaching out to tug on the ends of her hair. "Deal?"

Jordan looked at him and wondered how she had ever thought she could leave him again. She reached out, winced, but tugged his right back. "Deal."

The shrill ring of the room's phone had Owen breaking contact first. "Hello?" he said into the receiver. "Hey! How'd you get…oh. I see." He mumbled a few more responses before hanging up.

"Who was that?" Jordan asked. Owen fixed his green gaze on her. She could feel the blood drain from her face. "What. What is it?"

"It was Tully," he told her. "He found Parker."

About the Author

Crystal Bourque is an up and coming, new adult, urban fantasy author. She is obsessed with all things fantastical, so much so that she has a recurring dream about being a princess with a sword. When she's not busy writing, she loves trying new recipes, plotting her next travel destination, and singing loudly.

You can check out Crystal's website at: www.crystalbourque.com, or get in touch with her via email: hello@crystalbourque.com, or Instagram, @crystalbourqueauthor.